A GILDED
Death

~~~

CECELIA TICHI

A Gilded Death

ISBN 978-1-63972-518-2

Chapter One

Newport, 1898

THE AIR WAS SHARP, and I drew my cloak tighter around
my shoulders and peered down at the Newport harbor. The
jutting crags and rocks framed the waters below, where two
clumsy ferries rounded the breakwater at the lighthouse and
mixed with the sailboats and yachts. Narragansett Bay glittered
in the distance, and farther still, the ocean. I could see the naval
station on Goat Island and the walls of old Fort Adams, gray as
a prison. I was not here to sight see. I had agreed to meet my
friend Cassie at the edge of this granite cliff—so far, no sign of
her. The weather was clear, but a bad feeling hung in the air.

Cassie was overdue. Her footman came to me this morning, breathless, with a note "begging" me to meet her here
at this remote spot at three p.m. this afternoon. "Urgent—
About Auntie's death," she wrote. My friend's cursive was

1

crabbed and splotched, her note dashed off in haste. This summer Newport season depressed her, for the sudden death of her great-aunt last winter had plunged Cassie into mourning in leaden grays of body and mind.

Would I meet her? I instantly replied: "YES." It was now half-past three, and no sign of her. I glanced sideways at the gravel roadway. Still no carriage.

"See the burgee, ma'am? See it?" My driver, Noland, tried to be helpful. "That's Mr. J. P. Morgan's *Corsair* in the harbor, the 'greyhound of the sea,' near as fast as the Cunard liners. The red burgee with the crescent and cross."

The burgee? It was a flag, yes?—and for me, another word to translate, like "regatta," which meant a race. This was my third summer in Newport, and still it felt like another country. In my mind, open water meant lakes or rivers, and boats for prospectors on the Humboldt or Colorado Rivers. I understood canyons, arroyos, sagebrush and plunging rocky rapids. The cloud-white sails were still novel—even foreign.

A gust blew, and I tugged the lightweight wool cloak that Cassie had insisted I buy because the Newport air could be chilly and a fashionable cloak would help quiet gossip about me as Society's Wild West "Annie Oakley" who had "snagged" a New York gentleman. In this so-called Gilded Age, a snob named Ward McAllister insisted that Newport was "the place...to take root in." The social taproot was my husband, whose family had summered here for years. To me, summer was a season, not a verb, which said a good deal about my place in the Newport root system.

I thought the man might choke. His eyes widened, and patches of his cheeks turned red at my "impish" remark. We ladies were permitted endless wine, punch, and liqueurs, but cocktails? Never! The campaign for votes for women did not include votes for cocktails. This state of affairs must not continue. The Men's Café at the Waldorf Hotel begged to be challenged by thirsty ladies calling out, *cocktails!*, to demand action with a shaker and swizzle stick. In due course, I intend to lead the charge.

Colonel Twist had twisted to the left, freeing us both, and I gazed across the table. Cassie and I had a system of codes. Her arched brow was a signal shot across the damask tablecloth and bone china plates with our host's newly minted coat-of-arms, a tiny owl on a Viking ship to remind us that Edwin Glendorick's fortune had been amassed from shipping. Every lady at the table glittered with diamonds. Our hostess had added a tiara in tribute the guest of honor, a pale stripling of a bachelor who was introduced as a Baronet and the Sixth Earl of Cleave—or was it the Seventh?—who had pronounced himself delighted with his summer in Newport, from the croquet matches to the yachting parties.

The Earl's betrothal to the Glendoricks' daughter Emily was doubtless in negotiation, for all Newport knew that seventeen-year-old Emily Glendorick was soon to become one more of America's Dollar Princesses, destined to enter the British aristocratic House of Cleave upon her marriage to the impecunious Baronet. The Glendorick money would shore up the Baronet's family, while Emily, transformed into Lady Emily, would fulfill her parents' hearts' desire.

We had finished a wobbly tomato aspic and *consommé*, when another squad of footmen marched upon us, each gloved hand holding a gold-rimmed plate. Cassie's manicured index finger moved like a pointer for the implement with the little curve at the tip, my cue.

Of course, the fish knife.

I gripped the utensil meant for the flounder blanketed in cheese sauce, a sad substitute for the trout we caught in icy waters when I was a girl in the West. All that was before papa struck the Big Lode and I was sentenced to become a lady.

I met Cassie's gaze and winked my thanks to this best friend who looked out for me—just as I stood ready to help her. Growing up in mining camps with Papa, I had no playmates, and when we moved at last to Virginia City where I went to school, the girls' cliques barely tolerated the newcomer from the Rockies. This friendship with Cassie meant so much.... I hoped she felt comforted by my pre-dinner promise not to depart without the tête-à-tête about her late aunt.

If only my friend's scientist husband were here instead of digging fossils on some wind-swept rock in the Pacific Ocean. Or if her mother, Rowena (Rowena Van Schylar Fox) had not just taken a quick flying trip to the city, most likely to consult a lawyer about divorce. Cassie's father, Robert Fox, had been scandalously caught cuddling a Broadway chorus girl last spring—yet again. Some said Rowena's chilly

"Ma'am, if you please, step back. You're a bit close....
The rocks can loosen, and there's no surviving a fall here."

"Oh.... Thank you, Noland." I retreated. Was it proper
to say that heights both frightened and called me close, like
the Colorado Rockies of my childhood? Was it a breach of
etiquette to confide such thoughts to my coachman?

Cassie was never uncertain about matters of etiquette.
She did not dramatize in person or in writing. What was so
"urgent" about her late Auntie that we must meet on this
granite outcropping? Cassie—Cassandra Van Schylar Fox
Forster (Mrs. Dudley F.)—would not summon me here on
a whim. Why wasn't she here? She and I were to be guests
at a formal dinner this evening, though any chance at a
one-to-one confab in that scene would face long odds.

I was worried. A sudden, sharp gust of wind blew in, colder
than before, and Noland said, "A front's coming in, ma'am. We
don't get them often, but best get out of this weather."

My little Cartier watch said four p.m., and I drew my
cloak tight and stepped toward the carriage. Noland held
the reins, and I stroked the mare's neck, but her warmth
gave no comfort.

"Home, Noland, if you please."

☙

Theo Bulkeley was often pressed into service as my escort
when my husband Roddy—Roderick Windham DeVere—
was out of town to defend a bartender from the temperance

crowd or in demand to help blend a new cocktail for a café soon to open. Mark Twain, a western kindred spirit, had dubbed these years a *Gilded Age*, but my husband Roddy preferred *The Golden Age of Cocktails*. My husband's law school training and *bon vivant* hobby had made him a sought-after figure in courtrooms and barrooms, which we joked about when a telegram or telephone call beckoned him to the city.

"Is the Anti-Saloon League trying to shut down another bar?" I would ask. "Or does a new hotel need advice about their martini?"

Roddy would flash his handsome smile but keep me guessing. The courtroom dramas were on the public record, but my husband was often sworn to secrecy when called to consult on the cocktails that could make or break the reputation of a private club, a hotel bar, a resort, or a railroad club car. Our Newport cottage and New York household stocked countless bottles that Roddy called "libation foundations." Tipsy? We were not, but we had our fun.

Roddy insisted that I attend tonight's dinner this evening while he "toiled" in the July heat of New York City. Our friend, Theo Bulkeley called for me punctually in his brougham.

Tall and slender with pale blue eyes and narrow shoulders, the confirmed bachelor had been adopted into New York Society due to his impeccable Boston Brahmin ancestry, dating back to the Puritans. He and I were compatriots, though Theo was welcome, whereas my western upbringing in mining camps made me something of an exotic species to Society.

Theo's wit was often savage, and I relished it—most of the time. His membership in a half-dozen gentlemen's clubs in the city let him glean all sorts of useful hearsay. Tonight, however, from the moment of our arrival I wished the evening to end so I could hear Cassie's troubles. Just as I had feared, we swam too far apart in the general flurry of greetings and introductions at this great oceanfront palazzo of a cottage, Owls Roost, to have a private word. About this afternoon, Cassie managed to murmur only a quick "so sorry..." and add "dreadful news...terrifying," before we were forced to retreat into the general stream.

Our hosts, the shipping mogul Mr. Edwin D. Glendorick and his wife, Madeline, met us at the entrance hall, with its gold coffered ceiling and walls of floral silk appliqué. The gentlemen's hats and walking sticks were handed off to the valet and footmen, while maids touched up ladies' hair in an anteroom. We greeted one another as we stepped onto the oriental rugs in the Louis XV ballroom. Over the immense black marble fireplace loomed a tableau of cupids, cherubs, and a nest of owls, all executed by a famous Florentine sculptor—our host's point of pride. The oil portraits appeared to be ancestral, each one new and shiny.

I recognized most of the guests, Edith and Teddy Wharton, the Alderbachs, the Kents, Florence and Albert Dovedale. And there was silver-haired Archibald Romberg, a widower known as the "Beau Brummel" who pursued widows and certain single ladies. Here, too, were Colonel and Mrs. Twist, and many others, including Cassie's young uncle-by-marriage, the charming Sam Brush with his new bride.

We socialized while admiring—and assessing—the finery. The gentlemen were uniformed in white tie and swallowtail coats, but we ladies were to praise one another's gowns of brocade and chiffon, *peau de soie*, and lace and feather trimming. In the dusky evening summer light, Cassie Forster's ivory complexion glowed in a powder blue satin gown with its azure velvet neckline, although anyone who knew her well could see she was troubled. I too wore satin, mine a deep green. I hoped fervently to be united with my friend and, as good luck had it, we were seated across from one another.

At such gatherings, I looked to Cassie for cues about the gleaming array of sterling implements before me. By now, I recognized the bouillon spoon and knew not to sip the warm water with the lemon slice—a fingerbowl, not a soup. Our champagne was poured by a fleet of footmen in frogged tailcoats. Cassie had raised her glass. I took my first sip.

"Ah, chilled perfectly," said Colonel Twist who was seated to my left. "Hire an English butler, and your beverages will be at the proper temperature every time."

Cassie had suggested that I "read" the men's whiskers for my cues, and the colonel's remarkable muttonchops said *vanity*. I lowered my eyes and murmured, "So very true, Colonel. And my husband would agree…especially when a champagne cocktail calls for a sugar cube and a dash of Angostura bitters."

"I rest my case, Mrs. DeVere," Theo retorted. "Mrs. Roderick...Windham... DeVere...." He paced each syllable with slight mockery, this descendant of the Puritans.

The name on my calling cards does read, "Mrs. Roderick Windham DeVere," as Theo well knew. Born Valentine Louise Mackle on the fourteenth of February in Silverton, Colorado—"Val" to my the nearest and dearest—I was the only surviving offspring of Kathleen and Patrick Mackle, immigrants from Ireland's County Donegal, sadly both deceased. In their wildest dreams, old Rufus and Eleanor De Vere never imagined that their beloved only son and heir, Roderick— my Roddy—would fall in love with a western "gal" or that she would fall madly, head over western bootheels in love with him.

Was it Destiny, as Cassie insisted? Or was Rufus's addiction to hopeless investment and his son's interest in spirited beverages the root cause of our offbeat romance and marriage?

Here are the facts. As a New York boy, Roddy had often toured the downtown American Museum that showman P.T. Barnum stocked with wild animals and quirky exhibits. Later on, teenage Roddy found the lower Broadway museum far too dull, while a nearby bar offered intrigue worthy of an alchemist. No longer was whisky simply poured and drunk. A new era of spirits had dawned. The young man watched the barkeeper perform like a Svengali whose mysterious potions delighted patrons as he plied the liquor bottles, sliced fruit, glassware, silver utensils, and crystal-clear ice. Roddy was told that a certain "Thomas Alva Edison" of bartenders had formerly mixed drinks in this very site and had compiled a book of drinks "in endless variety." The author, "Professor" Jerry Thomas, had tended bar all over the United States and Europe. Bartenders revered him as their Founding Father.

The DeVere family crisis erupted when Roddy's parents found *The Bon- Vivant's Companion*, by Jerry Thomas, in their son's rooms. Alarmed, they were advised to hasten to the Arizona desert where their son could "dry out." Deaf to Roddy's insistence that he merely sipped and savored, Rufus and Eleanor virtually kidnapped Roddy and fled to a whitewashed adobe hacienda in a village crowded with cowboys, Indians, Mexicans, and swarthy foreigners with picks and shovels.

The "hacienda" year brought Roddy and me together. Without it, we would never have met. Rufus DeVere became intrigued by the sight of prospectors with their loaded pack mules and read stray copies of the Virginia City *Territorial Enterprise.* The gold rush was history, but silver still made fortunes—for a few. My own papa had become a Silver King, thanks to his great timing and hard toil.

Getting rich overnight was still an obsession, but the Lodes were nearing sundown even if mining stocks stayed high.

temperament had sent her husband into the warm embrace of dancers, a disputable point, but I could swear to the frostiness of Rowena Fox, whose fingers glittered with antique gemstones on every occasion.

"Is your friend all right?"

"All right?" From my elbow, Theo's voice interrupted my thoughts. "Cassandra, I mean. Is she well?"

"Why do you ask, Theo?"

"It's just…since her great aunt died."

I paused, a bit guarded. Cassie and her Auntie Georgina had been so very close. He late aunt supported Cassie with praise and encouragement. The two had formed a bond that never gelled between Georgina and her own chronically shy daughter, Sylvia, a spinster whom Cassie described as "bony" and "eccentric."

According to Cassie, cousin Sylvia Brush lived by herself in a shingle cottage in Tuxedo Park in the near mountains of New York. Tuxedo, said Cassie, was fashionable about ten years ago when families bought the cottages and imagined an exclusive American Cotswolds. But Tuxedo had quickly lost favor, though Sylvia settled in, a recluse who became the despair of her sociable mother. Invited to Van Schylar holiday dinners, she wrote her intention to "hold the thought" but never attended.

"Cassie is bearing up," I told Theo. To my eye, she looked fretful and distracted, though others would see an elegant young matron and mother of two young children chatting amiably with the gentlemen to her left and right, both in shirtfronts stiff as boards. On her left, Teddy Wharton doubtless regaled her with tales of his horses or dogs. Mrs. Wharton—Edith—was in view a few seats down, graciously icy as usual, most likely eyeing the furnishings in disdain.

"Cassie is as well as one can expect under the circumstances, Theo. See for yourself. She smiles, and Teddy Wharton is charmed. She's on the mend, coming up for air."

"Good to hear your reassuring words," Theo said in the mild voice that signaled something else on his mind. "We all understand that Cassandra is not herself this season." He put down his fork. "Have I heard something about séances?"

I hesitated. The currently popular fad had seduced my friend. Cassie tended toward feelings that her social circle called "superstition." Theo prodded, but I quickly changed the subject. "Let's not forget that Cassie and her aunt were very close."

"Oh, for certain. Her Auntie Georgina is missed by all. Few have such flair...all those 'causes'... police raids on gambling dens, statehood for Cuba, kennels for stray dogs." Theo sipped his wine. "Georgina ruled the croquet courts, didn't she? And that exit of hers, what perfect timing. The Broadway theatre couldn't have produced a more dramatic final curtain."

Between mirth and chagrin, I said nothing. Cassie's great-aunt's untimely death had been the shock of last winter, for Georgina Van Schylar Brush had collapsed and died at *the* social event of the New York season: Mrs. Astor's annual ball.

"The Brush fortune..." Theo murmured. He toyed with a spoon. "All due to the Log Lifter."

"Log what?"

"The machine that lifts logs onto rail cars. The Brush Log Lifter, Harry's biggest patent...his magic carpet, so to speak...and Georgina's by marriage."

The money question hovered, but I speared a green bean and said, "Cassandra's loss is heartbreaking, Theo. Georgina was like her beloved grandmother."

We said no more on that subject, but Fifth Avenue had been consumed by Georgina Brush's sudden demise. ("In perfect health two days before the ball.... Seen sleighing in the Park that afternoon... At the theatre only a week ago.") The newspapers went wild. Pulitzer's *World* and Hearst's *Journal* were bloated with lurid accounts—"DEATH STALKS SOCIETY BALL," "FATAL MOMENT CAPS LIFE OF WEALTH AND LUXURY... CROQUET COURT 'WICKED WITCH OF WICKET' COLLAPSES!!!"

For once, the press coverage of Mrs. Astor's annual Ball had more to report than the extravagant menu and inventories of the ladies' jewels. The deceased's lineage from Jon Van Schylar of colonial Knickerbocker New Amsterdam was recounted, as was her marriage before the Civil War to timber mogul Harry D. Brush of Bend, Oregon, and the survival of her daughter, Sylvia Ann Van Schylar Brush of Tuxedo Park, New York.

All Society had speculated on the terms of Georgina Brush's will, especially the question of what, if anything, was to be left to the reclusive Sylvia, who, to everyone's astonishment, was the major beneficiary of the Brush timber largesse, the forests, sawmills, lumber yards, railroad cars, and the log lifting device that Theo described.

Georgina's reason for bestowing such a fortune on her daughter had become the puzzle of the season. Some thought the mother was making amends for raising a recluse. Others believed the money was meant to catapult Sylvia into the causes that had received modest bequests. Time would tell. Meanwhile, Sylvia would be expected to don mourning clothes and stay close to home for a year, which should be second nature to the bereaved recluse even if pondering her lavish inheritance.

Theo put down his spoon. His voice was sly. "Would you like a bit of gossip, Valentine?" He leaned close. "I understand that Miss Sylvia Brush—or a lady who could be her twin—has been observed in the city this month…in the ladies shopping district, unescorted."

"Surely, mistaken identity," I said.

"And she refreshed herself at Macy's soda fountain."

"Ridiculous, Theo." I knew from Cassie that no lady in Society would be the city by herself in the summer season, much less a daughter in mourning. No one in Society was to be found in the city in the summer except for a quick trip for emergencies. A night or two at the St. Regis or Waldorf, and they were back at the summer places. The rumor was too extravagant.

"Whoever was shopping in the Ladies Mile, Theodore Bulkeley," I said, "it cannot have been Sylvia Brush."

disuse. Papa had more millions than he could count, and untold amounts of Mackle money replenished the DeVere coffers upon our nuptials. The Fifth Avenue mansion and Newport "cottage" were secure, and the DeVere's private rail car was no longer at risk of a forced sale. Papa's health, however, worsened, though he refused to leave Virginia City. His final resting place was the Silver Terrace Cemetery, where he lay in fellowship with the miners. I returned every year to his grave, and the Queen Anne now housed Fourth Ward School teachers, gratis the Mackle Trust. Roddy objected when I called myself an orphan of Virginia City, so I kept my home-sickness to myself. In truth, my Western eye often served as a sharp lens on the Four Hundred and its doings.

⁓∽

We had confronted the meat course, brownish gray roast beef as dry as wood. With the plates whisked away, the salad was served, and finally the dessert, a *Coupe Eugenie*, vanilla ice-cream with candied chestnuts and a sprinkling of crystallized violets. Cassie, I noticed, ate not one bite. The coffee was served, and the gentlemen prepared for cognac and cigars in the dining room, leaving us ladies to gather in a Louis Quinze drawing room for tea and the cigarettes which were the new fashion. Cassie eagerly—almost frantically—lighted one and drew smoke deeply into her lungs. It seemed to calm her. Another hour until the promised tête-à-tête.

In any case, the staid, buttoned-down Rufus DeVere got a bad case of silver "fever," convinced that the played-out Ophir Mine was due for another strike that could reclaim the DeVeres' sagging wealth in short order. He hustled his wife and son to the silver mining capital, Virginia City, Nevada, where the V&T Railroad wound up and around a mountain like an anaconda snake. By the time they checked into the Silver Queen Hotel & Saloon on "C" Street, they were breathless at nearly 6,000 feet above sea level and two flights of steep stairs to their rooms, but also breathless at the prospect of newest wealth.

After our nomadic years in the mining camps, Papa and I were now full-time residents of this improbable city, clapped against Mount Davidson in Nevada's Washoe Mountains. The weather was mostly awful, summers hot and dry, winters a mix of bone-chilling snow and rain and dust, plus roaring gale winds we call the Washoe Zephyr. Papa had built the two of us a Queen Anne style house on "B" Street with a decorative wraparound porch and gas lighting and running water and a coal-burning stove. After canvas tents and one-room mountain cabins, after winter nights shivering in itchy red wool Union suits, I thought Virginia City was heaven.

Roddy and I met in the Silver Queen Hotel dining room, where Papa and I often dined, when the DeVeres came for their evening meal. Conversation drifted from their table to ours. Papa swore to Rufus that the Ophir and all the other nearby mines were nearly played out, not one a worthwhile investment, but Roddy and I began our own conversation. In the lingo of the mines, I spoke of "winzes" and "drifts" and "chloride of silver." Roddy rejoined with rides in a "landau" in Central Park and "bathing" at Bailey's Beach in Newport. Neither of us knew what the other was talking about, but vocabulary mattered not a wit, for our eyes told each other everything. I could not take my eyes off him. To me, he looked like a Greek god, the ones I'd seen in picture books. His broad shoulders, deep blue eyes, and the wavy brown hair that dipped over his forehead…I nearly swooned.

He pointed to the bar at the other end of the dining room. "Jerry Thomas used to tend bar here," he said.

"Who?"

"The famous bartender…inventor of the Blue Blazer. Would you like to see a trick?"

Before I could answer, the young man sped to the bar, had a word with the bartender, and beckoned me and my papa. His parents sat stock still as we watched Roddy take hold of two silver mugs and pour whisky into one, water and sugar into the other. With the bartender's help, one mug was set afire, and Roddy DeVere held the entire dining room rapt as he poured blazing whisky back and forth from one mug to the other…streaming blue flames that drew oohs and ahhs from onlooking diners. Applause broke out. Roddy bowed. "My tribute to Professor Jerry Thomas," he said.

I decided to record the amazing drink in my diary, and Roddy recited the ingredients and directions that I took down in a notebook that was to become a journ years to come.

Blue Blazer

Ingredients:

- 2 silver mugs (with insulated handles)
- 1 or 2 ounces scotch whisky
- 4 ounces boiling water
- 2 lumps sugar Lemon peel

Directions:

1. Pour scotch into 1 mug.
2. Pour water and sugar into second mug.
3. Set scotch alight and allow to burn for minutes while pouring it into second m
4. Quickly pour lighted mixture back and from mug to mug.
5. When fire is extinguished, serve in one mugs with lemon peel. (Additional whi added.)

We married three years later. Roddy's "spiri and courtroom jousting in defense of the brewery ery, and the vineyard charmed me no end. And th adamant opposition to the match eventually cr

The last of the Virginia City booms had gone had gambled away most of his fortune on mine proved worthless and refining machinery that r

Amid the farewells, Cassie and I became separated. Ladies gathered their cloaks from the arms of maids, and gentlemen claimed the ebony walking sticks and top hats. The Glendoricks' butler orchestrated the departures, and the massive front doors of Owls Roost swung wide as carriages circled the crushed shell driveway to the entrance. Each liveried coachman held the reins tight as the butler announced the guests' carriages, and the grooms sprang to open their doors. Cassie and I were drawn hopelessly apart.

Suddenly, a cry. The train of Florence Dovedale's gown had been trampled, and concerned guests and servants clustered around her. In the confusion, a corridor opened between Cassie and me. In that instant, she hastened to my side and whispered something I couldn't quite hear. I tried repeating the words back to her to make sense of them, "—not her heart?"

"Aunt Georgina." Cassie's bosom heaved. "Not her heart. Not a stroke. We were wrong."

"Wrong?"

"Murdered. She was murdered. I'm afraid, Val. I'm so very afraid." Cassie's voice sounded half-strangled, half-drowned as she virtually cried out to me, "Val, golf tomorrow. Two p.m., just us two. The country club. Don't dare be late. Don't dare."

Chapter Two

FITFUL SLEEP DOGGED ME all night. Surely Cassie's declaration was a horrifying rumor, not a fact. Roddy had arrived home from the city in the depth of the night and was sound asleep in his bedroom, so I did not wake him with the dreadful news—knowing it could be hearsay. I was wide awake at the crack of dawn, dressed and ready to go by midmorning.

The hours dragged. What Cassie meant by the word "golf," I felt certain, must really mean afternoon tea in a quiet spot at the Newport Country Club. My friend was no athlete, and the notion that details of the supposed murder of Georgina Brush were to be confided on the links—totally daft. I approached the welcoming green-and-white striped awnings of the clubhouse at 1:45 sharp. It was another breezy day, though sunny, and I glimpsed Cassie's coachman, O'Boyle. With dark hair and eyes, he was so-called Black

Irish, a man in service to the Forster family for years. He tipped his hat as I entered the main lobby.

Cassie was not among the few members perched in the wicker settees that lined the vaulted lobby. I scanned the potted palms, the garlands and scrolls, and the arcaded balcony with its views to the ocean. The club welcomed ladies, and I nodded to a threesome of acquaintances who were departing. No Cassie in sight.

"Mrs. DeVere?" From behind, a young manager startled me, a sign of my nerves.

I turned. "Yes."

"Mrs. Forster expects to meet you at the teeing ground. The caddies are ready." He smiled and disappeared.

Golf, after all. What was she thinking? Or was she simply too upset to be sensible? In the ladies locker room I changed into the golfing clothes that I kept on hand for an occasional round, a loose blouse, Turkish trousers, and a belt, one of the few comfortable ladies' ensembles. Then golf hosiery, shoes, and the hat with its chin strap. The attendant offered to carry my clubs to the teeing ground, but I shouldered the load and went forth to meet my friend, who stood with two boys wearing matching knickers, jackets, neckties, and Eton caps—the caddies, Michael and Rory.

"Val, at last." Gloves on, Cassie held her driving wood. She wore a merino wrap skirt and cotton blouse. With her perfect "hour-glass" figure, her creamy complexion, her heart-shaped face and bright brown eyes, she was a portrait of delicate beauty. She could have been a Gibson Girl.

Today, a Gibson Girl in distress.

"I thought we would talk over tea," I said, and surrendered my bag to the eager Michael.

"This is better. We'll sit on the bench at the third hole and talk. Hardly anybody is out here."

She was right. Golf in Newport was often a morning game.

She nodded toward the Rory who teed up Cassie's "gutty," and she stepped up and attempted the stance that was drilled into the Newport ladies by the Scots golf tutor who had arrived from St. Andrews last year. Head down, shoulders natural on the back swing, wrists cocked, and Cassie's hickory shaft arced up and down. The iron clubhead met the gutta percha ball and sent it about twenty yards into the gorse shrubs. I took my own wood Brassie and addressed the next teed up "gutty," resolving to be a good sport, though my favorite game required a stringed racket, not a bagful of sticks.

Acquaintances called me "a natural," not really a compliment, though the game moved faster toward the crucial third hole today because my drives and putts were decent. The caddies had been warned not to keep score because Cassie's game took in the sand pits and the rough, and we needed no additional irritation. At last, we reached the third hole and its bench, making certain the caddies were far upwind, out of earshot.

"Tell me."

We were hip to hip on the slatted bench. "Georgina was poisoned."

I took her trembling hand in mine and started to ask, How do you know? but rephrased my question, "What makes you think so?"

Cassie's gloves were off, her perfect nails pearlescent. "Madame Riva told me."

"The manicurist." I might have guessed.

"Val, I thought we reached an understanding about Madame Riva."

"Your medium. Your spiritualist." I instantly regretted my harsh tone.

Séances to commune with the deceased had taken our country by storm. Even Old Cornelius Vanderbilt ("The Commodore") had hired a spiritualist to let him communicate with a dead business rival. According to reports, as he sat at a table, the medium had told him, "Jim Fisk is here," and Vanderbilt had asked Fisk's ghost for advice about the stock market—and got an answer!

That was nearly twenty-five years ago, but Ouija boards were now stocked in every Newport cottage and Fifth Avenue mansion, and trance mediums were much in demand. Roddy was a declared agnostic on the whole topic, but I will say this: the old Virginia City Washoe Club has become notorious for the ghosts of gun fight victims and gamblers who lost and vowed vengeance. Visitors say they hear cards being shuffled and smell gun powder.

Cassie's hand in mind felt like a little bird that was desperate to be calmed.

My effort on this bench was empathy for my friend—and persuasion. Cassie's terror that her Auntie had been murdered was apparently triggered by a flimflam *artiste* who made her morning rounds of the Newport cottages with nail files and creams and polishes. She bent over fingers and toes like an oracle by day, then doubled her fees by giving séances in the evening.

Cassie's voice was plaintive, desperate. "Remember her prophesy, Val?"

"I do." Last summer I, too, had once been manicured by Mme. Riva, who claimed Romanian royal ancestry and worked her emery boards and orange sticks with fingers flashing with fiery rings. She wore a turban, amulets and bead necklaces, a vivid peasant blouse and numerous skirts. With eyes half closed, she intoned, "You have work to do before you leave the earth. And you must rest, that you may be prepared to undertake it." One manicure by Mme. Riva was quite enough for me.

"Remember what she forecast for me last summer, Val? The 'spectres?'"

I did indeed, because Cassie decided that I, myself, Valentine Louise Mackle DeVere, was one such "spectre" prophesied by Mme. Riva. It was the very word that first sealed Cassie's and my friendship.

At the time, I was under the summer tutelage of one Mademoiselle Dureau who was hired (I insisted) to instruct me in the proper etiquette required for my new station in life. Roddy had qualms about her from the beginning. Her *"non!"*

was Napoleonic, and he begged me to oust "that French drill sergeant" from our home. "We can find you somebody nicer for this etiquette thing of yours, Val. Let's do."

Stubbornly, I stuck with Mlle. Dureau until the episode in a public tearoom, when a mistake with a spoon prompted a torrent of French censure. My eyes welled up, I admit, when a fashionable lady turned from the next table, faced the mademoiselle and loosed a slipstream of French in a low voice as commanding as it was eloquent. I didn't need to know the French language to understand that Mme. Dureau was scalded but good. The stranger then uttered *je le regret* and hastened us away before I could say thank you.

Not a week later, my thanks poured out in plainest English when, bicycling on Ocean Drive, I stopped to assist a woman who had taken a tumble when her back wheel blew a tire. We recognized one another at once and the newly wed Mrs. Roderick Windham DeVere, late of Virginia City, Nevada, was now formally acquainted with Cassandra Fox Forster, the lady with the hour-glass figure. We struck a chord.

Mme. Dureau was sent packing when Cassie promised henceforth to be my guide to Society's code of conduct. I became, in turn, a sister of sorts. Cassie told me later about her belief that I was among the "spectres" whom Madame Riva had insisted that she was destined to encounter. For my friend's sake—and my own—I would not be sorry if Mme. Riva took herself to Saratoga for the summer.

Cassie tightened her tremulous grip and quoted the full prophesy. "'Before you leave the Earth, you will see—"

"I know. 'Spectres.'"

"Yes, but there's more." She now imitated the manicurist's voice, more in reverence than well-deserved parody. "'You shall witness manifestations.'"

I reminded myself that Cassie's beloved childhood nanny, a Caribbean islander named Safira, had first led her into unseen worlds of spirits, ghosts, and prophetic premonitions. Cassie remembered oils and veils and a keening voice as Safira held her tight and rocked her into a trance-like sleep. She had loved the nanny, who was so warm and so unlike Cassie's ever-angry mother. When little Cassie began to see visions, however, the alarmed family sent Safira away, but her impact lingered in Cassie's life. My friend had learned to reveal her visions sparingly, lest she be thought demented. I sometimes wished to be spared one or another of Cassie's "views."

"Madame Riva's wording is very foggy, Cassie," I said, trying to be gentle. I reminded myself that my friend's parents were verging on a divorce and that her family home from childhood, however unhappy, was likely to crash like the Atlantic breakers we heard on this golf course by the ocean. Also, Cassie had two young children to oversee and a household largely under her command because her husband was away for months at a time. "It could be sailboats in the mist," I said, "or a steeplechase race here at the club. It could be anything."

"But yesterday morning Madam was quite specific, Val. She channeled the spirits." Cassie's head bent forward, and her temple touched mine...warm, even feverish. "Madam Riva said to me, 'A Borgia is amongst you.' I didn't understand her at first, Val. You know how she speaks in parables. She said, 'At the close of the first month beneath a shining waterfall, the deeds of a Borgia in this year of the Gregorian calendar.'"

That Riva woman and her calendars—the Caesarian, the Sumarian, the Babylonian. Never mind. I went for the Borgia reference. "Cassie, this is not Renaissance Italy. Lucrezia Borgia has not washed up on American shores."

She did not hear me. She could not. "Auntie was stricken on January thirty- first, the very date of Mrs. Astor's ball." Her voice was nearly strident.

At this moment I appreciated our solitude on this former site of a cow pasture known as Rocky Farm. If anyone in Society were to hear Cassandra Forster speak about her Auntie's death by poisoning in the same sentence as Mrs. Astor's hallowed annual ball, the echo chamber of gossip would be thunderous.

As new as I was to Society, that much was as clear as the water of Lake Tahoe in Nevada. My work was cut out for me. I must somehow free my friend from the hare-brained hokum instilled by the gypsy with the nail files.

"Cassie, let's consider... You're not quite yourself. So much on your mind...the recent turmoil... a person can only bear so much." Without further thought, I blurted,

"There's no such thing as a 'shining waterfall' in the city in January. Even Niagara Falls freezes up."

She didn't miss a beat. "Val, I've thought about it. Aunt Georgina collapsed at the ball during dinner...there were about forty small tables, and Auntie's was located under Mrs. Astor's crystal chandelier. Don't you see, a shining waterfall of crystal?"

I sighed. If not the chandelier, it would be the crystal goblets on the table. Or a lady's waterfall of diamonds. Or a glass salt cellar. Cassie's conviction defied logic.

Flummoxed, I paused. My friend's hand had become a tight fist. She was terrified. Completely at a loss for words, I was nonetheless resolved not to let her delusion stand unchallenged.

I was working up a suitable response when, suddenly, a piercing cry filled the air. The caddies were roused, arms waving as they jumped up, shouting.

Cassie and I both peered skyward just as two fat seagulls flew low over us and, so to speak, lightened their loads.

"Horrid!" "How terrible!"

"Disgusting!" The wet smear smelled like raw fish, but count on Cassie for the handkerchief plucked from a little pocket in her skirt. "Here, Val, let me help." She dabbed at my hat, her lap, both a mess. The caddies chased the birds in the distance and made animal growls to ward them off. Somehow, the scene struck us as comic. We both began to laugh, the contagious laughter that rolled deep and filled the chest and brought tears to the eyes. This was not the laughter of etiquette books, but full-throated gusts of hilarity.

"The gentlemen so fond of shooting pheasants and squab should bring their guns to the Country Club. Seagulls are always in season," Cassie said.

"A shotgun in the bag with the irons and woods.... 'Caddy, my twelve- gauge, if you please.'"

And we set off again until our ribs hurt. I was relieved that Madam Riva was out of mind for the moment but wished Cassie's beloved Dudley Forster were here with his wife and children.

The caddies had come back and apologized for the gulls. Cassie assured them no apology was necessary. Michael, the taller lad, suggested a falconer for the club. "Sure, ma'am, a hawk could be taking care no such bird would be bothering a body. If you or the gentlemen might be interested, I could be of service. My name is Keefe, Michael Keefe."

He made a little salute with his cap, nodded at Rory, and they reached for our bags, though the prospect of six more holes to play felt like drudgery. As it happened, fate intervened at that moment.

"Look, ma'am. Have a look." The second caddy, Rory, pointed at a distant figure hastening toward us, nearly at a run. "It's Mr. Swann, I do believe."

It was indeed. The butler of the Newport Country Club cut a comic figure on the links, the tails of his morning coat flapping in the breeze, his bald scalp shining in the sunlight as he trotted in our direction. Reaching us, he barely paused.

The man was winded, panting, his breath barely sufficient to speak. "Ladies... Mrs. DeVere, Mrs. Forster."

Cassie gestured to the bench. "Mister Swann, please do sit down."

"No, Madam, I have a message. The utmost importance... if you please..." He pulled an envelope from his vest pocket and handed it to Cassie, careful, I noticed, not to touch her hand. We all stood stock still, a tableau of the caddies, the butler, and myself as Cassie opened the envelope and read the message inside. In that instant, the friend who never forgot her manners nearly shrieked, "It's cousin Sylvia. She's in the city. She's ill. She's not expected to live."

Chapter Three

FOUR FLIGHTS UP, in a dark, one-room tenement apartment in the Lower East Side, Sylvia Brush lay face up on a tattered brocade divan. She was fully clothed in a russet linen daytime dress except for her bare feet. She did not stir when Cassie stepped close and cried softly, "Cousin Sylvia... Sylvia, it's Cassandra... Cassie." The blue eyes were open but milky, staring, fixed. Cassie took her hand, but the stiffness of the thin fingers told her it was too late.

"The lady is no longer with us," came a thunderous baritone voice that echoed off the walls. We had rushed up the stairs, guided by a young woman who apologized in frantic tones for the many steps, for the July heat, for the rank odors in the stairwell, the cramped living space—and the fact of Miss Sylvia Brush herself on the fourth floor of this dilapidated building. Evidently, the young woman was the apartment's tenant.

"No longer with us," once again boomed a portly man in heavy, rumpled tweeds who stepped forward as we crowded around the divan. He closed each eyelid of the deceased with a thick thumb before turning to face us, bowing slightly to Cassie and me and mopping his glistening face with a huge handkerchief that he crammed into his trousers pocket. Beside him on the floor lay a bulging portmanteau. As our eyes were adjusting to the dark, windowless room, he said, "You ladies must be family. I am Doctor Horace Hoffert."

Cassie drew herself up to her full height of five feet, five inches tall. For introductions. "—Mrs. Dudley Forster, Miss Brush's niece. And this is Mrs. Roderick DeVere." She did not extend her hand. Taking my cue, neither did I.

"And I am Annie Flowers. I sent the telegram about Miss Sylvia's illness."

For the moment, we had forgotten the young woman, who now spoke with certitude, as if to assert her very presence. Her dandelion yellow shirtwaist was the brightest object in sight, her skirt a dark muslin, and her well-worn street boots were clearly defeated by pavement struck long and hard. "Miss Sylvia was lightheaded," she said, "and I invited her to rest." She said no more. We all faced the divan in respectful quiet. Beneath the lightweight linen dress, Sylvia Brush's ribs were visible, her pelvis two knobs at the hipline. I recalled Cassie calling her reclusive cousin "bony."

"Perhaps a drapery to cover up....?" I broke off. Nothing in this room suggested an extra blanket or sheet. I unclasped my cloak and spread it over the deceased. It reached to the shins. We peered briefly at Sylvia Brush's naked feet, then turned away.

From Tuxedo Park to the Lower East Side, none of this made one bit of sense. When the fearsome news had arrived at the Newport club, we hastened to the city. Cassie hugged her little ones, promised toys from F. A. O. Schwarz, gave instructions to their nanny, and wired her parents to expect her at the St. Regis by evening, trusting that Rowena and Robert Fox would extend their flying trip to accommodate her.

Roddy traveled with us, a gentleman accompanying two ladies. Our haste from Newport by steamer and train and hansom cab from the terminal was a blur. Roddy stayed with us to the cabstand, paid the driver, and reluctantly (at my insistence) went off to register at the Waldorf and confer about a certain cocktail elsewhere in the city. Time enough for me to join him when Cassie and I had finished our—task. Yes, call it a task. Dispatched to porters, our light luggage awaited us at both hotels, and the hansom driver was stationed at the foot of this grimy building to convey us uptown to the St. Regis and Waldorf-Astoria, since ours, too, was to be a flying trip.

"You say she was lightheaded?" Cassie prompted Miss Flowers. "And so you welcomed Miss Brush to your…home." The word took effort. Our eyes had adjusted to a scene of barest necessity—a washstand with a pitcher, a coal oil lamp, a few wall pegs with a few sad items of female clothing dangling from them, and a pallet arrangement on the floor where Miss Flowers had obviously bedded down the past two nights. A cross was nailed to the wall, a Christian cross in Little Israel. I caught sight of an odd mechanical device propped in one corner, a sort of violin attached to piano keys and a crank. A large cardboard shingle leaned beside it.

"She was welcomed," Cassie said. "And then? What happened then?"

Miss Flowers pointed to a large tin cylinder by the divan. "An empty lard can," she said. "I borrowed it. I don't own a pail."

A moment passed. Cassie said, "So Miss Sylvia became ill. A pail was needed because she was ill."

"Sick," said Miss Flowers, "very sick. I tried to summon her own doctor. She gave me a name, but he couldn't come."

"He refused?"

"He was out of the city. Dr. Hoffert came instead. I sent the telegram when she got so sick."

"Thrice," said the physician. "I have tended—Miss Brush, is it?—three times over the past two days. I conclude that cardiac convolutions have proven fatal. Death was unavoidable."

Cassie tried to grasp his meaning, as did I. "Doctor Hoffert," she asked, "are you a medical doctor?"

"I practice electrical medicine."

We eyed the buckled portmanteau, no doubt packed with wires and batteries. So, Sylvia was lightheaded and nauseated, heaving over the lard pail, and for two days this man had been trying to shock her into a recovery. Annie Flowers's telegram had come too late.

At this news, I feared for Cassie. In case of faintness, ladies were encouraged to carry a tiny vial of smelling salts. I had forgotten mine but hoped my friend was supplied, though she looked more alert by the minute, no salts needed. She said, "We must arrange for an undertaker."

"Do permit me...." Hoffert slipped a card from his waist-coat as if waiting for this very moment: "R. S. Moreland, Undertaker, Livery, and Boarding Stables." Cassie returned the card in a flick of her fingers. "We prefer to make our own arrangements." Her voice was commanding as she turned to Miss Flowers and asked, "May I have the use of a telephone?" The request signaled her disordered thoughts. In this space, Mr. Bell's device was as improbable a convenience as Mr. Edison's lightbulbs or Mr. Otis's elevator. Without servants, we were two society ladies marooned in a Lower East Side slum with a quack doctor and the remains of Sylvia Ann Van Schylar Brush.

I stepped in and took charge, starting with Western Union. Miss Flowers would send the telegrams I dictated, and within an hour, Mr. Alfred Frear of Lanham & Frear, Undertakers, had arrived with his workers who efficiently descended the four flights of stairs with a wrapped burden that might have been mistaken for a rolled-up rug.

Hoffert signed the death certificate with a flourish as "Doctor." When he suggested the matter of fees, I reminded him that ladies did not carry cash money and therefore he must invoice Mr. Dudley Forster of New York City and Newport. I declined to take back my cloak.

As we stood on the threshold to leave, Annie Flowers approached us to request one favor, that she might keep Miss Brush's shoes. "As a keepsake."

Chapter Four

"KEEPSAKE, INDEED, RODDY. THEY'RE probably on her feet at this moment. If you'd seen her pitiful shoes... how she lives in that airless warren. The pushcarts jamming the street.... A tiny girl clawed at our cab to sell artificial violets, and boys played near the carcass of a dead horse. I shielded Cassie from the sight."

My husband and I were seated at one of the four occupied tables in the Waldorf Palm Court. The others were filled with businessmen, their explosive laughter ringing in this cavernous space. It was humid, and I unfolded my fan to cool us both.

Cassie was now at the St. Regis with her parents, and the Fox-Forster family planned to spend another day in the city to make funeral arrangements. The DeVeres—Roddy and I—would return to Newport in the morning but come back for the funeral in Trinity Church.

The Palm Court was a cool respite. "Hold the entrées, if you will," Roddy said to our waiter. "And Moet and Chandon for the lady—the year 1884, if you have it chilled." Roddy's tenor had the ease of authority. "For me, a Manhattan."

The waiter stiffened. "Mr. DeVere," he said, "our head bartender was taken ill. We waiters would like to help, but the proportions...your very own recipe, sir....the bartender keeps it to himself."

"Then, a light Irish whiskey and soda."

"Yes, sir."

The drinks arrived. We toasted and sipped. Roddy leaned close and spoke softly but sternly. "You ladies must never go there again, not ever again. I should have gone with you. Promise me, Val. That useless snake oil doctor, and who knows what killed Sylvia Brush. A woman as thin as you say—"

"Rail thin."

"It might have been consumption. She might have died from a contagion that overtook her in hours. You and Cassandra have put yourselves at risk." My husband sipped his whiskey, savoring the taste. "Between Sylvia's home in Tuxedo Park and the city's Lower East Side," he said, what possible connection? Miss Flowers, Val...is she one of the city's new 'working girls?'"

"Doubtful, Roddy. I can't see Annie Flowers behind a counter at Macy's or Lord and Taylor or A. T. Stewart. She's not stylish like department store clerks." I added, "For that matter, I can't see her taking dictation as an office stenographer. Nor kneeling to scrub a floor nor standing at a sink peeling a family's potatoes. She's evidently as poor as a church mouse, but somewhat of a puzzle."

"You're certain that she did not work for Sylvia? As an employee?"

"I don't think so. Cassie asked her. 'Your acquaintance with Miss Brush,' she asked, 'has it been a relation of employment?'"

"And she said—?"

"At first, she was evasive. She said, 'Miss Brush and I both have employed energies for greater good.'"

"What greater good?"

The news I was about to disclose was fundamentally as mysterious to me as it would be to my husband. "Roddy, we learned a good deal about Sylvia's recent activities in the hour while we waited for the undertaker, Mr. Frear. Annie Flowers told us that in recent months, Sylvia was often busy in the city."

Roddy sipped his whiskey. "Go on."

"Theo's rumors about Sylvia, evidently, are true. She often came in from Tuxedo Park to meet with...." I paused. "Are you familiar with a musical instrument that looks like a stunted piano keyboard attached to a violin?"

"You mean a hurdy-gurdy?"

"So, you do know."

He smiled, squeezing my hand. "Men crank them on the street in front of cigar stores and barbershops. They bring along little chained monkeys that are taught to beg for coins. It's a tin cup enterprise."

"Only men play them?" I asked. Roddy nodded.

"Yes. The hurdy-gurdy man is a fixture in every city from Boston to Washington, D.C. Why do you ask?" In the silence that followed, Roddy's brow furrowed, as it did when he scanned clouds for the weather. I sipped my champagne and enjoyed my husband's handsome face.

"Roddy, Sylvia Brush has been turning the crank."

His jaw dropped. "A hurdy-gurdy?" I nodded. "In the Lower East Side?"

I shook my head. "Uptown. At the park."

"Our park? Central Park? You're sure?"

"But not for coins."

"Then what—?"

"For attention. She and Miss Flowers go together, especially on Sunday afternoons."

"The workers' holiday? When it's crowded with laborers?" Roddy sounded impatient and incredulous too.

"Yes." I pushed on. "She and Miss Flowers are partners. One of them cranks while the other holds the sign."

"What sign?"

"A large cardboard placard. I saw it in the room while... while we tended to our task. I managed to read the words."

"Like advertising?"

"Not exactly."

Now he was impatient. "And the cardboard sign says—?"

"The sign says, '**THE HURDY-GURDY IN NEW YORK MAKES PEOPLE THINK _SUFFRAGE_, SO WE PLAY THE HURDY-GURDY!**'"

He sipped his drink and said slowly, "So, Sylvia Brush, the heiress to the Brush fortune, has cranked a hurdy-gurdy... to promote votes-for-women?"

"A suffragist."

"Out in the public street in plain view...with a sign!" Roddy gripped his whiskey glass. The ice rattled, and he laughed. The waiter asked whether we wished to proceed with dinner. Roddy declined another whiskey, but I welcomed a second champagne.

Roddy said, "The papers call Sunday afternoons in Central Park one giant labor-union picnic. Frankly, I doubt that laboring men or the women who earn a living by wiring feathers on ladies' hats will fight for women at the ballet box. Wages, yes, and labor unions too, but women voting... Val, you have to agree it's far-fetched. Besides, the political powers-that-be are nowhere near the park on summer afternoons."

I might agree, except for one final point of information. "Roddy, Miss Flowers says that the summer Sundays at the park with Sylvia Brush have only been rehearsals."

"For what? hurdy-gurdy vaudeville?"

"For the coming seasons." I paused to enjoy the bubbly wine as if to ready myself for my next words. "They plan to march up Fifth Avenue. And they plan suffrage demonstrations at other events," I said. "Like the Coaching Club parade next May."

It took my husband a moment to absorb this point before his face registered astonishment. "The first Saturday in May? The New York Coaching Club? The annual meet?"

I nodded. Joseph Pulitzer's *World* put it bluntly nearly twenty years ago, and his words rang true today: "This is the aristocracy of Central Park." To me, the event was silly, though Roddy loved the yearly festivity, riding high atop a coach drawn by four spanking black horses (and so handsome in his gray top hat and a green coat with a boutonniere). In my youth in Colorado and Nevada, the stagecoaches were serious business, with teams of draft horses pulling freight and passengers over roads often rutted or washed out in flashfloods or blocked from rockslides. The driver in his buckskin—the "brother whip"—looked larger-than-life to my youthful eye. The privileged passengers traveling by stagecoach always sat inside, while those on top were dismissed as "hangers-on."

In Central Park in May, Mrs. Roderick DeVere, like the other ladies in Society, wore a crisp summer gown, the straw "leghorn" hat pinned tightly to my head. Even the horses wore rosettes behind their ears as we circled the park all afternoon before dining at the Brunswick Hotel on Twenty-sixth Street. Roddy was in discussion about a special cocktail before next year's dinner, and I planned to urge that ladies be included.

Roddy faced me and spoke slowly as if reciting a new lesson. "To be clear," he said, "this person, Miss Flowers, recruited Sylvia Brush to join the suffrage cabal—"

"Women, Roddy, not a cabal. And I'm not sure the word 'recruited' is quite right."

He did not hesitate. "Women who are crusading to change the law." I waited for him to continue. Roddy had studied law, as gentlemen of Society were expected to do, and he tended to summarize a given situation as a "case," to point out the gaps in an argument and chinks in the logic.

"So, to be clear...," he began, "a campaign to change the Constitution of the United States would supposedly gain momentum next May as the members of the New York Coaching Club enjoy themselves during their annual procession in the Park." He paused, to be certain of my attention. "Hearing the hurdy-gurdy, we would all look down from the top of our coaches, read the sign in passing, and immediately become persuaded to secure votes for women." Roddy mimicked dusting his palms. "Just like that."

"Of course not, Roddy. It's a long campaign." But my back was up now. "The suffrage women," I added, "might be the new pioneers, pioneering women in the city. It's considered a sisterhood."

He leaned close. "Val, it is likely that you ladies will get your vote at some point in the twentieth century. If so, you will have the opportunity to make the same confounding errors that have nearly wrecked the Republic in our lifetimes." He looked into my eyes and held his gaze. "Meanwhile, in our circle, your close friend Cassandra is once again made distraught by a death in the family, a death occurring in a very strange place, involving a Miss Emily Flowers."

"Annie."

"Annie. If the woman is nearly destitute, as you believe, how did she acquire a hurdy-gurdy? How did she become acquainted with Sylvia Brush, and how did the heiress of the Brush fortune get involved? And why? As for Sylvia Van Schylar Brush..." He fell silent as waiters come toward us with silver-domed dishes, and I realized how very hungry I was, until Roddy added, "As for Miss Brush, let us also ask what, exactly, has led her death. Why did she die? What caused her death? Who might have information about events leading to the death of an heiress whose mother so suddenly collapsed and died just months ago?"

Chapter Five

DUTIFULLY, ON CUE, SOCIETY instructed the maids and valets to bring out the ladies' and gentlemen's blackest dull silks and wools for the funeral of Sylvia Ann Van Schylar Brush. The black-edged invitations were delivered by private messengers who scurried along Bellevue Avenue like court clerks with summonses, while the telegraph key in the Western Union office tapped staccato commands to the distant resorts:

Yourself and Family are invited to attend the funeral of
Miss Sylvia Ann Van Schylar Brush
From Trinity Church, Wall Street and Broadway
To proceed to Forestlawn Cemetery.

The phrase, "from Trinity Church," signaled that Sylvia's funeral service would not take place at her home, sparing everyone the trek up the Hudson Valley to Tuxedo Park. Sylvia's housekeeper, however, was instructed by telegram to hang a crepe streamer on the front doorknob of the cottage to signal a death in the household. The door badges, as they are called, alert visitors that the household is in mourning and the family ought to be left in peace while arrangements are underway. Sylvia's housekeeper, Maude Gowdy, was also ordered to take care that all furnishings and papers remain exactly in place as they were when her mistress was last in the cottage. The badge now had a function beyond funeral etiquette. It would deter anyone who might innocently disrupt a scene that held information about Sylvia Brush's death.

Newport's lovely colonial-era Trinity Church was far more convenient for funeral guests, but Lanham & Frear strongly advised that the ceremony proceed with all deliberate speed in the city, considering the July heat. Rowena and Robert, Cassie's parents, needed no persuasion.

Sam Brush, however, had questions. He hastened to the city by himself to help with plans. Always on the side of modern machine progress, Sam asked why it was not possible to transport the remains of Miss Brush to Newport and the cemetery mainly by rail, since Mr. Swift and Mr. Armour proved that fresh beef could be shipped across the country in refrigerated cars. He offered to underwrite the costs of such a car. Mr. Frear was tactful but persuasive, pointing out that railroad box cars were not equipped to accommodate the witness who must, by law, accompany the body. The new patented cooling coffins were remarkable, he said, but the circumstances in this case called for expeditious dignity. Sam agreed.

All this was reported to me by Cassie in a short conversation while the town made its preparations for the city. Roddy's ominous questions at our Palm Court dinner still lingered. What, exactly, killed Sylvia Brush? What stopped her heart?

The so-called doctor, Hoffert, certified "cardiac convolutions," but what did that mean? Sylvia's light-headedness and day-and-night retching were not normally preludes to a heart attack. Did she exhibit other symptoms, perhaps a rash or lesions that were concealed by her clothing. Was she fevered? Did a deadly germ attack her underweight body?

Roddy agreed that Sylvia's housekeeper might be helpful. That's "Maude Gowdy," I said. "I persuaded Cassie to insist that nothing in the cottage be disturbed."

"Good idea. And also, the family ought to schedule a talk with Frear, the undertaker."

"Roddy, it's a funeral, not an autopsy."

My husband stayed patient. "An undertaker, Val, is like a doctor in certain respects, something like a coroner. Cassie's family ought to ask whether Herbert Frear detected something out of the ordinary when he prepared for the funeral. Sam could ask. He's always interested in mechanics. The heart is a pump. Sam Brush is just the man to talk to Frear. Didn't he put the death notice in the papers?"

He did. Sam placed the announcement of Sylvia's death in the newspapers with the obligatory information. She had died on July 18 following a brief illness, and her funeral would take place on July 21 at Trinity Church, a "simple service for relatives and intimate friends of the family," after which her body would be taken to Forestlawn Cemetery, Bronx, New York. Wisely, Sam omitted all else about Sylvia's demise, and we hoped the newspapers would not get wind of the recent doings of the rich Tuxedo Park recluse. The less in print, the better for a quiet inquiry into the background of the heiress's death.

Questions multiplied, but they went unspoken in the maelstrom of funeral arrangements. Cassie declined to expose her four- and six-year-old children, Bea and Charlie, to what Charlie called "Cousin Sylvia's Funner roll." With no notion of "Aunt Sylvia" in life, the children were asked to kneel for a moment of prayer, to hope that "Cousin Sylvia" was now in heaven, as was Cleo, a recently expired goldfish.

The collective migration to the city was undertaken grudgingly. Theo Bulkeley relayed overheard waspish comments when he imitated voices I recognized from parties and balls. I promised not to tell Cassie when Theo quoted: "Such a nuisance in the belly of the summer," "never laid eyes on the woman," "d—d rotten time to kick the bucket," "sacrifice a full day at the bridge table," "six feet under from the day she was born." These "gems," Theo reported, were heard from the country club to The Reading Room to the Casino, the recreational center devoted to my favorite game, tennis.

"Of course, everyone is annoyed, Val," Theo said. "It's another brush with the Brush bunch. It's wearisome, and just months since we all filed into Trinity for Georgina—and only days after Mrs. Astor's ball. The ladies hadn't finished locking up their jewels or sniping about which crème de la crème guests were chosen to join Caroline Astor on her throne."

I smiled. Mrs. Astor presided over her annual ball from an elevated sofa that is strikingly like a throne. I tried tactfully to ask whether Theo had heard rumors about Sylvia's health in recent weeks.

His smile was sly. "You mean, did she exhaust herself making up for lost time, looking for fun in the metropolis? The Nickelodeon? Coney Island?"

"I'm serious, Theo." I tried to prod his memory, but he knew nothing of the details of Sylvia's death, the Lower East Side, the tenement, or Annie Flowers. "I mean, have you heard anything new?"

His mood was antic. "Heiress as thrill seeker? Macy's soda fountain too tame, so she goes finds opium den in Chinatown and expires in vaporous rapture." He saw that I might possibly take this seriously. "Just joking, Val. I hear the woman nearly starved herself to death. She's nowhere near as interesting as her mother. Georgina was a hoot."

I remained silent about the day-and-night retching that led to Sylvia's death. "In case you happen to hear something, Theo, feel free to pass it on." He winked a "yes." As we parted, he turned to ask, "Did she have a will?"

"I... I don't know." The question stopped me. So logical, so obvious, and yet nowhere in mind. The horrors of the death, my friend's well-being, my talk with Roddy about the Suffrage business—it was all so much. The thought of Sylvia Brush's last will and testament had not entered my mind.

Or Cassie's?

Or her family's?

Of course, the question of the Brush fortune would be everyone's mind by the time we gathered for the funeral. Like all of Newport, Theo would attend.

Whatever the grab bag of private feelings, the Van Schylar lineage and the Brush fortune demanded attendance at Sylvia's funeral.

New York City's Trinity Church was amazingly convenient to Newport. A number of steam yachts would sail from the Newport Harbor to anchorages in lower Manhattan, which was quite near both to Wall Street and the church in which Sylvia would be commemorated. A motor launch would ferry Roddy, me, and numerous guests to the city on Mr. Howard Gould's *Niagara*, the new steam yacht we boarded in Newport. The *Niagara*, Mr. Gould boasted, features twin screw propellers that might make its sails obsolete.

Underway from a predawn hour, we were a study in contrasts, the passengers dutifully head-to-toe in black, and the captain and crew in gleaming whites. The stewards served coffee and champagne, but spirits rose in pleasure that Roderick DeVere had agreed to preside over a French punch involving wine, sugar, and lemons which he oversaw in sufficient quantities for the *Niagara* party:

WINE A LA FRANCAISE   Vin á la Française

Put eight oz. of sugar into a salad-bowl, and sprinkle on a few tablespoons of water; that it may dissolve. Add one bottle of excellent Bordeaux wine or red Burgundy, and the half of a lemon cut into thin slices. Stir well with a silver spoon and serve with a slice of lemon in each glass.

We stirred and sipped, braced for the somber ritual ahead. All references to last winter's funeral for Georgina Brush and the coincidental, all-too-soon funeral for her daughter were avoided as companions from dinners and balls clustered on the decks. The Dovedales were aboard, and Colonel and Mrs. Twist and the Townsends (Mary and Frederick). Cassie and the Van Schylar contingent were already in the city.

I welcomed the opportunity to eavesdrop on conversations that might offer insight about Sylvia, but the chit-chat veered to the colonel's regret that Ed Glendorick fired up his own steam yacht, *Viking*, instead of sailing with us so he could strong-arm guests about the U.S. keeping Cuba now that the war was over. Fred Townsend chimed in to say that Glendorick's newest yacht, currently under construction in a Belfast shipyard, would soon surpass anything currently afloat.

Mary Townsend hoped guests on the new vessel would not be subjected to well-done roast beef.

Amid the light chit-chat, the croquet devotée, Mr. Archibald Romberg, sought out a Newport widow, Henrietta Deems, and tried without success to be enchanting. Newly out of mourning herself, Henrietta rebuffed "Beau Brummel" Romberg's attentions, and he soon stopped at the bar for another glass of Roddy's punch. The various children enjoyed lemonade, as did the nannies. The water was calm. No one felt ill.

The sunny morning turned overcast by 9:45 a.m., when Roddy took my arm to enter Trinity Church for the service. We nodded to Mr. Frear, who stood guard, so to speak, at the rich bronze doors at the entrance and would supervise the cortege of carriages lining up at the curb for the journey to the cemetery. The coachmen wore black broadcloth livery with coats and vests buttoned up to the neck. No matter what time of year, custom dictated linen shirts, black silk ties, and top hats.

A half dozen policemen patrolled the sidewalk in dark blue uniforms with bright brass buttons and domed helmets, ready to disperse gawkers with batons if necessary. In the vestibule, Roddy signed the funeral visitors' book for both of us, and Mr. and Ms. Roderick Windham DeVere were ushered down the aisle of polished parquet woods.

Trinity was beautiful. The clerestory light bathed the sanctuary in a soft glow, and the stained glass above the altar was a visual feast. The vaulted beams criss-crossed as in a medieval cathedral, and every chord of Bach's chorales lifted the spirit and hushed voices. Roddy and I took our seats in a Van Schylar pew at the invitation of Cassie's parents and Sam Brush, who appeared distressed as he escorted his lovely wife, Evalina, into the pew, a southern beauty who now attended a memorial for someone who declined to attend her wedding.

We strained for breath in the floral hothouse of roses, asters, orange birds of paradise, creamy calla lilies, dahlias, and others on wire stands, in vases, on pedestals leading to the casket we would file past in due course.

The church filled. Cassie's parents, Robert and Rowena Fox, hid annoyance at the presence of one another. They sat without touching, the father slightly slouched and the mother, Rowena, ramrod straight with a gaze to match. Robert Fox's ginger moustache twitched, and Rowena repeatedly fingered a strand of hair that escaped its jeweled pin. Nearby were several Van Schylars who had come from Bar Harbor, Maine, as well as Newport. Some younger adults could be Cassie's distant cousins. They nodded to three elderly Van Schylar ladies who were ushered slowly to a pew.

An acolyte lighted the candles, the organ softened to a close, and the service began with "Dearest Lord..." from Episcopal Bishop Henry C. Potter. As prizefighters might say, Bishop Potter was a heavyweight. He had presided at Georgina's funeral in this church last January. A frequent dinner guest in Society, the Bishop asked many blessings in tones that rolled from the heavens to the mountains and valleys. His very presence at the altar signaled a Christian ritual that was infused by serious wealth, a reminder that this funeral was to be followed by questions of inheritance.

I glanced about. Certain individuals represented entire families. John Jacob Astor for his mother, Caroline Astor (the Mrs. Astor) and the entire Astor family, just as Mr. C. Winthrop stood in for the Winthrops and individuals represented the Chanlers , the Cuttings, the Webbs, and others. Sprinkled among the mourners, however, were individuals I could not identify, apart from servants of the Van Schylar and Brush households, the familiar butlers, footmen, maids, and coachmen.

About others, questions rose. Newcomers had entered Sylvia's orbit in the past months, but who were they, and what was their connection to her? I recalled none of them from Georgina's funeral. Who was the clean-shaven man in the tan corduroy suit who appeared to be chewing gum while rolling the brim of his bowler hat in both hands? His cheeks look reddened by the sun, or by a saloon? Seated in a far right pew, he appeared to be alone.

At the far left was a more striking figure, a man we called a "dandy." His vest was a black-on-black basket weave, his cravat a shiny black satin—or sateen. His coat reminded me of lithographs of riverboat gamblers. Diamond rings on his fingers flashed when he reached for *The Book of Common Prayer*. Whatever his connection to Sylvia Brush, I could not imagine. He too was alone.

Two women who marched down the center aisle in lockstep were easier to identify. They must be suffragists, both wearing blazer-style suits of black serge with straw hats barely trimmed but new. Unlike Annie Flowers, neither appeared to be poor. Were they acquainted with her? If she was here, I had not seen her.

One more figure caught my attention, a man whose posture and facial expression reminded me of the captain of the *Niagara* on our journey this morning. He looked vigilant, as if scanning a horizon to scope out bad weather. I guessed his age to be nearly forty, though his trim dark moustache and beard showed no graying. Wearing a close-fitting dark blue coat and tightly knotted neck scarf, he seemed like a uniformed military officer. I pictured gold braid around his coat cuffs and epaulettes on his shoulders. He turned in my direction, his eyes a stone-cold, chilling stare that caught me unaware. I looked away but felt his eyes upon me.

The service moved from the prayers to the commemoration of Sylvia Brush's life. "'A time to be born and a time to die,'" resounded from Bishop Potter, who slightly lowered his head. "...and we mourn Sylvia Ann Van Schylar Brush...."

I lost track of the message until the bishop proclaimed that "God has bestowed upon us certain powers and gifts which wealth puts into operation." Some of us surely remembered the same line spoken at Georgina's funeral. "God's own instruments... Christians of wealth...." Bishop Potter was now in double *forte*. "God has need of rich Christians to do His work on earth, and we know in our hearts that He doth make them. And so Sylvia Ann...."

Rowena Fox pushed back her hair, and her husband's moustache continued to twitch. Cassie was not in sight, nor Theo. I looked again at the strange guests— the dandy whose diamond ringed fingers were now tightly laced, and the gum- chewer whose jaws had stopped still. The suffragists' hats, side by side, were immobile. The naval captain, as I imagined him, continued to scan the horizon for storms. Having seen the death notice in every newspaper, were these people paying respects? Not one struck me as a summer resident of the resorts frequented by the Van Schylars, nor the Brush family.

Who were they? Why were they here?

Bishop Potter sat down, and Sam Brush came forward to offer the obligatory personal reminiscence on the character of the deceased. Last January, he paid heartfelt tribute to his sister-in-law, Georgina, and his affection and good humor were underscored in every sentence. But Sylvia? How daunting the task. How personal could he possibly be, since she shunned social gatherings, including his wedding?

At the pulpit, Sam struck notes of kindness. "...a lady who knew that life is best lived in earthly places that uphold the spirit...the stone walls of Tuxedo...the spiritual value of solitude...."

The bishop rose for prayer, a hymn was sung, the service concluded, and we all filed past the casket. The emaciated figure on the tattered divan in the Lower East Side bore no relation to the figure basking in the deep red velvet plush at the transept of Trinity Church. In death, Sylvia Brush looked ready to awake from a nap, thanks to the magic of Lanham & Frear. Her face and figure appeared ready for a leisurely day on a terrace or in a drawing room. She had been dressed in a pale blue summer silk suit I recognized from Rowena's wardrobe. We filed along at a respectful but efficient pace as the organ played a recessional.

What happened next was shocking but, in hindsight, perhaps predictable. This age of celebrity and vast wealth stirred the public into frenzy in our cities. People roused, and mobs swarmed. Outside Trinity Church on this July 21, 1898, a ruckus erupted that became a major topic of conversation for months.

Mr. Frear of Lanham & Frear, Undertakers, could not be held responsible. The firm met its obligations according to the best practices of our time. By now, a Lanham & Frear hearse signaled a funeral of distinction. The signature weeping willow pictured on the side of the jet black hearse was now a trademark of loss and bereavement among the rich. Lanham & Frear guaranteed a signature hearse that was pulled by teams of ebony black horses, perfectly matched, the brass fittings on the harness burnished like gold.

Not to get ahead of events, but Society could not confine itself solely to its gated mansions, so police kept the crowds in check at the entrances of homes, concert halls, and Episcopal churches at which, with few exceptions, the Four Hundred worshipped. On this late Thursday morning, the sight of a Lanham & Frear hearse and a series of black coaches along the curb began to attract bystanders. The crowd, however, grew enormously at the sight of eight black ostrich feather plumes that waved atop the hearse roof. The New York funeral customs required these plumes, which were unknown to me in the West. While two plumes might signify a deceased person of modest means, the maximum of eight, like herald trumpet fanfares, proclaimed that the deceased was a person of the greatest wealth. An eight-plume funeral was a crowd's siren song.

In minutes, it was obvious that Mr. Frear had under-estimated the number of police needed for a dignified conclusion to Sylvia Brush's funeral. Last winter, whole squadrons of officers managed the crowds at Georgina's funeral. It snowed, and we bundled up in furs and muffs. Cassie's husband, Dudley, was at home, a great comfort at the time. Outside the church, the crowds gathered despite the cold because Georgina Van Schylar Brush was news-worthy, both because she died at Mrs. Astor's ball and was a "character" in Society, but also because "Brush" was a name nearly as famous as Carnegie or Rockefeller. Or Astor. Even though Sylvia never made headlines for fashion or for hosting a legendary party, she was automatically notable as a Brush. The fact was known to Mr. Frear, but he misjudged.

As Roddy and I neared the church doors to be led to a cortege coach that would go to the cemetery, we were pushed by an oncoming human tide. Grim-jawed women and a few hard-eyed men surged down the aisles to lunge for souvenir flowers on stands, in vases. Dignity gave way to a scuffle for mementoes, a tug-of-war for wreaths and standing sprays. Bouquets were shredded, and petals fell to the floor to be smeared underfoot. Nannies shielded bewildered children while shepherding them to the door. Gentlemen took firm hold of ladies' arms, moving sideways to the open door but knocked by strangers' shoulders and stepped on by high-heeled boots. The aromas of incense and fragrances gave way to the sourness of unwashed bodies and foul breath at close range. I looked up to see a familiar garment, a cloak similar to one of mine.

It was mine—the cloak that draped Sylvia's body in the apartment, the cloak I left behind. It was draping a familiar figure, Annie Flowers. She held a single yellow rose, and she disappeared before I could catch up to her. In minutes, Roddy and I were seated in our assigned coach in the cortege. Moving up Broadway, we peered out at bystanders who paused to gawk. Men doffed their hats in respect, and a mounted police escort kept order. We all looked forward to returning to Newport, but in these next long, hot, tedious hours riding to the Forestlawn Cemetery, my thoughts circled around two funerals and two deaths, both from "causes" that appeared to be related to the heart. The question remained unanswered: what killed Sylvia Brush? A second question began to hover as well. What, exactly, had killed her mother almost six months ago to the very day?

Chapter Six

IT WAS STIFLING HOT on our return from Forestlawn. Clothing stuck to our skin, and fans were useless. The graveside service had been mercifully short. My husband had served as an honorary pallbearer while I stood by Cassie for support.

Roddy lowered the roll-down leather curtains of the coach for a hint of breeze as we entered the city. Immediately we were assaulted by thick, fetid air and the cries of newsboys on every corner. Peering out of the coach, we could read the huge headlines: "BRUSH HEIRESS DEAD AT FORTY!" "SUDDEN DEATH OF AN HEIRESS" .... "CASUALTY OF BRUSH FORTUNE." "Read all about it!" A few of the cheekiest boys approached our coach, calling. "Get your *Journal*... your *World*... your *Herald*.... Two cents...." We refused for the sake of propriety, but make no mistake, we were tempted. Boarding the motor runabout to ferry us to the *Niagara*, we felt we had run a gauntlet.

The New York papers were at our cottage by the next morning, and I ordered the dog-cart and a fast pony and drove the two miles along Ocean Drive from our cottage, Drumcliffe, to the Forsters' Seabright, quickly turning over the reins to O'Boyle at the entrance. It was not yet ten-thirty.

Cassie's butler, Hayes, met me at the door and offered to carry my package. I thanked him but toted the parcel to the breakfast room myself. Out West, we could enter a room and get to the point, but here decorum ruled.

"Mrs. DeVere to see you, ma'am."

"Thank you, Hayes. Please advise any callers that I am not at home today. Mrs. DeVere and I will be here in the breakfast room until further notice." A portly figure in a morning coat, Hayes bowed and withdrew. A uniformed footman was removing plates from the breakfast table, the butter, the marmalade, the toast that all looked untouched at Cassie's plate. Also, the emptied porridge bowls and cups from the children's places.

"We will have tea," Cassie said to the footman. "Do sit here at the table, Val. The children are going to the beach. They want to tell you themselves." Wearing a crème colored morning sacque, Cassie looked as sleepless as I felt. What a matched pair we were this morning. Roddy feared I was too fatigued to control the pony, but I insisted on donning a casual white duck suit and taking the reins. I sat on a needlepoint cushioned chair and put my bundle on the seat beside me.

Cara, the children's nanny, appeared with Bea and Charlie for their outing. To her credit, Cassie allowed her children to be kids, as we called them in the West, insisting that her children's arms and legs move freely. Today, Charlie wore a navy sailor suit, and his sister, Bea, a skirt with blue jacket embroidered at the hemline.

"Say 'Good morning' to Auntie Val."

They chorused, "Good morning," then burst to tell the day's adventures. "Auntie Val, we are going to the beach!"

"—into the water!"

"And Carstairs is bringing us lunch!"

I recognized the footman's name. "What will you have to eat?"

"A pic-nic," said little Bea. "And a sand castle,"

"Crabs!" her brother proclaimed. "I trap crabs in a bucket." Charlie's face became very serious, his pronunciation careful and slow. "Daddy says they are *callinectes sapidus.* From the Greek, he says. It means beautiful swimmer...and tasty. It also means tasty."

Bea made a face and a noise. "Now, Beatrice!" said Cassie.

"Children, shall we go?" Cara reached for their hands. "O'Boyle has hitched Lucky to the cariole. And the children will change at the bathhouse, ma'am."

"And Carstairs will deliver lunch at noon. Say good-bye to Auntie Val, children." So they did, and off they went. Cassie's children sometimes filled my mind with thoughts

of a possible family of my own—but not today. I reached
for the bundle beside me.

Cassie needed a moment. "Val, just a word before...
before we step into the mud. Whatever dirty gossip comes
from the city, you and I both know that Newport has its
own... its own swill."

"You mean *Town Topics*."

She shuddered. "I do."

She was one hundred percent right. *Town Topics* was
the scandal sheet that Society both deplored and devoured.
Every Newport family dreaded finding its own name among
the rumored scandals. It was *Town Topics* that informed
Cassie's mother, Rowena (and all of Newport) of her husband's dalliances with a dancers at a restaurant called
Murray's Roman Gardens.

"Another attack on our family... Val, how can I bear it?"

"Cassie, consider the adage, 'No way to it, but through
it.'" I reached beside me for the bundle and spread the contents on the table. Every New York newspaper was before
us. "Here we go."

In minutes we scanned the two warring papers, Joseph
Pulitzer's *New York World* and William Randolph Hearst's
Journal, both notorious for flashy prose that raised pulses
and bedazzled the public. Facts might be sprinkled in, but
fiction sold papers.

I held up the front page of the *World* to show Cassie
a photograph. "When last did you see Sylvia?" I asked. "I
mean, when she was alive?"

"I asked myself that question all yesterday at the funeral."

"The caption says 'Sylvia Van Schylar Brush.'" From head to bosom, the woman in the photograph was resplendent in jewels—diamonds at her ears and a multi-strand pearl necklace nearly concealing all flesh at the neck. I counted eight strands. "Is this Sylvia?"

"I don't know. Look at this one." Cassie lifted the first page of the *Journal* to show a charcoal pencil portrait in profile. The woman's hair was upswept, her cheekbone prominent, her nose sharp, and a suggestion of weakness at the jawline. "Is this the same woman?"

"I...I don't think so."

"Which one is Sylvia?"

"Suppose... suppose neither...." The moment was quiet as we absorbed this possibility. Page one of the *World*, I noticed, also featured a photograph of the war hero Admiral George Dewey. Countless pictures of him had been published since the Battle of Manila and the victory last spring. With his perfectly groomed brushy white moustache, he always looked the same, a dignified military officer. A huge celebration was planned to honor him next year in the city. "Here's Admiral Dewey," I said. "He looks like...like Admiral Dewey."

"And here's Colonel Roosevelt in the *Journal*," said Cassie. "He's with the Rough Riders in Cuba, the colonel wearing spectacles and a cavalry hat."

"And that droopy moustache." We chuckled, then focused again on the newspaper portraits of Sylvia—the alleged Sylvia. Cassie remembered that, years ago, she might have seen her cousin dressed to attend a debutante ball at Delmonico's. "I was about four, perhaps five years old. I remember a spotted tulle gown trimmed with feathers." She shook her head. "Val, the gown is more memorable than the young woman."

We concluded only one point: that neither of the newspaper pictures bore any resemblance to the deceased woman in the Lower East Side tenement apartment. Nor did either one resemble the figure in the casket at Trinity Church. So, we took deep breaths and read what the reporters for Messrs. Hearst and Pulitzer had fed to the public.

"'Body of Heiress Found in Bowery.'"

"The Bowery? Not the Lower East Side?"

Cassie shook her head no and read on. "The *World* says, 'naked to the waist, the body of Brush wood heiress…. found in a gutter…. bullet-riddled….'"

"Bullets?"

"'Victim of outrage!!!'"

"What sort of 'outrage?'" I asked.

Cassie leaned forward and whispered, "A violation of the most intimate kind."

"Oh!" I cringed and read from the *Journal*: "'stalked by killer …. strangled…. clothing ripped asunder… police in search….' Cassie, this is total fiction."

"Agreed. Do you see any mention of Annie Flowers?"

"No."

"The Lower East Side?"

"No... wait, here's a sidebar." I read aloud, "'The beloved Sylvia, from childhood a virtual orphan in the Brush mansion... lonely, friendless... a solitary child on the beaches of Newport, a tragic figure amidst the palatial riches of the Wood King... her life destined for tragedy.'"

Cassie asked, "Who said that?"

I held up the paper to show the headline and flashy layout: "CLOSE BRUSH FAMILY ASSOCIATE SPEAKS OUT."

"What 'close associate?'"

I read further. "Someone named... Riviana Slovyak."

We quieted as the maid appeared with tea service—linen napkins, sterling spoons in the intricate Forster pattern, teapot, strainer, cups, saucers, a honey pot, and lemon halves tied in net bags, to strain out seeds. The maid disappeared.

At last I repeated, "Riviana Slovyak. I believe that is—"

"Madame Riva. Oh, no!"

My friend's mood—raging high dudgeon—may it continue. Cassie poured us tea, her hand trembling. My guess was this: Mme. Riva was finished at Newport. No more nails or séances for her.

But I was wrong. Yes, Cassie was upset that the manicurist had spoken to reporters. She was more disturbed, however, to think that Mme. Riva had foretold Sylvia's death.

"'Destined for tragedy,'" she repeated. "Oh, Val, just to think—"

I sipped my tea...way too hot. "Cassie, anyone's life that is cut short can be labeled 'destined for tragedy.' My Mama died in her twenties. She got diphtheria. Papa did everything he could. She never recovered." My cup rattled in the saucer. "She got sick and died. No 'destiny' was involved."

We faced one another across a gulf of misery and misunderstanding, but bonded in mutual pain. We clasped hands. I felt my friend's pulse and believe she felt mine. We silently asked ourselves and one another, Where do we go from here?

The quiet was broken by the Forster butler, Hayes, who appeared with a card on a silver tray. "My apologies, ma'am. A gentleman has come to call. I informed him that you are not at home, but he strongly requests that I present his card."

Cassie took it from the tray, read it quickly, and showed me the blocky masculine script of Mr. Samuel D. Brush. "It's Sam. Shall we, Val?" I nodded a firm yes. Cassie turned to her butler. "Thank you, Hayes. Please show Mr. Brush to the blue drawing room and say that we will join him presently."

I finished my tea while Cassie dashed upstairs to change into a white tailor-made shirtwaist and violet summer wool skirt. Together we headed to the drawing room.

"Ladies, good morning...." Sam rose, as a gentleman must when a lady enters the space. At full height, he was well below six feet, but his deep chest and fitness spoke of strength. Sam had wrestled at Harvard, and the summer often found him rowing along the shoreline. The white straw skimmer hat in his left hand thumped against his trouser leg, and his thick dark curly hair had not been combed. Normally merry, his hazel eyes were dark. His new wedding band twinkled in the light.

"Let's do sit down," said Cassie. "Tea, Sam? Or coffee? I must remember that you prefer—"

A polite "no," and we all sat. "You've seen the papers?" he asked. We nodded. "The trash they print, it's unforgiveable. Evalina says there's nothing like it in Charleston." He went on. "Hearst and that gang, their 'yellow press,' and the public eats it up. I remember what Hearst did when my brother passed."

Roddy had told me that Harry Brush, "Mister Timber," was a rough-hewn lout that no one mourned except Sam, who revered his older brother as a father figure, insisting Harry Brush's foresight had built a nation. ("Rockefeller gave America oil, and Harry Brush gave the country lumber!") The widowed Georgina dutifully donned lusterless silks, but it was Sam who grieved. The phrase, "So unlike his older brother," was heard most often about Sam Brush.

On the loveseat, he looked ready to wrestle the cushions. Cassie and I perched on Chippendale chairs on either side of him. "About Sylvia—" Cassie said.

But Sam's blast at the press Lord was not to be stopped. "Hearst's frontpage story of the deranged girl with her hair on fire—remember that one? Or the boy who blew himself to smithereens when he mistook a stick of dynamite for candy? Any catastrophe will do, the bigger the better. How about a war in Cuba?"

Sam's normally robust voice sounded half strangled as he went on. "Too peaceful in Havana? Revolution stalled? Never mind that Cuban patriots put their own lives on the line for years, risked death to oust imperial Spain from their island homeland. No, the kingpin of the American press will beat the war drums. Let Hearst blow up the *USS Maine*, 274 sailors and officers killed."

Then I remembered. One of Sam's closest friends from college was an officer on the *Maine.*

"Sabotage a US naval vessel, and let's have a war. Hearst's war. He said it publicly, 'I'll furnish the war.' The US military fought to free Cuba, but Hearst is a war monger. There's blood on his hands."

Neither Cassie nor I dared to suggest that the cause of the explosion had not been proven, that the battleship tragedy might have been an accident. For Sam, the proof was that his friend had died in the explosion last February, just two weeks after Georgina Brush collapsed at Mrs. Astor's ball and died. For Sam Brush, newly married, the first two months of 1898 had brought a double blow.

He had stopped, taken a breath, and dabbed his forehead with a handkerchief from the pocket of his blazer. "Ladies, apologies. I fear that my strong feelings... like a boiler ready to burst...."

Cassie's kindly face absolved him of any and all offences. "We are all struggling, Sam. That melée in the church yesterday, and the heat in the coaches...."

"Completely unnecessary. Electrical fans could make all the difference. Air-cooled coaches, think of it." Cassie eyed me, relieved to see Sam seeming more like himself. We both felt better. Every new gadget, he was convinced, improved lives measurably. "It's a matter of distributing air by passing it over ice," he said, "and of course containing the meltage. Now that electric fans have caught on, the design for coaches ought to be simple. In due course, I'll have a word with Frear. He may be interested in a partnership for a patent."

I recalled Roddy's advice that Herbert Frear be questioned about the condition of Sylvia's body. This was not the moment to offer the suggestion. It occurred to me, however, that we had never talked about the facts of Sylvia's death. The newspapers' lies and distortions, yes, but not the facts.

Cassie leaned forward, a prelude to a difficult topic. She moistened her lips. "Sam, not to be hasty, but do we know anything about…about Sylvia's estate?"

He shrugged. "The Tuxedo Park place? The housekeeper is still there, and of course, the disposition of Brush Industries is the main thing. Otherwise, I wouldn't know. I suppose we'll hear from the lawyer, what's-his-name—Phillips, isn't it? It's all in the lawyers' hands, I should think. I can't imagine that Sylvia left a will." He faced us both. "I regret I never made the effort to know her, to help her."

"None of us did." The moment sagged. Cassie and Sam looked sheepish. Somewhere in the cottage a clock chimed the hour. Cassie moistened her lips once again. "Sam, as a favor, would you please have a word with…with Mr. Mann?"

The mood was suddenly electric. Sam snapped, "That *Town Topics* serpent in the garden."

I held my breath, hoping the name did not restart his fury. E. D. Mann was the owner and publisher of the weekly scandal sheet.

Sam rose. "It's my next stop of the day, a talk backed up with muscle."

"Nothing physical, Sam. Please promise...."

He managed a short laugh. "I don't mean fisticuffs, but If I can stop his bilge...everything in my power, Cassie."

My friend walked Sam toward the door, and Hayes appeared, on cue, to see him out. Neither she nor I had the heart to return to the sordid newspapers. Perhaps our thoughts converged, but it was Cassie who said, "Someone must go to Tuxedo Park. Someone needs to talk to the housekeeper."

I nodded. "Maude Gowdy." We both knew that Sam was the likely candidate. We were reminded, however, of his words, "'a boiler ready to burst.'"

Cassie nodded. "First Georgina and then his friend on the *Maine* and now... and his new bride, not even a year since their wedding. All too much."

Back and forth we went, but the decision had been reached minutes before we said it aloud to each other. Cassie and I would go together to Tuxedo Park.

Chapter Seven

"I'LL BE HERE TO meet your late-afternoon return train," Cassie's father, Robert, assured us, "and we'll go home to Newport together." He had escorted us from Newport to Penn Station, where we would board the train for Tuxedo. He claimed an important appointment with an attorney, which we guessed concerned his divorce from Rowena.

He handed us train tickets with a reminder that a Tuxedo Park omnibus would take us into the gated park. "Do assure the housekeeper that her position and wages will continue until further notice."

We nodded, boarded the train, and soon slipped through the tunnel under Manhattan and into the industrial zone outside the city. I watched factories slide by in the sunshine, the scene brightened by sumac trees. There was something appealing about life that thrived in hostile places. Two recent deaths in the Brush family—was that nature at its most hostile?

"Val? Hello, Val...."

"I'm right here, Cassie. I'm with you." I turned from the window and smoothed my skirt. We both wore walking suits with double-breasted jackets that pinched at the waistline and flared over the hips—perfect for Cassie's hour-glass figure but somewhat of a trial for me. The etiquette guides advised a business woman to choose clothing that permitted "easy locomotion" and "should display no two incongruous colors." Cassie combined scarlet and slate. For me, it was green and blue. And gloves and hats.

The train soon entered the Hudson Valley where everything was green. "Beautiful here," I said, watching a deer leap into a grove in the distance.

"I have mixed feelings, Val," Cassie replied. "We had a cottage in Tuxedo Park when I was a little girl. Father tried to hunt and fish, but he lost patience, and mother called it the ends of the earth. They sold the cottage when I was seven or eight. Father said it didn't suit us, but the real reason was the market."

"The stock market?"

She nodded. "Stocks fell, and the cottage had to go. And our yacht. Now it's in the Newport Harbor under another name, another owner." She bit her lip. "My father hates boats of any size. He's much better off without the *Sycamore*. But mother has never forgiven him." Cassie imitated her mother's frosty voice. "'People will believe us reduced in circumstances, Robert. How could you?'

"The market bounced back," she continued, "but mother cherishes her grievances. My poor father. You should have seen him try to calm her when news came that Sylvia was the major beneficiary of Aunt Georgina's will." Cassie twisted her gloves. "My fondest memory of Tuxedo Park is feeding bread to the ducks in a pond, away from my storming parents."

The locomotive whistle moaned softly as our train slowed, and we pulled our kid gloves tight as the conductor announced, "Tuxedo Park Station" and assisted us onto the platform.

The omnibus waited, manned by a top-hatted, gray-haired, rosy-cheeked driver who helped us to our seats. We ignored the aroma of gin and the silver cap of a flask that poked from his frayed coat pocket. He took the reins of two matched black Shires whose coats glistened from hours under a curry comb and a dandy brush. The horses' rhythmic hooves on the packed earth roadway might have lulled us to a doze, except for the task ahead. We passed through the gate.

The sight of Sylvia's Highland Cottage was chilling on this hot summer day. On a hillside, encircled by thick dark trees, stood the somber stone structure with sharp-pitched gables and an overhanging roof that pulled downward, as if gravity might eventually collapse the whole thing. A rock foundation supported walls of dark shingles in the rustic style that had been popular for some years now. Light from the leaded, diamond-shaped windowpanes shone like little beacons. We caught our breath at the top of a short flight of stone steps before Cassie reached for the brass door knocker and rapped twice.

"Ladies, good day. I am Maude Gowdy."

The housekeeper must have seen us coming, for the door swept open, and she stood aside to let us pass inside. A black door badge lay on a foyer table, obviously removed after the funeral but not yet put away. Our eyes adjusted to the dark, cool, interior where the silhouettes of furnishings in the great room were lightened by highly polished silver—candlesticks, pitchers, tea service, platters, trays gleaming on every dark surface. Wall sconces cast gloomy pools of ochre light, and when the door closed, we saw a surprisingly young Maude Gowdy, who stood before us wearing a long gray housekeeper's dress with a ring of keys suspended from her belt. Her fair complexion contrasted with pitch-black eyebrows and hair. Her thick-soled shoes were suited for sweeping indoors and out. She spoke to us in the lilt of her native Ireland.

"Ladies, won't you please follow me to the inglenook."

She led us to a blue and white Delft-tiled fireplace. The chairs flanking the hearth were long out of fashion and defied comfort, but we sat down and accepted the house-keeper's offer of tea.

"And perhaps a bite, ladies? Miss Sylvia liked to offer callers a cup of tea and a bite of lunch."

What callers? Before we could ask, the housekeeper disappeared. Cassie opened the little watch she wore on a gold neck chain. "We have about two hours, Val."

"We'll make the most of it, a quick cup and a bite while we ask Maude Gowdy some questions. I'm famished."

"Likewise."

The housekeeper returned with a short outburst, as if she hadn't spoken to another soul in days. "Irish breakfast tea, ladies, a favorite of my home, County Cork, which is surrounded by Counties Kerry, Limerick, and Waterford. I do hope you like the tea and Irish soda bread and jam, all favorites of Miss Sylvia. She so enjoyed it, she permitted no other."

Maude Gowdy put the tray down, the ornate silver spotless, gleaming, as were the creamer and sugar bowl, the knives and spoons. "And here's your butter and the cream and sugar, ladies. And the jam. I hope you like strawberry— and I'd allow the tea to steep a bit." Having delivered her oration, the housekeeper began to step away.

"A moment, if you will, Gowdy," said Cassie.

"Indeed, ma'am, at your service." Her feet together, standing straight, the housekeeper stood at attention.

"Your service with Miss Sylvia," Cassie began, "has your employment here been long?"

"Just over a year, ma'am. Before that, Miss Brush employed an older couple. The cold weather troubled the missus's bones, and they went into service in your southland. I myself am accustomed to the cold and damp. What I miss in America is a peat bog fire."

Cassie looked puzzled. I would tell her how my papa spoke of the peat bog fires in Ireland, how fragrant the aroma that filled every tiny cottage no matter how poor.

"You mentioned callers," Cassie went on. "The family understands that Miss Sylvia preferred solitude."

"Oh, there's an Anglican priest that came calling, but some others handed in their cards. Miss Sylvia offered a cup of tea and a bite in the side room, but she didn't receive them."

"I don't understand," said Cassie. "She extended hospitality but did not receive her callers?"

"Ma'am, she felt they traveled this far and talked their way through the Tuxedo Park gate and should go off fortified."

"But did she receive callers?"

The housekeeper seemed on the edge of exasperation. "I took the calling cards to Miss Sylvia on a silver tray. She read them and said yes or no. The ones that were 'yes' got tea and toast. The others were sent away. I was instructed to tell them 'Miss Brush is not at home,' and I did so."

She paused, as if deciding whether to go on. "I expect they all hoped for money," she said. "They didn't look like beggars, no they did not. There was a man that chewed gum the whole time he drank his tea. Another had diamond rings and patent leather boots."

With a slice of soda bread poised in mid-air to be buttered, I stopped still, recalling the two men in Trinity Church at Sylvia Brush's funeral. "The man with diamond rings," I said, "did Miss Sylvia possibly speak with him? And what about the man with chewing gum?"

She flushed. "I cannot recall about the chewing gum man, but Miss Sylvia perhaps spoke with the diamond ring gentleman with the patent leather boots. There was quite a few at the door over the whole year. I'm kept busy with the house, you see, even to the kitchen. For sure, we could have used more hands hereabouts, but Miss Sylvia wouldn't hear of it. I did clean the snow from the patent leather boots and warmed them by the fire. Patent leather is no good in winter."

"Can you tell us whose name was on his card? Or any other cards?"

She looked affronted. "Ma'am, my duty was to present the card on a tray, not to read the name. My duty was to polish the tray, and that I did." Maude Gowdy's bosom seemed to swell at these words. "I kept the trays—all the silver— shining with a mixture of my own devising, and Miss Sylvia was most pleased."

The housekeeper gazed at a gleaming wall sconce. "'Maude Gowdy,' she said to me, 'your silver cream must go to market. Keep it a secret. You will not be in service long. You will have a household of your own. Your silver cream is your passage. You may depend upon my support. One way or another, you may depend upon it.' Those were her words. She said, 'I will document my promise.'"

The housekeeper stood tall, a domestic sergeant major. "If you ladies wish, I can open the safe in the kitchen and show you the work of my silver cream on the Brush family silver. I'd be pleased to present a piece that shows the benefits of my silver cream. Miss Sylvia entrusted the combination of the safe to me. 'Your cream is better than a chamois or rouge cloth.' Miss Sylvia said so many times."

We thanked her but declined. Cassie had confided that the custom Brush silver pattern was an overly ornate mélange by Tiffany, too heavy by far. We sipped and listened as Miss Gowdy continued her narration.

"We all three came to America together, you see, my two brothers and me. And they were to work in the livery stables, but a contract man offered a silver dollar to go to the mines. They went into the coal mines in West Virginia. A tunnel fell in on them, and I pray to the Virgin Mary that both my brothers are in Heaven."

What should we say? Offer condolences for the brothers? Regret that a mine shaft had failed. I thought of my papa, his constant care for the miners, his fear of fire and calamity in the depths of the silver mines. It seemed somehow indecent to eat at this moment, though hunger gnawed, and we ate our bread and jam discreetly. The hour pressed.

"Will that be all, ma'am?"

"One moment, Gowdy," Cassie put down her cup. "I want to assure you that the family appreciates your service at this difficult moment. We hope your duties are manageable, and we will do everything possible to help you secure a new position at the appropriate time."

The housekeeper merely nodded. If she had other plans in mind for her future, she did not voice them to Cassandra Forster this afternoon.

"One more question," Cassie said. "We understand that Miss Brush visited the city in the months before...before we lost her."

The housekeeper was silent. "A friend believes he saw someone in the department store area called Ladies Mile," I said. "Someone who resembled Miss Brush."

Maude Gowdy shook her head and said reproachfully, "Miss Sylvia did not confide unnecessarily in her housekeeper."

"But was she ill?" I nearly blurted. "She was terribly thin."

"I made porridge and good Irish stew for her. Lamb with carrots and potatoes. Porridge every morning, and the stewpot was always warming."

In her own way, the housekeeper dodged the question of whether Sylvia Brush was a wraith whose health was at serious risk. I pressed on, "I believe that Mrs. Forster wishes to...examine Miss Brush's personal effects."

Cassie put down her tea, and we went upstairs by ourselves to enter a bedroom that was chaste but not monastic. Cassie sniffed, as if testing the air. "Gowdy has been in this room in the last hours, Val. Otherwise, it would be stuffy. These cottage bedrooms are poorly ventilated."

"You assume it was Maude Gowdy," I said. "Who else would it be?"

"...an open question."

We managed a little laugh, then looked around at wallpaper featuring bluebirds and a navy quilted spread over a narrow four-poster bed. A dressing table and chest of drawers stood against a side wall, and a coal fireplace reminder that Tuxedo Park winters were long and severe. Cassie lifted a corner of the spread to examine the bedding. "Clean sheets," she said.

An accent pillow embroidered with pink roses lay on the bed pillow. "Pink roses," said Cassie, "mean chastity in the language of flowers. I believe mother did this for Sylvia—or 'to' her. She was intentionally pointing out that her niece was an old maid. That gift was a little harpoon."

I turned. "Cassie, look at those pictures." We stepped closer to see paintings of dogs hung in neat rows on the walls. There was a toast-brown collie, a black hound on a pedestal, brindle boxers, terriers, dachshunds, a beagle….

All the portraits were signed in the lower right corner by the same artist, R. Rudd. Another wall displayed photographs of dogs of no discernable breed. "Your cousin's bedroom is a canine gallery," I said, "but notice, the pedigrees have one wall—and mutts the other one."

"Kennels for strays," Cassie said, "one of Auntie Georgina's favorite causes.

Perhaps Sylvia took it up in daughterly devotion."

"Cassie, look here." I pointed to an empty space among the oil paintings, a tiny hole where a small nail had been driven. "A hook was right here," I said, "but it's gone. Painting and hook, gone."

"Maybe Sylvia didn't like the painting. Or she didn't like the dog. Maybe she gave the picture as a gift—but not to Annie Flowers. Miss Flowers didn't even have a calendar on her walls."

We moved to the bureau. "What's this on the top?" I asked. A little silk flag… red-white-and-blue with a single star sprouted from a stand. "A yacht club? A gentlemen's club?"

Cassie wasn't sure. "Let's peek inside the drawers."

Neatly folded underclothing filled the top drawer, but the others were crammed with papers of all sorts, some tied in packets. "Val, look at these— unopened invitations." Cassie almost gasped. "They go back three, no, four years."

The unopened social invitations could take all afternoon. "What about the business envelopes?" I asked.

Cassie opened one to find invoices paid by the firm of Hester, Phillips, and Lee. "They're a law firm, Val. They handle a good many of the Brush Industries documents and family matters too. Mr. Phillips usually is on hand to answer questions and offer advice. He's very conservative. My father trusts him completely."

She unfolded several sheets. "Look at these... items purchased by Sylvia Van Schylar Brush and paid to Lord & Taylor and Macy's, all from March through May of this year....ceramic teapot, Waltham clock, rubber bathing shoes.... And look, here's a postal card with the Atlantic City boardwalk, Val. 'Having fine time, see you soon.' It's signed 'Annie.'"

"Annie Flowers? How could she possibly afford a seaside vacation?"

"—unless Sylvia funded it. There's no date."

"Let's take the card with us," I suggested.

She nodded and opened another of the mailings from Hester, Phillips, and Lee. "Look at this—$100.00 for Sisters in Suffrage."

"To Annie Flowers?"

Cassie shook her head. "To a P.O. box, but the recipient is not named." Here's another one. $150.00 for *Liberacion de Cuba.*"

"The Cuban revolution... your Auntie Georgina had promoted statehood for Cuba, hadn't she?"

"Yes, but she died before the war heated up last April."

"Before Colonel Roosevelt charged up San Juan Hill," I said. "Cuba is a US colony now, isn't it? Or a Territory? Don't we own it?" Neither of us knew. The newspapers reported peace talks, but the print was so small, the diplomacy so tangled.

Cassie bent to open the bottom drawer, then cried out softly, "No... Oh, no, no..." as she rose clasping pottery shards in each palm.

"What is it?" My friend held the shards as though they might shatter once again.

"It was a lovely old pitcher. My mother smashed it when Auntie Georgina's will was read. It was horrid. Mother threatened to contest the will. She hinted about a row with Sylvia. We needed to give her smelling salts." Cassie's grip tightened on the pieces of pottery. Her eyes welled up.

"Your poor father. Was he able to calm her down?"

"No, it was Sam. It's always Sam." She dabbed her eyes with a handkerchief from her skirt pocket. "I remember a terrible scene at one Thanksgiving dinner table when my mother compared the Lorillard tobacco business to Brush wood." Cassie clutched the handkerchief, her knuckles white.

"That Thanksgiving Mother ranted on through the turkey and vegetables, how the Lorillards benefit from every cigar and pipe that's lighted—or when I puff a cigarette." Cassie leaned closer. "She wasn't talking about tobacco, Val. It was money on her mind."

I understood her discomfort. Roddy had taught me the golden rule of Society. It was bad taste—actually forbidden—to speak directly about money.

"Sam put things right, Val. He pointed out that tobacco demanded brutal field labor and exhausted the soil, and the leaves of tobacco plants burned away to ash in pipes and cigars. But forests of timber, he said, were God's gift to anyone with an axe or a saw and the energy to use the trees for houses to shelter us."

She smiled at the recollection. "It brought the whole tableful of Brush and Van Schylar and Fox family members back around to the idea of giving thanks. Of course, the wood won out over tobacco, and Samuel David Brush proved the point. I hope to heaven that Evalina knows what a gem of a husband she has married."

I gently opened Cassie's fingers, replaced the pottery shards in the drawer and closed it, afraid my friend might weep if I asked how the smashed pitcher got into Sylvia's bedroom bureau. I changed the subject. "Should we see the bathroom?"

The blinding white tiles on the walls and floor signaled a recent renovation.

The porcelain tub, the sink and commode were hospital white, as were the towels. "Dudley talked about doing our bathroom like this," Cassie said, "replacing the marble tub with porcelain—for the children and for me. On expeditions, he bathes as soldiers do in battle," she continued. "His pith helmet becomes his basin. I think he secretly likes it." She ran one palm along the sink. "Look at the soap dish—Ivory soap. Bea and Charlie love it because it floats."

I leaned in closely. "It's a brand new bar, Cassie. No one has bathed with it." The soap, the pristine towels and fresh bedsheets… it's as if the cottage awaited Sylvia's return. How ironic that Sylvia should install this shrine to hygiene in her home while courting a fatal illness in the squalid germ field of the Lower East Side. So far, the woman was a mass of contradictions.

I rested my hand on the wall as I straightened up, my hand brushing a tile that appeared to be ajar. At my touch, it loosened and fell, and I found myself peering into a hollow—a cavity that reached back as far as my elbow. It felt smooth to the touch, like the zinc on a cook's tabletop in the kitchen.

"What are you doing?"

"Cassie, it feels like…like a little hiding place. Like the safe deposit boxes for ladies' jewels."

"In the bathroom? Surely not."

"It's about the same size. Put your hand in."

"I'd rather not."

I held my breath, groped in the space, and pulled out a large flat envelope. There was no address, no stamp, no dated postmark, no identification of any kind. The flap was torn as if the contents had been hastily plucked out.

Cassie took the envelope from my hands and opened it. It was empty, but a scrap of paper had stuck to the glue on the flap. No more than an inch or two in length, it was an off-white color with gold embossing. Cassie held it between her thumb and forefinger.

"Can you guess what that was—?"

"No. Can you?"

"It looks engraved, like the corner of a diploma. Why would Sylvia have this?" Cassie did not know. "Don't throw it away," I said.

"I'll put it inside with the Atlantic City postal card to take along."

She opened the casing of her gold watch. "We really must be off. There's just enough time to meet the omnibus for our return train." My friend was right, but I suspected her haste was a sign of a worry more than necessity.

Outdoors, as we readied for the journey back to Newport, the cloud cover and darkening sky matched our mood. Instead of daylight and clarity, the Tuxedo Park sojourn had brought confusion, doubt, disappointment—and no better grasp on whatever had sent Sylvia Brush to an early grave in Woodlawn Cemetery beside her mother.

Chapter Eight

WHEN RODDY AND I exchanged testy "words," we usually cooled down quickly, found a mutual interest, and put the mild disagreement behind us. At the moment, however, we were reduced to bare civility on the matter of Tuxedo Park, the late Sylvia Brush, and my foray with Cassie the previous day. Polite with one another, yes indeed we were, but every sentence thus far today had been frosty. ("Please do pass the cream, if it's not too much trouble.... No trouble whatsoever.")

I had hoped for better spirits by this afternoon here at Drumcliffe, but the atmosphere in our home had remained cool from last night's tiff with Roddy. He was awake and fretful when a Fox family coach brought me home after midnight, exhausted. In nightclothes, Roddy opened the door himself. Instead of receiving a welcome, I felt accosted.

91

"You might have sent a telegram, Val. For all I knew, you were lost in the Ramapo Mountains."

"Tuxedo Park," I replied, "is hardly in that sort of mountain range." I could have referenced the Rockies in Colorado or the Washoe in Nevada. "Besides," I said, "there wasn't time. Mr. Fox met us at Penn Station and hurried us to the steamer, and then his coachmen met us here at the wharf and drove me—"

In response, Roddy yanked at the sash of the silk paisley dressing gown that I had given him for his birthday and muttered that Robert Fox had much to answer for. Our servants, he said, were dismissed for the night. "—including Calista. If you need help undressing, I will assist."

We trooped upstairs to my bedroom suite, and silently Roddy unlaced my summer corset and disappeared down the hall to his bedroom. This morning we breakfasted mostly in silence.

After coffee, I dressed in bloomers, ordered my bicycle from the carriage house, and defiantly pedaled against the wind the entire way from Ocean Drive to the Casino, the premier social and sports center for Newport. In the heart of the Village, the Casino also drew shoppers, and I noticed a few stares when lifting my racquet from the bicycle basket at 10:55 a.m.

My tennis lesson on a newly flattened grass court— Court Number Three, the ladies' court—began at eleven o'clock and ended, mercifully, at noon.

I was too vexed from yesterday's outing to Sylvia's cottage, too tired from strenuous cycling, and too irritated with my husband to serve or volley reliably during the endless hour on the court. My forearm was sluggish, and my racquet could not find the "sweet" spot for a return. My serves were hopeless.

"Eye on the ball, Mrs. DeVere," my instructor had urged, more than once. "I am trying, Mr. Thatford," I replied. The tennis champion Richard ("Dickie") Thatford had won numerous tournaments in Philadelphia and now spent summer weeks teaching amateurs the fine points of the serve, the backhand, and the forehand with a certain spin that made the ball clear the net, bounce, and die before an opponent could reach it. Amply compensated for his time, Mr. Thatford nonetheless appeared pained to be in service to Court Number Three and probably counted the hours before his return to the US Nationals.

"Not your day, Mrs. DeVere."

"Next time, Mr. Thatford." And I meant it.

My return trip to Drumcliffe could not have escaped Roddy's attention. Faced with cycling back home, perspiring, and every muscle played out, I had flagged down a delivery wagon from the Tisdall grocery store, requested the driver to fit my bicycle amid his crates and cartons, and took my seat beside him all the way to our cottage. I stared straight ahead, acknowledging no one among the social gauntlet of raised eyebrows and gaping mouths along the Village sidewalks, on the faces of kitchen staff at the cottages awaiting their deliveries, or from the recesses of the carriages proceeding along Ocean Drive.

"Helpful lesson, was it?" my husband asked. We stood facing one another in the conservatory, usually one of our favorite spaces in the cottage because the green plants and the indoor splashing fountain were so cheerful. With his hair neatly brushed and cheeks freshly shaved, Roddy was wearing spotless white trousers and a sack blazer from Brooks Brothers. Disheveled and hungry, I was in no mood for pleasantries.

"Very helpful," I replied.

"Val, we need to talk." Roddy's tone was softer, a bid to melt the ice.

I was happy to relent. "Let's sit for a moment, Roddy. I know you have a croquet match, but sit with me just for a moment?"

He put aside his mallet, a gift of custom hardwood that I had ordered from New Zealand as a holiday surprise. We sat side by side on a chaise by a lemon tree planted in a jardiniere.

"You know, my dear, I'm only concerned about your wellbeing," Roddy said. "And your safety."

"I am perfectly safe."

He took my hand. "No one is 'perfectly' safe. Boats collide, bathers drown...."

"Stop, please." Roddy was doubtless thinking of a young man who had recently crashed his boat, fell overboard fully clothed, and drowned in Narragansett Bay. Neither of us knew him or his family, but the Newport *Daily News* had been full of the story. Tragic, yes, but not our tragedy, which is the point I now brought up. "Our breakfast room," I said, "would get us off to a better start without the *Daily News*. That poor young man has nothing to do with us."

"Val, you are exactly right. I'm so relieved that you see my point—that family matters are best handled by families. The drowned young man has his people. As for your Cassandra, she has her husband—"

"Who is halfway around the world."

"Which is not our concern." Roddy ran his fingers through his hair in frustration. I managed not to interrupt, a habit that I was trying to break. But it dawned on me that we were speaking at cross-purposes.

"Cassandra's parents are at hand," he said, "and so is Sam Brush. She is very fortunate to have her aunt Georgina's young brother-in-law so close by, and so caring. And his wife's relatives are also in the family circle, now that he has wed."

"Evalina," I said, "from North Carolina. Or is it South—?"

"No matter." Fixed on his message, Roddy was not distracted by the distinction between southern states. "Her family goes back to colonial times in Newport," he said. "My point is, Evalina Brush's family is now a part of the Van Schylar and Fox and Forster families."

He hadn't finished. "They are all bound by blood and by marriage, Val. They are the ones to deal with the settlement of Sylvia's estate. It is up to them to handle whatever matters arise."

Roddy reached for his croquet mallet and stood. "Cassandra is blessed, my dearest, to have in you the best friend a lady can have. And I am blessed to have you as my bride." He leaned forward, his arm around my perspiration-damp shoulder, and kissed me softly on the cheek. "Please think about what I just said."

I promised.

At the conservatory doorway he turned and, departing for the afternoon, added, "Remember, Val, this evening we're at Beechwood."

"Beechwood?"

He echoed the word and was gone.

Meant to buoy my spirits, the name pricked like a hat pin in a balloon.

Hoping for a quiet evening with a new novel and one of Roddy's special cocktails, I must instead prepare for dinner at the cottage of Mrs. William Backhouse Astor, Jr., known simply as Mrs. Astor. Her villa, the Italianate Beechwood, was the summer palace of the Queen of Society. Her Majesty, Caroline Astor, was a most gracious hostess, but her invitation was a command. Attendance was mandatory. No sudden "headaches" could permit one to beg off.

Was this evening to be a formal dinner? Surely not a ball... but what did the invitation say, and where was it? When did it arrive? Roddy must have responded, although it was my duty as the lady of the house to attend to social matters.

Vexed, I searched the silver salver by the front entrance where calling cards were deposited. No, the salver was swept clean.

Up the marble grand staircase, I took the steps two at a time, my path lighted from above by the La Farge stained glass skylight depicting the goddess Diana, but at the moment I hadn't time to enjoy the image of the huntress poised to release the golden arrow from her bow. Going toward Roddy's study, I passed a tall bronze candle stand of mythic gods fighting off serpents, a loathsome *objet d'art* from Roddy's mother.

It took a moment for my eyes to adjust to the dim light in my husband's study, decorated in deepest reds by the celebrated Allard & Sons of Paris. On top of the leather blotter on the rosewood desk sat letters from the Newport Country Club and a notice from The Reading Club. No invitation.

Cassie would never be at a loss for the whereabouts of invitations to dinners, garden parties, balls, and all the rest. Her social secretary met with her every morning to help supervise the schedule. Roddy had urged me to hire a secretary, but I resisted. Cassie had children to oversee, so she needed help.

Besides, we had enough servants. They seemed to be everywhere in our cottage. Couldn't I enjoy breakfast in peace without the intrusion of a secretary? Perhaps Sylvia Van Schylar Brush had made a sensible decision to leave it all behind for Tuxedo Park. Then again, she had entangled herself in affairs of the city, affairs that may have proved deadly.

It was now nearly three p.m., and I bowed to necessity and called Calista for help choosing an ensemble for this evening. In minutes she joined me in my bedroom suite, the quiet efficiency of her trim figure so reassuring.

"Ma'am?"

"Mr. DeVere and I are invited to Beechwood cottage this evening."

"Yes, ma'am."

I tried to seem calm and collected in the presence of a woman who was a few years my junior, but oversaw my wardrobe, and much else besides. Calista Adrianakis was formerly employed as a stewardess on a coastal steamer. Her letter of reference assured me that whatever the crisis of the moment, a popped button or a passenger prone to imbibe, she kept her wits about her, a trait I increasingly valued. Her preferred dress—shirtwaists and skirts with clean lines— filled me with envy for the simplicity that was impossible for the wife of Roderick Windham DeVere.

"I seem to have mislaid the invitation," I said.

"I believe the evening includes dinner and an entertainment." At my quizzical look, she explained, "Sands had a word with me."

Sands had been the DeVeres' butler since Roddy was a boy. He was English, of course. All Society employed butlers from the United Kingdom. Their household management skills were believed to be superior, and his ultra-British voice reminded me of stage plays with Papa at Piper's Opera House in Virginia City.

"Might the invitation be available?" I asked.

Calista magically produced it, the heavy cream stationery bent but not creased, from a side skirt pocket. It was dated July twelfth.

596 Bellevue Avenue

Mrs. Astor Requests the pleasure of Mr. & Mrs. Roderick DeVere's Company at dinner and an entertainment on Tuesday, July the twenty-sixth, at eight o'clock.

I paused for a moment to reflect that the invitation would have been delivered by a footman nearly two weeks ago, well before Cassie's hysteria about Georgina's death by "poisoning" and the sudden, shocking death of Sylvia in a Lower East Side slum. The funeral with two fresh graves—the daughter buried beside her mother—and the day trip to Tuxedo Park…. The whole mad series of events made the invitation seem like a relic from another time, another world.

"May I assist you, ma'am?"

I nodded, jolted into the present. "What would you say to the embroidered crepe dress?"

"I should think a gown instead, ma'am."

A gown, of course, the fine distinction that was honored religiously.

"The entertainment, ma'am, do you have any idea…are animals involved?"

"I wish I knew." Calista was no doubt remembering that two favorite gowns had been ruined by bird droppings, despite assurance that hundreds of hummingbirds or turtle doves released over a courtyard were a delightful surprise, and entirely harmless. My golfing clothes, destroyed last week by the seagulls, had been replaced.

We agreed on a deep lavender China silk gown with a *princesse* back, recommended by the couturier for its "sweep and magnitude." Calista would lay out the gown, the undergarments, the hosiery and evening slippers, even the jewelry, help me dress and style my hair. "May I suggest, ma'am, that you take a nice bath this afternoon. You'll feel better. With verbena salts, yes?"

Yes. Filled to the brim with scented warm water, my deep marble tub let me sink to my neck and relax every tense muscle for long moments. The fact of the bathroom, however, stirred thoughts of Tuxedo Park and the gleaming white tiles— the empty slot with the empty envelope and an embossed scrap of paper. What to make of any of it, the little flag, the postal card, and the pictures of the dogs?

How I yearned to lay it all out before Roddy and ask him to think along with me. And to ponder the evasive Maude Gowdy who seemed willfully ignorant of Sylvia's trips into the city, as if a warm pot of stew met all obligations.

If only Roddy hadn't determined to keep us clear of the affairs of the Van Schylar-Brush clan. Surely, he would understand my friend's plight if reminded that Robert and Rowena Fox were divorcing and the heavy toll on Cassie from Robert's nervousness and Rowena's icy temper. As for Sam Brush, his devotion to the family was not in question, but a newly married man must prove fidelity to his bride by constant devotion. Evalina would expect—and deserved—his full attention. I agreed that Dudley Forster ought to come home, but for now he was beyond the reach of cable, telegraph, and steamship.

All this could possibly move Roddy, if he were in the right frame of mind. Some ladies were geniuses at sculpting their husbands' moods. As yet, I was not among them. The light in my bathroom had shifted to signal the waning afternoon. I reached for the bar of French milled soap, knowing for the moment that nothing could go forward.

Guests' names were announced in a deep baritone fanfare at the entrance to Beechwood: "Mr. and Mrs. Stuyvesant Fish…. Mr. and Mrs. Ogden Goelet…."

Each carriage inched up the driveway, and with each name, the carriage door was opened by Mrs. Astor's groom, and Society stepped toward the grand foyer in high style. Roddy had ordered the matched pair of French trotters and our coachman Noland expertly held the reins. Entering and stepping down from our Barouche in a floor-length gown was easily done.

"Mr. and Mrs. Roderick Windham DeVere."

The door opened, and Roddy stepped out to assist, along with two grooms. Footmen in powdered wigs hovered nearby to prevent mishaps. The evening was pleasantly warm and clear. In white tie and tails, Roddy glowed, and my China silk gown was reasonably comfortable. Calista had styled my hair in finger waves and fastened a diamond and sapphire aigrette, the fan-like spray of jewels substituting for the huge hats that I detested. I took Roddy's arm, and we moved inside the cottage. Mrs. Astor greeted her guests by name, regal in her white satin gown with a long train and a diadem of diamonds. "So happy to have you here at Beechwood...."

"Mr. and Mrs. Harry Lehr.... Mr. Reese Osborn.... Colonel and Mrs. John Jacob Astor IV...." The colonel himself, Mrs. Astor's son.

And then, "Mr. and Mrs. Robert J. Fox...."

Cassie's parents, officially still together, moved as a pair, Rowena on Robert's arm. I had never noticed how much taller she was than her husband— her soon-to-be ex-husband. Perhaps she was deliberately wearing high heeled pumps to loom above him. As usual, Cassie's mother displayed antique jeweled rings on every finger. Her eyebrows and close-set eyes gave her a permanent frown. I had assumed that Cassie would be here with one of the couples, but I had not seen her.

"Mr. Theodore Mather Bulkeley."

Theo—excellent! He saw me, winked with a conspiratorial short bow, and joined the gentlemen to await the name of the lady to be escorted to dinner. By the rules of etiquette, married couples would dine apart. At my ear, Roddy whispered how much he would love to have dinner at my side. In fact, we had hardly spoken since he returned from the croquet lawn and we prepared for the evening. Dressing took such an enormous amount of time, even with a lady's maid and a gentleman's valet. Roddy now drew a card to learn that his dinner partner was Mrs. Victor Philbrick, a longtime family friend of the DeVeres. He stepped away.

"Mrs. DeVere?"

I turned to see a sloe-eyed officer in the formal uniform of the United States Army. His hair was parted in the center, and his light brown moustache flared with precision. The gold braid, brass buttons and shoulder boards of his tunic were dazzling. "Colonel Astor," I said.

He took my arm. "Shall we dine?"

Mrs. Astor's cottage had had been extensively renovated by Richard Morris Hunt, one of the fashionable architects who opened up terraces and French doors to allow soft breezes. The ballroom itself was set with numerous round tables for eight, our place cards and menus ready at each setting. We would dine upon Mrs. Astor's famed gold service.

Colonel Astor guided me to our table, held my chair, and we were seated along with Edwin (Ed) Glendorick and Mrs. Stuyvesant Fish—Mamie. Old New Amsterdam was represented at our table by Mrs. John King Van Rensselaer, who was partnered with Edward Berwind, the coal baron. Here came Cassie's mother, Rowena, being seated at our table to the left of her dinner partner, Edward (Teddy) Wharton, which meant that Edith was somewhere in the room, probably taking mental notes for a mean-spirited novel she planned to write.

A string quartet played table music, and introductions followed, although most of the guests had known one another for years. Nodding in my direction, Rowena remarked that I was very nearly regarded as her own stepdaughter because of my close friendship with her Cassandra. "Very nearly," she repeated in her chilly voice. I managed a smile.

Our first course, *Rillettes de Tours* (cold paté in little ramekins) was placed before us. Let the conversation begin.

"I understand we are to be entertained after dinner," said Ed Glendorick, "outdoors on the lawn."

"A young dancer," said Teddy Wharton. "I hear she leaps like a gazelle."

"A gazelle in Mrs. Astor's gazebo? How droll." This from Mamie Fish. "I hear she never has set foot in a ballet studio, not once."

"*Au naturelle...*"

"*Quelle sauvage!*"

"What is her name?" I asked.

"Isabel... no, wait, it's Isadora. Isadora Duncan."

"From San Francisco." "The Wild, Wild West."

Sneering laughter followed, and I bit my tongue. Luck had put me in range of Cassie's mother, and I planned to draw out Rowena and learn as much as possible during dinner. Perhaps she knew something useful about Sylvia's habits in the months before her death. Perhaps a slip of Rowena's tongue would explain her rage at the news of

Sylvia's inheritance, for Rowena Van Schylar Fox was already a woman of considerable wealth. I would open the topic of Tuxedo Park in the most general terms, which would surely prompt some helpful remark. Perhaps Mrs. Van Rensselaer would speak up, or Edward Berwind.

Mamie Fish, however, had eyed me across the table and seized the moment. "I happened to peer out from Crossways just after lunch today," she said, trusting everyone to know the Fish cottage by name. "And before my eyes was a most remarkable sight on the roadway. Most remarkable."

"Oh, do tell," said Rowena.

"The Tisdall grocery wagon," Mamie continued, "and seated beside the delivery man was a female figure holding an implement, probably a carpet beater, so I thought at first. But I was mistaken...."

"Mistaken?" said Mrs. Van Rensselaer.

"One's eyesight mustn't be trusted in the midday sun," said Mamie Fish, "but an opera glass told the story.... The carpet beater was in fact—"

"—a tennis racquet," I said, hoping that my voice rang clear as a bell. A sip of wine gave me a moment to gather my wits. "Indeed," I said, "I was thankful for the grocery man's willingness to take a lady passenger who was quite wilted after a strenuous tennis lesson and a morning of bicycling."

I smiled broadly, hoping to look amusing. "Such excellent sport, cycling, but I confess that I overdid it today. The Tisdall wagon shipped my bicycle and ferried me to

Drumcliffe. I happily sat among the crates of carrots and sacks of flour and chatted with Mr. Tisdall...most pleasant."

Mamie Fish was not prepared to let go. "Dear pet," she said, "the next time a tradesman's vehicle is tempting, I am sure your Roderick will send a dog-cart for you." Her fork raised, she speared her paté and quickly went on. "If Rufus and Eleanor DeVere were to see their daughter-in-law on display atop a grocery wagon.... Well, whatever might we expect next here in Newport? If the last ferry has left one stranded on the dock, would one hail a lobster smack?"

As a few of my dinner companions chortled, Colonel Astor came to my defense. "You must join us for a bicycling tea in the fall when the weather cools, Mrs. DeVere," he said. "And by the by, it happens that this year, I hold a new patent on a bicycle brake."

I wanted to hear more, but Edward Berwind chimed in. "Commendable, sir. A West Pointer couldn't do better, and I say this as a Navy man." The table was wreathed in smiles. Everyone knew that Berwind coal fueled the US Navy from sea to shining sea.

Our soup, *crème d'Asperges Vertes*, was served. Spoons were raised. Ed Glendorick took the opportunity to salute Colonel Astor for his recent wartime service. "Understand you've seen action in the Philippine Islands, Colonel."

The colonel nodded. "The Spanish empire is done for, at long last."

"And you also fought in the Santiago campaign in Cuba. The 'Astor Battalion,' wasn't it?"

"'Astor Battery,' sir." The colonel seemed amused.

It was a relief that my friend Theo, seated at another table, could not hear our conversation. Glendorick's obsession with Cuba had driven him nearly mad. Theo had cornered me in an oak grove at an afternoon ice cream social two days ago and had let loose about Glendorick's mania about the Caribbean island. "The man has become Newport's worst bore," Theo said, "worse than the old codgers who rant on about the Civil War. The battle of Nashville, Manassus, Gettysburg... no one wants to hear about it. When I see one of them at a club in the city, I duck right out."

I replied that, unfortunately, we ladies had no city club to duck out of, but Theo's dander was up. "Glendorick and Cuba," he continued as his ice cream melted, "downright insufferable. Cuba, what has it got, sugar cane? Our Sandwich Islands send us plenty of sugar. We don't need to own more islands. I tell you, if Glendorick doesn't stop buttonholing every uniformed military man in sight, some of us will send 'regrets' when the wedding invitations arrive."

Now, here at our table, Glendorick pushed on, "The Philippine Islands and the island of Cuba, so important, so far apart. And infested with rebellion, both of them. Am I right?"

The colonel did not immediately answer.

"That fellow in the Philippines and what's-his-name in Cuba...Marti?" The soup plates were whisked away and replaced with the entrée. "Am I right?" The conversation seemed far too serious, beyond the bounds of dinnertime light banter.

"Yes, correct." Colonel Astor slowly sliced his filet, seeming reluctant to stay on the topic.

Ed Glendorick clutched his dinner knife. "Cuban plotters, they never know when to stop. Cuba ought to be annexed to us. Annex the whole island. Don't you agree?"

"Always trouble with human beings," Teddy Wharton said, "always good reason for dogs and horses." His effort to lighten the mood went nowhere. The rest of us feigned great interest in our filet—except for Ed Glendorick who signaled the footman for red wine, his beef untouched. At Owls Roost, I recalled, the roast was dry as tinder. "Don't you agree about Cuba?"

Colonel Astor carefully put down his knife and fork and looked around the table. "Ladies and gentlemen," he said, "you are the first to know that I will be mustered out of the US Army this autumn. Resuming civilian life, I will be free to express political opinions. Until then, however, I must remain a neutral party.... Ah, here is our salad. I confess that officers' mess in wartime gives one great appreciation for my mother's table."

And I for the perfect manners of John Jacob Astor IV I thought to myself at that moment.

We arrived without further incident at dessert, to be served on the lawn during the evening's entertainment. "A garden party under the stars! How novel, how very Newport," the guests cooed. But the move from the dinner table to the semicircles of lawn chairs was the death knell for my plan. Mamie Fish's tongue lashing and Edwin Glendorick's boorish carping about Cuba had reduced the evening to time served for nothing. Any chance to glean information about Sylvia, any chance that an evening at Beechwood could help Cassie—dashed. Seated on the lawn with dessert plates of *Crème St. Honoré* and printed programs on our laps, we watched the young, sylph-like Isadora Duncan dance barefooted to her mother's piano arrangement of a recent piece by a new French composer, Claude somebody's *Prélude à l'après-midi d'un faune.*

The murmured comments suggested that a lovely evening had been crimped by the oddest of entertainments. But the exciting Isadora—I would remember her name. The departures were soon announced as carriages and coaches stood ready to receive their owners. "Mr. and Mrs. Cornelius Vanderbilt.... Mr. and Mrs. Armand Cartwright and Mrs. Dudley Forster...."

I watched Cassie disappear into a coach with the Cartwrights and vanish into the night.

"Mr. Theodore Mather Bulkeley..."

Away went Theo, gone. I had not had a chance to speak with either of them. It was nearly one o'clock in the morning.

"Mr. and Mrs. Roderick Windham DeVere...."

Consumed with fatigue and frustration, I braced myself for banalities on the ride home. Instead, when we reached Drumcliffe and stepped inside, I was completely taken aback by Roddy's words—words that kept us up all night long and upended everything.

Chapter Nine

I FELT MORE SUMMONED than invited when Roddy said, "Join me for a drink, Val? In the library, please."

We walked in silence to the gloomy dark brown library. I suspected that word had gotten around about my ride from the Casino on a grocery wagon, and my husband had felt obliged at dinner to defend my "honor." Not that Roddy would ally with the viperous Mamie Fish, but he might remind me that his Wild West wife on a delivery wagon went too far for Newport. Divorces abounded in Society these days, but fraternizing with tradesmen was strictly forbidden—which made me decide to ride with Mr. Tisdall a few more times this summer and to wave at Mamie Fish when the wagon passed in front of the Fish cottage, Crossways. Personally, I wished the Four Hundred had spent a few weeks in the mining towns out West. They'd be thankful for any wagon ride—by mule, horse, or oxen—that spared their soft tender feet.

Prepared for a scolding, I entered the room with walls the color of mud. Dark leather-bound books buried in glass-front cases lined two walls flanking a massive fireplace framed in black stone, and dragons snarled from the andirons. Roddy called the library his summertime laboratory where he kept a stock of liquors and flavorings to try out different cocktails. An ice box—one of several in the cottage—was resupplied weekly, so I expected a chilled drink on this hot summer night.

My husband lighted the electrical sconces and began to select bottles and glasses while I settled into a well-cushioned armchair. In minutes, he handed me a cocktail. Ready for a scolding, I felt confused. Roddy's expression was tenderly apologetic. "Salud, Val," he said. We touched glasses and sipped. "Do you like it?"

"Delicious," I said. "What do you call it?"

He winked. "You and Cassandra rode the Erie Railroad on your sleuthing field trip, and the Erie has named this cocktail for the gated park you ladies visited."

I paused. "Not... the Tuxedo?"

He grinned and nodded. "The Tuxedo."

"And you invented it?"

"I'll never tell. Client privilege. But the drink tonight is my peace offering to my wife...my lover."

The Tuxedo

Ingredients:

- 2/3 ounce Plymouth gin (chilled)

- 1/3 ounce sherry
- Dash of orange bitters

Directions:
1. Add gin and sherry to cocktail glass.
2. Stir.
3. Add bitters and serve.

We kissed, and Roddy pulled up a chair so close that our knees nearly touched. He shed his formal coat and loosened his tie. I took off my shoes. We sipped our drinks. A clock somewhere in the library struck one a.m.

"I know it's late," he said, "but I've learned a few things... information that is possibly of serious concern." Roddy spoke carefully, a trait he doubtless learned from law school. I waited for whatever was coming.

At last, he said, "You know my views on tending to one's own business, but we cannot live by iron-bound rules." He looked quite serious. "Val, with concern for Cassandra's welfare...there are matters that may have serious consequences for her...and must be made known to her, and soon."

I put down my drink and sat up to listen. Suddenly, the mood of the moment grew somber.

"The croquet lawn, Val, is not a calm and placid scene. Nowadays, tapping colored balls through wire wickets on grass seems quaint, but players can be vicious. Yesterday afternoon, I learned of a certain wager."

"At the Casino?"

"Yes."

"By its members?"

Roddy nodded. Despite its name, gambling was forbidden at the Casino. Apart from tennis courts and croquet lawns, there was a card room, billiards, a theater, wide verandas for strolling.

"Anyone we know?"

"In a manner of speaking, yes."

"Surely not Cassie," I said. "Her golfing is well meant, but she won't come near a sport that requires a racquet or ball. Or a shuttlecock." Roddy did not smile. Whatever Casino betting might have involved Cassie felt far-fetched, and trivial.

"It's about Archibald Romberg," Roddy said.

"The Beau Brummel widower," I said, "who thinks he's a gift to the ladies...though so far, the ladies won't play Juliette to his aging Romeo."

Roddy did not smile. "Remember his mood at the celebration for Georgina last summer at Stone Point?"

"Indeed, I do," I said. "He turned purple when Sam awarded Georgina the silver loving cup for 'Excellence in Croquet.'"

Roddy looked strangely grim. "We thought Romberg might lose his temper."

"A sore loser," I said. "I watched him try to woo Henrietta Deems on the *Niagara* deck on the way to Sylvia's funeral. She turned her back on him. You were busy mixing punch, but I saw it."

Roddy sipped his drink, still serious. "Today," he said, "I learned of Romberg's wagers last summer with Georgina Brush."

"Cassie's late auntie...who beat him badly. The 'wicked witch of the wicket,' Georgina Brush...."

"There's more to it, Val. I've learned the two of them bet against one another, Georgina against Archie. Two avid competitors, and each kept raising the ante. The sums multiplied. Romberg lost a very substantial amount of money at croquet...so much that his properties risk forfeiture in a sale, perhaps an auction."

"I don't understand."

Roddy's thumbnail flicked against the cocktail glass, which chimed softly. "Romberg bet sums that he could not cover."

"Meaning...?"

"Meaning the fortune from the old Romberg flour mills is gone. Archie Romberg is broke, and it's no surprise. Romberg Mills lost touch with the times when Gold Medal and Pillsbury took over, and Wall Street approved of flour in sealed sacks instead of scooped from a barrel. Romberg lost customers, and the stock fell, but Archie was too busy wining and dining to pay attention. General Mills might take it over, but the sale will be pennies on the dollar. When bankruptcy documents are signed, *The Wall Street Journal* will report it."

"...and foxy reporters will trace Romberg's loss to Georgina Brush," I said, "a minor blot on the Van Schylar family name." I picked up my drink and sipped. "I don't see what this has to do with Cassie. I suppose the Romberg story will show up in *Town Topics*." 'No scandal unreported,' isn't that its promise? Anyway, Roddy…shall we go upstairs?" I nudged my toes against his ankle, eager for the mood that had started with a Tuxedo cocktail.

But Roddy's voice was firm. "There's something more to tell you."

"My dear, I am listening."

"It is my understanding, Val, that Archie Romberg visited Tuxedo Park late this past spring."

I needed to catch my breath.

"Possibly more than once."

"To see Sylvia?"

"We don't know. Romberg might own a cottage and want to sell it fast to raise cash. Someone might have seen him, perhaps a groundskeeper or…."

"Or Sylvia's housekeeper, Maude Gowdy." If she'll tell the truth, I thought to myself, though why wouldn't she? "Or the omnibus driver," I said, "though his recollection might be hazy. He had a pocket flask and a florid, rosy red complexion. The aroma, I believe, was juniper berry."

"Gin." Roddy took my empty glass and put it down beside his, true to our one-cocktail-at-a-time custom. "I will look into all this, Val. If there were visits to Sylvia Brush, the purpose—or purposes—are not known. We must not make hasty assumptions."

"I understand."

"And I ask for your patience."

"I'll try." Patience was never my strength. "I promise."

"And something else." His tone was almost grave. "I learned something else...at dinner."

"Oh?"

"About Mrs. Brush—"

"Miss? Or Missus?"

"Georgina... the late Georgina..." He paused. "My dinner partner tonight at Beechwood, Mrs. Philbrick...Gladys." Roddy's voice tightened. "Maybe you noticed her, with the snow-white hair? She was a close friend of Georgina. She was at Mrs. Astor's ball when Georgina collapsed.... She did not pass away immediately."

"We know all that, Roddy. She lingered."

"The cause of death—"

"—a heart attack," I said. "Or a stroke. The newspapers said so."

"Newspapers, indeed. We know better, Val. Hearst and Pulitzer for the truth? Really?"

"The death certificate," I said, "Cassie told me about the death certificate. A stroke or heart attack, one or the other."

Roddy took a deep breath. "Those are reasonable causes, aren't they? Nobody thinks twice about a stroke or a heart that stops beating when a person is well along in her sixties. The newspapers got their front-page headline because a very rich and prominent lady collapsed in the middle of Mrs. Astor's annual ball. They did not pursue the cause of death. Why would they?"

"Roddy, what are you saying?"

"That I learned something very different about Mrs. Brush's last days. Mrs. Philbrick took my arm after dinner and asked to pause as we stepped outdoors to see the dancer on the lawn. Of course, I agreed."

"Of course."

"She begged for a moment's conversation." Roddy paused to make certain I was listening. "She wanted me to know that she and Victor—her husband—had attended the Astor ball last January, as they have done for years, and that she was seated at a ballroom table across from her friend, Georgina Van Schylar Brush."

On the edge of my chair, I nodded.

"She was upset, Val. I tried to calm her. I offered reassurance about the value of her friendship with Mrs. Brush. I feared she might make a scene, embarrass herself. Guests were already on the lawn with their desserts.

"But she was insistent. Gladys Philbrick wanted to speak about that night at the ball—and the days afterward. She remembered the crackling fires in Mrs. Astor's ballroom on that bitter cold Monday night. The dinner was served from 1:00 a.m. as usual, and the guests began to dine. When her friend felt lightheaded, she said, other guests at their table kindly exchanged seats.

Georgina's eyes, she thought, were sensitive to light, and her chair was directly beneath the most brilliant crystal chandelier…. Val, are you listening?"

"Crystal chandelier...." I repeated. In my mind, a cascade of faceted crystal. "Something I just thought of, but no... sorry, please go on."

Roddy spoke faster. "As we know, the new seating arrangement was no use. When she fainted, Georgina's satin gown slid up past her knees, a point Mrs. Philbrick remembered. The gentlemen guests tried to help, and Mrs. Astor's footmen took charge. Georgina was immediately taken home to the Brush mansion where she lingered for two days before her death."

"Roddy, don't we already know all this?"

He forged on. "Before her death, she suffered two days of agony. Two days."

"What sort of 'agony'?"

He chose his words. "Violent upheaval."

It took a minute. "You mean nausea. You mean—"

"Yes, vomiting. It started from the moment the carriage brought her to the Brush front door. The butler had to fetch an ice bucket."

A silver ice bucket for the heaving Georgina. I recalled the lard pail for Sylvia. "How does Mrs. Philbrick know all this?"

"She was worried, and she paid several calls during Mrs. Brush's final two days."

"She saw Georgina? In bed?"

"Not exactly. The butler took her card but would not admit her, not past the foyer. He stood his ground."

I nodded. Our Sands would do the same.

"But here's this: Mrs. Philbrick says that she heard Georgina's distress."

"I don't understand, Roddy. No lady's boudoir suite is ever near the front entrance of such a home as the Brush mansion. Even I know...."

"They didn't move her upstairs, Val. She was too sick. The butler said she was made as comfortable as possible on a *chaise longue* in a first floor salon. From the foyer, Mrs. Philbrick could hear...her throes."

"For two days?"

He nodded. "The doctor's carriage was at the curbstone. She assumes he was constantly at Mrs. Brush's side...until the end."

"But the doctor was helpless."

"So it seems."

The library clock struck two a.m. From the windows a nearly full moon cast the night sky into tones of dark gray. I was wide awake.

"Roddy, why did Gladys Philbrick confide all this? Why to you?"

"I asked myself that all the way back from Beechwood. Sometimes a person needs to tell a tale that's so powerful and haunting that it just bursts forth. Of course, the DeVeres have been family friends of the Philbricks for generations, so that's part of it. And Mrs. Philbrick said her husband does not want to hear about it. He told her not to ask questions."

"Meaning what?"

Roddy rubbed his eyes. "Whether the food at the ball might have been spoiled."

"But nobody else got sick, right? If they did, we'd all know because the *World* and *Journal* would have pounced on that story, and *Town Topics* for sure." I imitated a newsboy voice. "'Read all about it—New York City's Four Hundred Poisoned at Mrs. Astor's Ball.'"

The air was warm, but a chill ran up my spine. "Roddy, one more question before we go upstairs, if you please?"

My husband stood to arrange the sherry and bitters bottles and put them back on the library shelves. The gin went into the ice box. "A footman will see to the glasses in the morning," he said, ready to turn off the electrical lights.

"One more question?"

"My dear, the floor is yours."

A sensible wife would have put this off until we both had rested. "Roddy," I began, "everything you have told me over a delicious drink in this wee hour of the morning is very...."

Do I say, 'Disturbing?' 'Frightening?' Do I remind him that Sylvia, too, died after two horrendous days of an identical agony?

"...complicated," I said. "But my dear, you could have kept it all to yourself. Why have you told me all this?"

Roddy took my hand and stood so close that our bodies touched, his chest to my bosom, our hips.....

"It's crucial you know all this, Val, because forces beyond us are in play, and your friend Cassandra will need your help."

I heard him exhale deeply, felt his warm breath. "And because another rumor was circulating last night at Beechwood—that a will has surfaced, a last will and testament of Sylvia Brush. Most of all, Cassie will need you because you see things with a western eye. You alone have a different angle of vision."

Chapter Ten

THE LAST WILL AND testament of Sylvia Ann Van Schylar Brush was scheduled to be read on Tuesday, July 26, at two p.m. at Stone Point, the Newport cottage of Mr. and Mrs. Samuel D. Brush.

"Shouldn't the reading be here at Seabright?" I had asked Cassie. "Wouldn't your own cottage be more... comfortable?"

"Of course it would."

"It's not too late to change—"

"I made a mistake, Val. I admit it, a mistake. Sam offered Stone Point, and I accepted right away."

I strolled the Seabright gardens side by side with Cassie on this hot, steamy Monday midmorning, trying to sound calm. We both wore shirtwaists with walking skirts that cleared the gravel of the garden paths. This was not a casual visit. Cassie was a friend in need, so I came right away, knowing my part doubled down to a "friend in deed." My questions must stop short of an inquisition.

Cassie, however, might harbor information that could help—or hurt—her and the children. "Cassie," I asked softly, "How were you notified about the existence of the will?"

"My mother." She swatted at a fly as if the insect had flown directly from Rowena to torment her daughter.

"And who informed your mother?" I asked. "Do you know?"

"I didn't ask. It was...so sudden. Then the telegram came from Mr. Phillips, so I didn't pursue it."

I remembered the lawyer whose firm paid Sylvia's bills. "Delivered here to your cottage? The telegram made it... official?" She nodded. I hoped Cassie would show me the telegram or quote it from memory. She was silent.

"Yes."

We passed the boxwoods, so green and fragrant. "Who in the world might have guessed that Sylvia prepared a will?" I tried to strike a note of wonder at the very notion. By law, ladies had limited legal rights in Rhode Island and New York, though not in an appalling number of other states of the Union where their signatures would bear no legal weight against not the large inky scrawls of men in authority.

"I have no idea about Sylvia's will, Val, or I'd have told you. We would have talked about it. All those drawers in her Tuxedo Park bedroom...we looked carefully, didn't we... as much as time allowed?"

"Very carefully," I replied. "No hint of a will."

"No hint...." The secret compartment in the Highland Cottage bathroom came to mind, and the empty envelope— the emptied envelope with the torn scrap. The envelope was rolled up inside the tiled enclosure. Should I mention it as we strolled the garden?

Should I tell my friend right now that both Sylvia and her Auntie Georgina evidently suffered identical throes of agony before their deaths? Would it help? Uncertain, I kept quiet for the moment as Cassie tugged her skirt clear of the thorns on a rose bush. Nearby, a gardener with clippers and a basket was cutting fresh flowers for the household. "The will," she said, "has come out of nowhere, out of the blue."

"Suppose that Sylvia told someone about it before she got sick?" I suggested. "Someone beside the lawyer. Maybe Annie Flowers? That postal card from Atlantic City was signed 'Annie.' We could try to find her and ask..."

"Just...just out of the blue," Cassie murmured. Unwilling to speculate, she peered at the ocean and held her gaze. In the distance was the unspoken wish that Dudley Forster would magically appear on the horizon and see her through this new episode in the Van Schylar family drama.

Or melodrama? Or tragedy?

Whichever it might be, I shared that wish. Dudley was an upstanding gentleman who was forthright and honest. Cassie had known she was marrying a man committed to science that would lure him halfway around the world.

Acceptance at face value, however, differed radically from the lived experience, as she was learning. "What would

Dudley do?" was a question that begged the question. Cassie had no idea what her husband would do. As if to mock her wish, an outbound yacht sped under full sail to join the others already in the far distance, their sails appearing as the tiniest white triangles at the line where the sea met the sky.

"Have you any idea what the terms might be?" I meant to steer my friend gently toward the event tomorrow afternoon. Inviting me to this morning's walk, she had already told me that the will was to be brought and read by Mr. Alfred Phillips, Esq. of the law firm of Hester, Phillips, and Lee. He was scheduled to arrive from New York City on the Fall River steamer at 12:10 p.m. "The terms," I asked, "can you guess?"

"Guess?" Cassie snatched a handful of heart-shaped, pink flowers from a nearby shrub. "Guessing is for charades in the evenings. I have no idea." She dropped the flowers one by one. "Did you know these are called bleeding hearts?" Having seen them at Drumcliffe, I had never asked the name. "They fade at this time of year, but they are resilient. To appear delicate, but to be resilient, that's my thought today, Val." She turned to me. "Isn't that best?"

Of course, I agreed. "But if the reading would be preferable here at Seabright…"

"I was caught off guard, Val. I saw Sylvia lying dead in that tenement, the horrible doctor closing her eyes with his fat thumb. And I thought to myself, spare my Bea and Charlie. The last thing children ought to see in their home is a grim- faced attorney with the manner of a funeral director. Truly, Mr. Phillips looks more mournful than Mr. Frear."

We managed to chuckle, and Cassie pushed a hairpin into place. "I was too hasty, I didn't think," she continued. "Of course, I could have sent the children to the beach with Cara. Or I could have rescheduled their lessons."

Her children were at a riding lesson this morning, a blessing for a young mother in need of a calming few hours. In some quarters of Society, I suspected, the contest between horsemanship and literacy went to the saddle and reins. The English saddle, that is. Never a western saddle more suited for a day's work.

"I'm sure it's not too late to arrange the reading here," I said. "Sam would understand."

"Sam, yes, but not Evalina. She would feel slighted. She's ordered special preparations as if it's a social occasion... afternoon tea, and the footmen are rearranging furniture. If I request that we gather here, she'll misunderstand and pout. No, Val. Sylvia's will is to be read at Stone Point. So, let well enough alone."

We turned along the path and sat for a few moments on a filigreed iron bench that overlooked a garden whose layout was peculiar for Newport. French or English gardens, said Cassie, were *de rigueur*. But Seabright featured a hybrid of English plants mixed with native grasses, wildflowers, and a hut that resembled native housing in the South Sea Islands. Dudley insisted that nature also have its way. Rowena had declared her daughter's garden to be incoherent and predicted harm would come to the children. ("Their taste will be debased, mark my words.") My friend's own view of the compromise had evolved, I noticed, into tolerance verging on acceptance. The children played hide-and-seek in the grasses and shared secrets in the hut.

Fearing to roil the moment, I nonetheless wanted to verify who, exactly, would attend the reading of Sylvia's will. I said, "It's kind of you to consider Evalina's feelings."

"Really, Val, it's Sam's feelings. A sulking bride is no joy."

"My dear friend, we both might understand that point."

Cassie managed a brief smile, then grew quiet for a moment. "I mustn't be unfair to Evalina. It's that Sam and his gadgets can be, well, a bit overwhelming."

At this, I was unsure whether to laugh or sympathize. Stone Point was Sam's pride, but often a trial to dinner guests, who could feel more like ticketed visitors on a guided tour as their host demonstrated electric motors and mechanical devices that powered everything from the dumb waiter to a reclining Morris chair.

Cassie said, "We love him, but I think the World's Fair in Chicago turned his head. Sam went to oversee the Brush wood panels at the fair, but the machinery on display hypnotized him. It was like…like opium."

A startling word, but Cassie smiled. "Do you know he tried to borrow a suit of armor from Oliver Belmont's collection? He wanted to motorize the arms and legs to make it walk, just for a party…."

"I doubt that he will show off his machinery tomorrow, Cassie. It won't be a party."

"No."

"He will be kind and considerate."

"Yes."

"And Evalina will do her best."

"I hope so."

"And the family members who are expected tomorrow, of course, your parents...."

Cassie cringed. I should have started with Sam and Evalina. "I didn't mean—"

"That's all right, Val." Cassie sat up very straight on the iron bench. "Delicate and resilient—my watchwords." She spoke as if announcing guests at a formal gathering. "To attend tomorrow afternoon: Mr. and Mrs. Samuel D. Brush, Mr. and Mrs. Robert Fox, and Mrs. Dudley Forster, née Cassandra Van Schylar Fox Forster." Her voice softened. "Also, some Van Schylar cousins. You remember the elderly ladies at Sylvia's funeral, the ladies with canes?"

"I do."

"And the younger Van Schylar women? They didn't all sit together, but some summer in Bar Harbor, others at Saratoga."

I recognized the two resorts. Roddy had promised an early autumn visit to Maine one day to visit Bar Harbor, but Saratoga in western New York was on his blacklist from boyhood when his parents had forced him to drink the spa water for health. "The cousins," I asked, "do you know them?"

Cassie shook her head. "Not really. They live in the Hudson Valley instead of the city. One of the Van Schylars moored a small yacht in the river to commute to his Wall Street office."

My next question was delicate, since matters of money must be phrased indirectly, even with a close friend. "I wonder whether Sylvia ever visited the relatives in the Hudson Valley?" I asked. "Perhaps for a weekend now and then?"

Cassie's knitted her brow. "You needn't be coy, Val. You are trying to ask politely whether the Van Schylar cousins stand to inherit some of the Brush fortune."

"I suppose."

"You are! Let's. Let's agree, we must be truthful."

"In that case, 'delicate,'" I said. "And 'resilient.'"

I waved away a bee. Tomorrow at this time Cassie would be dressing in preparation to drive to Stone Point. She would wear lusterless silks and a black straw hat whose decoration had been stripped of bright floral clusters. Her gloves would be a muted dark kidskin, and her stockings and suede boots, both black.

Driven by O'Boyle, she would sit alone in the Victoria carriage all the way to the Brush cottage, Stone Point, each mile of Ocean Drive in view of the rolling sea that would remind her of her absent husband. No friend could accompany her on this journey.

We stood and clasped hands. My palm was dry, Cassie's damp. Was it heat or anxiety? "Cassie, I wish I could help."

"Val, I will count on you."

"I'll think about you tomorrow afternoon. Tomorrow's best wishes, Cassie, all for you."

⟳

Tuesday at 2:00 p.m. found me in the mezzanine study at Drumcliffe with the latest issues of *Town & Country* and *Vogue*. I was too distracted for a book.

Roddy would join me presently. His inspection of a carriage axle repair was taking longer than expected. He insisted on seeing the work for himself. Our coachman, Noland, relayed this information to our butler, Sands, who in turn asked our housekeeper, Mrs. Thwait (a woman I instinctively disliked) to instruct Calista to tell me.

"Will that be all, Ma'am?"

"I think so...no, one more thing, Calista. A plate of molasses crisps for Mr. DeVere. He will join me here in the mezzanine in a few minutes."

"Yes, ma'am."

"And please bring an ice bucket...and tea."

It felt like hours, not minutes, when I heard familiar footsteps, and felt my husband's kiss on my cheek. "I thought you'd be here."

"My hiding place," I said, supposedly out of 'world-and-time,' but at the moment, it isn't working."

"How could it?" Roddy pulled up a cushioned chair to sit near me. "How do you feel? Have you lunched?"

"No. I'm on edge, braced for shocks. It's like in Colorado when Papa warned us to look out for timber rattlers."

Roddy laughed, but I was not amused. "On your advice, Mr. DeVere, I've opened my Western eye to see what I can see. "Right now, I picture the scene at Stone Point where the last will and testament of Sylvia Ann Van Schylar Brush is being read...is it a ceremony? A ritual? My papa filed his will in Nevada. What is the law in New York?"

"Actually, Val, the law says very little." Roddy sat back. "The document must be located, of course. It might be filed in a law office or a bank. It might be secured in a residential safe along with family silver. Or it might be—"

"—stuffed in a shoe. Or a cigar box...or the hollow of a tree?"

"More or less. I know what you're thinking. The bathroom nook in Tuxedo Park—"

I had told Roddy the details of my visit with Cassie. "Quite possibly," I said. "A formal will in New York, Roddy... is it usually engraved, like a diploma?"

"No. It would be copied by a clerk in a law office, a man trained in penmanship." Our silence measured the gap that law had not filled. "Once located," Roddy said, "the will is put into the hands of an executor for execution... which is the reading." Guessing my next question, he went on. "Val, the law on the reading takes second place to...frankly, to etiquette." He paused, seeing my frown. "I know, it's the word you love to hate."

"But a word I must respect.'" In the West we called it behaving ourselves. "Does it need a witness?"

"That depends on the jurisdiction. It helps for clarification if the will is contested."

I tried not to picture Sylvia's heirs at war...and Cassie's distress. "Can a person write her own will? Just sit down with a piece of paper and pen and go to it?"

"Pretty much. If the will is prepared in a law office, of course, a clerk will make sure the paper is durable."

"But no curlicues or embossing?"

"No curlicues. The attorney is a witness, so is the clerk."

"But if a person...."

We were interrupted as Calista knocked softly and came in, balancing a tray with plates, a platter, napkins, a teapot, glasses, mint leaves, and an ice bucket. "Sir, ma'am...." I gestured to a table, and the tray was set down. "Shall I pour?" She looked uncertain. A lady's maid did not serve food or beverages. Mrs. Thwait would not approve. "Ma'am, Mr. DeVere...If you wish...?"

"Please, Calista."

"By all means," said Roddy.

We watched the former coastal stewardess deftly take the tongs, grip chunks of ice for each glass, fill both with tea, and pop mint sprigs at the rims. Her fingers moved with the skill of the bartender at the Palm Court. As a woman, of course, such a profession was out of the question at this time, but not when the next century turned. "Thank you, Calista. I'll ring for a footman when we're finished."

The door closed, and Roddy took a handful of the molasses crisps. We lifted our glasses and signaled a toast. The cool tea was delicious. Darjeeling, I thought. Or Oolong. It was hard to keep them straight.

"Where did we last have this?" Roddy asked. He held up his glass. "Tea with ice… was it at Rosecliff? Ochre Court?"

"It was Stone Point, Roddy. Evalina ordered it for a luncheon a few weeks ago. Don't you remember? She went on and about the famous iced tea in the South, and she gave every guest a copy of *Housekeeping in Old Virginia*, that cookbook she loves. She said it made her feel at home."

He bit a cookie. "Very tasty. Goes with the tea."

Another bite, probably his substitute for lunch, but I felt annoyed.

"I'll wager that all Newport will soon be drinking tea that's iced," he said. "Probably a spiked version too, with some fetching name, like Whiskey Tea Sling, or Lightning Tea Smash. I'll get to work on it."

My eyes began to fill, from frustration. "Roddy, at this very minute, a lawyer about two miles from here is reading a document that might very well have a profound impact on my friend—our friend, for better or worse. And you… you are preoccupied with cookies and tea inventing names for your cocktails. At this minute, people's fates are being dictated at Stone Point, while the master of Drumcliffe is absorbed in…in whisky."

"Val, don't misunderstand." Roddy rose and came to my side. "Don't you see, I'm deliberately trying not the think about Stone Point this afternoon. It will only rankle us to imagine the contents of a document that no one—presumably no one—has seen. Or knew existed. Sylvia Brush's death…no one was prepared. To learn that she died under the same circumstances as her mother just a few months earlier…this raises life-and-death questions that we cannot answer at this time. We have no choice but to wait."

How long we waited, I have no idea. We sat together in the mezzanine study, me on the divan, Roddy in the well-upholstered chair. He dozed briefly, then paged through a book called *The Flowing Bowl: Where and What to Drink.* I leafed through *Vogue.* The cookie plate held crumbs, and the ice had melted.

It was a sharp rap at the study door that roused us both. Already dressed for evening, Sands stood before us. "Mr. DeVere…Mrs. DeVere, my apologies for this intrusion, but Mrs. Forster is at the entrance. May I say, she does not look well. She has not offered her card but wishes to see you at the earliest possible moment. The very earliest."

Chapter Eleven

FRAMED AGAINST THE GLARING sunlight at the entrance to our cottage, Cassie Forster looked like a cut-out silhouette that grew into a life-size figure, jet black in the lap of summer.

"Cassie…." Breathless, I gasped her name. My friend's dark hair had fallen loose from its many pins. She gripped her black straw hat tightly in both hands, as if it were a talisman to ward off the world.

"Come in. Join us." I put out my hand, but she seemed frozen. Two of our footmen hovered, awaiting orders. Sands stood at the entrance like a sentinel. Cassie looked like a refugee.

Roddy's voice broke the spell. "Let's do sit down."

"Thank you." Her voice was weak. She stepped inside.

"We'll go into the—" Too many rooms, too many high-ceilinged caverns with over-sized furniture. "Into the music room," I said.

We flanked our friend, who halted but found her footing. The soft blue music room felt calm despite the mantle lined with marble busts of wild-haired composers. A harp stood by the window next to the grand piano that badly needed tuning. Nobody played either instrument.

"Let's sit over there, by the loveseat and chairs," I said.

We passed the piano and settled Cassie on the loveseat. I sat down in a matching armchair, but Roddy hesitated. "Cassandra," he said, "your coachman—"

"O'Boyle?" She looked confused.

"I believe he is waiting. If I may, I would like to send him back to Seabright. Mrs. DeVere and I will see you home."

"Yes, thank you." She kept a tight grip on her hat. Roddy stepped out of the room, murmured to Sands, and the music room echoed briefly with the sounds of hooves and carriage wheels. Then the strange quiet. Was my friend well enough to have the conversation we expected?

"Your hat…" I began. It was tugged and pulled, a misshapen black straw that Cassie reluctantly put on the seat beside her. It would never be worn again.

"We hope you will be comfortable," Roddy said, his voice soothing. "Let me order something. I'll ring." Grateful for a task, he went to the call button on a side wall. "May I suggest beef tea, Cassandra?" Roddy said.

"Beef tea," she said. "Oh yes, perfect, thank you."

To me, the term meant a pond where cattle drank, but Cassie brightened at a beverage. Our silence was slipping from calm to awkward.

Roddy said, "Quite an afternoon," his voice as sympathetic as when Papa came down with the cough from the mines. The footman returned with cups and a kettle on a tray. He poured out a tan liquid that smelled like grilled steak. Roddy and Cassie raised their cups and drank quietly.

I was about to test the odd brew when Cassie at last burst out, "It came to me."

"I beg your pardon—"

"All of it. Sylvia left nearly all of it to me." The air seemed to crackle.

"—not sure I understand," Roddy began.

Cassie's waved her arm, spilling the beef tea. She did not notice. "I don't even want it. It's not fair. And my mother was...she was monstrous."

"Discourteous?" Roddy asked.

"Another smashed vase... it's uncalled for. Father is right, she's a thunderstorm." Cassie took another sip of tea, her cup shaking. "Evalina was furious, and Sam pretended it was an accident. My mother will contest the terms...oh, she will contest them. She threatened to go to court, stop the probate."

"But if Sylvia's signature in pen and ink are clear as day, the terms are legally binding." Roddy's words about daylight and law seemed to fall on deaf ears.

"Cassie," I asked, what is the '*it*'?" Sylvia left you 'nearly all of it?' What is the '*it*?'"

She looked exasperated, as though we must already understand. Roddy said, "Take your good time, Cassandra. We are here. We have no plans for the evening."

Which was not true. We had been expected at the harbor for an evening sail on the Goelets' yacht, *Mayflower*. Roddy was expected to surprise everyone with a crafted punch for ladies and gentlemen. I assumed that he had sent a messenger with our excuses. If my husband had canceled a social obligation, he took Cassie's plight very seriously indeed.

"Could we start at the beginning?" Roddy asked, his voice honeyed. "We will try our best to understand, won't we, Val?"

I nodded, fearing my voice might sound too insistent. To sit beside my friend, to take her hand, comfort her—that's what I yearned to do. But if Cassie sobbed on my shoulder, we would learn nothing. For her own benefit, she must sit alone on the loveseat.

"The weather was so fine this afternoon," Roddy said, his voice like syrup. "Pleasant for one and all. And we assume that everyone assembled in good order?" Roddy continued, "Convenient travel makes such a difference, whether one chooses an open carriage or prefers to be shaded from the sun."

My shoulders tightened at the trivial talk when the urgent matter was Sylvia's will.

He went on, "Or whether one prefers to enjoy the deck or an inside cabin on the ferry."

"Or the steamer," Cassie said. She seemed calmer. "Yes, the good weather helped everyone. The cousins from Saratoga feared *mal de mer*, but they arrived in good health."

"A great benefit," Roddy said, "for everyone who was expected this afternoon."

Cassie nodded, and I realized that Roddy was tactically easing her into the recollection that was so raw. My husband was born and bred into Society with its tempo so different from the West, and I must take my cue, although it felt like another country. I said, "I would guess the cousins found Stone Point cottage to be beautifully landscaped... its delightful gardens."

"They did enjoy the gardens."

"And found the interior to be...most interesting?"

She managed a short smile. "One of the cousins is attempting to write a novel. She said the cottage furnished remarkable new ideas for her setting."

"From the sight of the tapestry?"

"Oh, by all means, that tapestry."

Cassie and I had often rolled our eyes at the custom-ordered tapestry that Sam inherited from his brother Harry, a huge weaving of a forester beside felled trees against a background of bright brown stumps. The forester's shirt was flaming red, the head of his axe of silver thread. "Gaudy," I pronounced it. Cassie said "*de trop*."

Roddy's face signaled the moment to move on, "So Cassie...." Roddy lifted his cup and sipped. "Everyone was welcomed—"

"And offered tea and teacakes," I added.

"And seated..." said Roddy.

"In new bronze chairs," Cassie said quickly. "Evalina ordered them for the dining room and had them put into the morning room where we gathered. So heavy two footmen were needed to move each one."

"But everyone was made comfortable?" I sensed Roddy trying to speed up the pace, narrow the focus.

"Quite comfortable," Cassie said. "And it was cheerful to have the little dog on the loose."

"What little dog?" I asked. It was Roddy's turn to look a bit irritated.

"A French bulldog. It's a new breed. Evalina named her Velvet because her fur is so soft. She's a smart little dog, really charming."

"Would you like your beef tea warmed, Cassandra?" Roddy asked. "Or another? And are you comfortable? The late afternoon sunlight not too strong?"

No, said Cassie, the light was fine, the seat perfectly comfortable. The tattered hat on the loveseat cushion told how much my close friend would rather talk about anything except Sylvia's will.

Roddy set down his cup with a click, a signal that we must come to terms.

He would take the lead, reining in Cassie from these distractions, from the tapestry to the chairs to the dog. Roddy did not practice law, except to defend taverns against the temperance "crusaders" in city courtrooms, but I imagined my husband in court preparing to cross-examine a witness.

"You used the word 'nearly,'" he said softly to her, as if sharing a secret. "As you said a few minutes ago, 'nearly' everything came to you."

Cassie reached for the hat. She said, "Yes, nearly."

"Then others have benefitted from your cousin's will, have they not? "Who else Cassandra? Can you tell us? In strictest confidence, of course." He looked to me to underscore the point. I nodded with a certain exaggeration as if in pantomime.

"The church," Cassie said. "St. Mary's Episcopal Church. Fifty thousand dollars."

"A handsome sum for the church in which she worshiped," Roddy said.

No surprise there, I thought. Cassie gazed over my shoulder toward the piano but seemed not to see me. A footman came to lower the draperies, but Roddy waved him off. "And were other memorable gifts provided for those who are in range of 'nearly?'"

"And for Maude Gowdy," she said, "five thousand dollars."

"The housekeeper at Tuxedo Park," I said to Roddy. "We remember her, don't we, Cassie?" I tried to keep my friend focused. "...Sylvia's promise for her housekeeper's 'well-being?'"

My friend seemed to imitate the lawyer's voice. "'—upon my death, in support of her enterprise.'"

"Her secret silver polish," I said. "It has to be her silver polish. Cassie, you remember how the cottage looked like a silversmith's show room."

"And the 'enterprise,'" Roddy broke in, "is to be funded only upon Sylvia Brush's death? Is that correct? Only 'upon my death?'" She nodded and fingered her damaged hat.

Evening shadows lengthened across the Persian rug, the busts of Beethoven and Mozart merged in light grays on the floral rug. Roddy took another sip of the beef tea, which had to be stone cold. Was he pondering his next move?

Cassie began to rise. "I really ought to be going. Would you be so kind?"

Gentleman that he was, Roddy promptly stood. "If you wish, Cassandra, I will order a carriage, but we mustn't send you off without an invitation to dine. Please do not permit us to be so rude."

The fact was, right now my friend was both brittle and fragile, but Roddy and I needed to know something more in order to help her. The two Van Schylar Brush women's deaths—mother and daughter—under identical circumstances within a few months felt more and more beyond coincidence. Those two bequests, it appeared, were the only exceptions to "nearly everything." We would soon learn more about the terms of the will from Sam, of course, but the urgency was here and now.

"A moment more, a few more minutes," Roddy said. "Val, won't you join Cassandra on the little sofa? Just briefly."

My husband, the tactician. I went to the loveseat, pushed aside the mangled straw hat, took my friend's hand, and sat us down. "We won't keep you a minute longer than needed," I said, "but can you help us understand Sylvia's last wishes, your inheritance—what she has left you?"

At that, Cassie's shoulders went limp, "Hartshorn," she murmured.

"Smelling salts," I said, ignoring the more polite word. It was doubtful that my friend had eaten a meal today. "Roddy," I said, "please have a footman bring hot chocolate and buttered toast for all of us." We waited several awkward minutes until the toast and cocoa arrived. Cassie nibbled, drank, and seemed to stare at nothing.

Perhaps it was my turn. "Last will and testament—" I began. "And the main beneficiary is a person who is...listen to me, Cassie. Can you hear me?" She nodded. I twisted around to look her in the eye. "The main beneficiary," I said slowly and carefully, "is delicate and resilient."

"Resilient," Cassie echoed, with just enough resolve in her syllables.

"And she can tell her very good friend—who is sitting at her side at this moment—exactly what she has inherited." I repeated, "Exactly."

As if reciting in a schoolroom, her voice tremulous but constant, Cassie spoke in a monotone. "....'my property and all assets I bequeath to Cassandra Van Schylar Fox Forster.'" She added, "'in accordance with and pursuant to the interests of my mother, Georgina Rose Van Schylar Brush.'"

Roddy stood, quiet and motionless, listening.

"So, you have inherited Aunt Georgina's...projects," I said. "Your favorite Auntie." My mind briefly conjured up the list, Cuba, the dog kennels, suffrage. Georgina had taken up the cause, and Sylvia followed. Now it was Cassie's turn.

Did her aunt and cousin die as a consequence of a cause? Causes? And Cassie? Was it her turn now?

"And Tuxedo Park too. That too...." Cassie said it solemnly, as if the shingled cottage was as onerous as the movement for women's votes, weighing as heavily on her mind as the entire Brush fortune. Overwhelmed. She was overwhelmed.

We three spent the next few minutes nibbling toast points and sipping hot chocolate, snacks that neither Roddy nor I normally cared to have at this hour, our cocktail hour. Shadows deepened on the carpet where the composers' heads became a wide blur.

Cassie replaced her cup. "Now, I will be off," she said. "Just in time to read bedtime stories to the children. These evenings we turn the pages of *Peter Rabbit*...I love reading to Bea and Charlie."

We all rose. Roddy would order a carriage. Our coach-man Noland would drive her to Seabright. My husband, however, had another word to say before we parted. He looked serious. No, he looked grave.

"Cassandra," he said, "we are fortunate to enjoy summers within a certain set of friends here in Newport. One feels there is safety in numbers among us." Cassie nodded. I had no idea what he intended to say.

"Some of our fortunes are a well-kept secret. Consider the Bradley Martins." We did. It was well known that Mrs. Martin's father, Isaac Sherman, had quietly amassed a huge fortune and surprised his daughter at his death. No one knew that Sherman was quite rich.

Roddy went on, "Others of us, however, are known quite publicly for the businesses they've founded. Consider Mr. Carnegie...."

Yes, the name synonymous with steel.

"Or consider the name, Brush."

Cassie and I murmured, "Wood."

Roddy continued, "And the newspaper stories, the reporters at every rail station, every depot, every entrance to hotels, theaters, churches...."

We nodded like schoolgirls, though Cassie was eager to depart and began to fidget. I too was becoming impatient.

"And recall the unfortunate conclusion to your cousin's funeral service...."

Neither of us welcomed this reminder of the havoc that broke out as we left Trinity Church, the mob, the fear. Cassie turned pale. I took her hand, furious at Roddy.

"Here at Newport," he went on, "we have a fine constabulary. The police are diligent, responsible, and protective of the citizens."

What was Roddy getting at?

"But Newport is not solely Bellevue Avenue and Ocean Drive. The many side streets, Franklin, Prospect Hill, Mann...." Cassie looked numbed. Why the geography lesson? I was stupefied.

"The Newport police cannot be everywhere at all times. They are not a private force." He stepped close, out of range of servants' ears. "Cassandra, from now on, you will be known as the principal heir to the Brush fortune. Here at

Newport, life will seem to go on as usual, but the newspapers will publicize your name. Strangers will attempt to reach you, and not all of them will wish you well. You must have private protection."

So this was it—bodyguards. Cassie's hand turned clammy in mine.

"Your name will be in the papers, your picture as well. And the names of your children. If your Dudley were with us, I am confident that he would support my proposal. On behalf of your husband, I recommend the Pinkerton agency."

"Pinkerton detectives," Cassie was alarmed. "Surely not. I do not need detectives. No, no...."

Roddy's voice was tempered steel. "I will telegraph the agency the first thing in the morning. This is not the time for polite quibbling. Pinkerton men ought to be at your service day and night. I'm certain that Dudley would insist. This is no time to dally. There is no time to lose."

Chapter Twelve

"PINKERTON MEN! PINKERTONS AT Newport, here in our very own social capital? Really and truly, Pinkertons? 'The Eye That Never Sleeps.' Sam Brush intoned the detective agency's motto in a comic basso voice. His mockery was unsettling, the volume of his voice alarming in our vestibule at Drumcliffe. It was one hour from lunchtime, and I had not yet heard today from Cassie.

Sam had arrived on horseback moments ago just as Roddy returned from the telegraph office where he had sent a message to the Pinkerton Agency office in the city. Tying his horse to our gatepost, Sam came inside and handed his derby hat to Sands. At the sound of Roddy's low murmur and Sam's booming decibels, I quickly joined them with a finger across my lips to signal, "Hush." Servants abounded, from the butler to the kitchen sculleries, supposedly hearing nothing, sworn to secrecy and threatened with discharge upon violation. Still....

Sam turned to me, lightly shook my hand and lowered his voice. "Dear Mrs. DeVere—Valentine—my apologies. Every cottage vestibule in Newport needs acoustical engineering." He had a quicksilver glint in his eye. "Please do lead us to the drawing room where we can best speak in privacy."

The heat of the day was rising, and Sam's upper lip was dewy from his ride and from the weight of his houndstooth jacket and snug riding britches. I took us to a small reception room whose heavy draperies dampened voices, a room that felt cooler because the large paintings featured pleasant summer seashore scenes in France. Or was it Italy? The pictures were already on these walls when I became mistress of Drumcliffe, as was the heavy Empire period furniture that I intended to replace. Leaving the echo chamber of a vestibule, we were impatient to hear Sam tell us the details of Sylvia's will.

"Sam," I asked, "will you stay to lunch?"

"Thank you, no. I breakfasted on chestnut pastries that Evalina served yesterday afternoon. I may not dine for another week."

We laughed a bit, and I ordered luncheon held. "And if a message should arrive from Mrs. Forster at Seabright cottage, please do inform me immediately. We'll be in the...." The name of the room escaped me. So many rooms named by Roddy's mother."

"The *Peintures de Plage* room, ma'am?"

Beach pictures, that's it. I nodded and held my questions while we enacted our usual social overture.

"Evalina sends her warmest regards," Sam said, adding that his bride was "held captive" at Stone Point, fearing their footmen might reassemble the dining room in helter-skelter confusion. "She wanted nothing more than to visit Drumcliffe, but she sent me on her behalf while each bronze chair is hoisted back to its place," he added. "I had proposed we install an electrical lift in our cottage, but my bride would not hear of it. I'm sure the staff would disagree." Sam turned toward Roddy. "About these Pinkertons, Roderick…. Shall I raise a glass or wag a finger?"

Roddy hid his annoyance at our good friend's boisterous mood. The notion of the nationally famous private detective agency had struck Sam, it seems, as a joke. I had first learned about Pinkerton men from Papa. They caught train robbers out West, sent a few embezzling conductors to prison, and broke up the Butch Cassidy gang, though some recent ventures were more controversial.

Would a drink soothe or stimulate this guest whose jovial mood was jarring us? Roddy's glance told me Sam Brush must be properly hosted. "What is your pleasure, Sam? Let us raise a glass. The hour calls for a bracing milk punch."

A footman was sent for one of Roddy's wheeled bar carts, and we paused to watch my husband mix milk with rum and brandy and ice chips, all with the skills that hinted of a secret dream to tend bar in London or Paris. Or San Francisco. He strained the drinks into glasses, grated nutmeg over the tops, and presented one to Sam. For me, a sip of Roddy's drink and a mineral water. The cocktails my husband and I shared together were between us, a semi-secret.

Milk Punch

Ingredients:

- 8 ounces milk
- 2/3 ounce Santa Cruz rum
- 1/3 ounce brandy
- 1 dash vanilla extract 1 teaspoon sugar Ice chips
- Nutmeg (if desired)

Directions:

1. In large glass or shaker, add milk.
2. Add all other ingredients.
3. Shake well, strain and serve.

"Here's to our very own Newport," said Sam, raising his glass. "Whisky and cool milk and a sprinkling of nutmeg, a gift of the gods." He toasted in my direction. "And to the human ingenuity that carbonates water—a gift of modern science." We all drank, though Roddy barely sipped.

Sam went on. "I have been on the run since dawn today," he said. "The Van Schylar cousins were sent off in a brougham to the harbor, then the Fall River line, on to Penn Station and—miracle of modern speed—they will be in Saratoga by evening. No dawdling." He drank again. "Roderick, Valentine…you are no doubt eager to hear about the event of yesterday afternoon at Stone Point."

"As much as you wish to say," Roddy said.

Sam paused, looked from Roddy to me. "Yesterday afternoon nearly did us in...worse than tiresome. Phillips droned on and on and reread entire passages.... He must be in his later eighties by now. Lank cheeks, a sunken eye, a haggard man. Too many years spent in the company of legal documents." Sam smiled. "It's what they'll say about me if I live that long. 'Old Sam Brush, too many years tinkering with machines. Gave it all to gear wheels and sprocket arms.' One interesting point—Miss Sylvia's will was typewritten. Very modern. I'm planning on getting a typewriting machine myself."

"That is interesting, Sam," I said, "Do you know anything about who might have typed the will?"

He shrugged. "Probably a clerk in Phillips's office. Maybe they're spending a few dollars to modernize now that old Hester is gone, by all accounts a tightwad." He looked at our faces, realizing the topic of the moment was far from the machinery that never failed to captivate him. He sighed and drank his punch. "Apologies once again to you, my friends." He looked sheepish.

"Cassie visited us here at Drumcliffe after the reading," I said. "She was...not herself."

"How could she be, really?" Sam looked dismayed at the recollection. "Her mother is a harridan. Rowena has worn out every welcome in Newport. A vase smashed to smithereens, very rare, Qing Dynasty. Evalina expects a replacement, and if I know my bride, she'll get it. The notorious Mamie Fish is no match for Rowena's outbursts. The sooner Robert Fox is a free man, the better for all of us." Sam reached for his glass as if to settle his feelings. He now seemed rueful. "And to think, the woman is a sister to Georgina, my dear late sister-in-law. How can one be alive while the other...." He broke off.

"Our impression is that Cassie is most upset by the terms of her cousin's will," Roddy said.

"Upset? You put it mildly. If Evalina's little dog hadn't been in the room to divert us, we'd have felt like it was another funeral."

"Yes, we've heard about the dog," Roddy said, doubtless to get past the topic.

"Evalina plans to raise these little dogs, with the pointy ears," Sam said. "'Bat ears,' they're called. I'm going to design a kennel with mechanized water and feeding stations. It will all be very modern."

He drank his punch. "About Cassandra and the will," Roddy prompted, "was there confusion?"

"Not at first. The church, the housekeeper at Tuxedo Park...I saw Cassandra nod approval. At least, I thought I did. Then Phillips got to the main bequest, the language about Cassandra continuing Georgina's work, and I saw her go very pale. One of the Van Schylar cousins gave her smelling salts."

Roddy and I exchanged a glance.

"She'll be fine. It was a jolt, of course, like an electrical shock when a person is not grounded. But she'll find ways to deal with it. We'll all help. I have ideas." He looked my way. "I know she counts on you, Valentine." He sipped and turned to Roddy. "Now, what's this about Pinkertons?"

Roddy drew his deepest breath for this conversation. "For Cassandra's protection," he began, "with Dudley so far away and the publicity that's certain to be drawn to her."

"Of course. Full agreement on that score. We've all endured the press and low-lifes that spit on us on public streets. And crazy anarchists with knives and pistols. Think of what happened to Frick."

We paused to think. Six years ago, the newspapers were full of the anarchist who tried to assassinate Henry Clay Frick, the ruling "king" of the process that turned coal into coke for the steel industry. Fortunately, Mr. Frick survived the gunshots. The episode made headlines for weeks at a time.

"And consider what one single stick of dynamite can do," Sam went on, "a cardboard cylinder packed with nitro-glycerin, the whole thing tucked into a pocket.... Strike a wood match, touch the flame to the wick...think of the Haymarket riot in 'eighty-six."

Another fearsome thought. Someone had thrown a bomb at a labor rally in Chicago. I was a girl back then, and Sam a young boy, but the adults had talked of nothing but dynamite.

Roddy had barely touched his punch. "No offense, Sam, but let's not dredge up every misuse of explosives or a firearm."

Sam loosened his necktie. "Apologies once again." He bit his lip. "I trust you friends can understand that, for me, some very foul thoughts have crowded into my mind of late, although I try to be as cheerful as a newly-married man can be." He added, "A man with a beautiful bride who is bringing elegance to Stone Point." Somehow the last words sounded more dutiful than heartfelt.

He paused, reaching for his glass. "But my brother's loss is always haunting, and my friend lost on the *Maine*, and then Georgina…and now Sylvia. I barely knew her, but the sudden shock…explosive, personal dynamite." He almost gulped the punch and held the glass in both hands. "To stand at the pulpit at Trinity Church and eulogize a lady who was a member of our family but died of neglect…our neglect." He looked miserable.

Perhaps he would also be open to the question shadowing Roddy and me— why two women, mother and daughter, would die agonizing deaths under identical circumstances within a few months' time. Was it wise to bring it up now? Sam had alluded to Sylvia's sorry physical state. If he had a quick "flying" trip to the city scheduled in the next few weeks, perhaps he could inquire further at Lanham & Frear about the condition of her body, find out something that might explain her strange untimely death. Across the chair cushions, Roddy could be thinking these same thoughts. We both looked ready to speak, when Sam abruptly put down his glass, sat up straight and spoke with such resolve that, for the moment, we both stayed quiet.

"Please don't misunderstand, Roderick and Valentine," he said. "I didn't intend to scoff at the idea of Pinkerton agents. In fact, the Van Schylar and Brush families owe a great deal to the Pinkerton enterprise. Perhaps you remember the Brush labor strike?"

I did not. Roddy was obviously searching his memory.

"The Wisconsin lumber mills? The wood shingle plant in Maine? My brother Harry, God rest his soul—Harry Brush would never let labor unions infest the wood business. 'Tree beetles,' he called them. When the wood workers' 'brotherhood' went on strike, he called in the Pinkertons. They went to Maine, they went to Wisconsin. Armed squadrons, bayonets on their rifles. No more union 'brotherhood' in Brush Industries."

Roddy said, "About Cassandra...of course there's no need for an armed squadron with bayonets. But she is alone with the children at Seabright until the season ends. Dudley is not due back in the States until autumn. Early October, I believe, before the winter storms."

"So, we gentlemen must act on Dudley's behalf." Sam sat forward, arms outstretched, his wrestling days at Harvard echoed in his posture. He looked energized.

It seemed impossible now to bring up our concerns about Georgina and Sylvia's similar deaths.

"It's not the Pinkerton armed gendarmes that worry me," Sam said, "but Pinkerton is making a great deal of money on divorce cases these days."

"Spying on unfaithful spouses?" I asked.

"'Divorce detectives,' they're called. Right now, it's the most profitable unit of the company. The detectives spy, even fabricate evidence. Imagine—phony evidence to break up homes." We all shook our heads. "And surely, you have heard rumors here in Newport about husbands and wives, the married daughters and sons. *Town Topics* feeds them and feeds on them. Not to be a prude. I am a modern man, after all. Divorce happens. Alva Vanderbilt divorced Willy K. and married Oliver Belmont. And Robert Fox is soon to be permanently free of Rowena. Life goes on. Divorce is perfectly acceptable these days, but scandal is…."

"Scandalous?" I quipped.

"In Cassandra's case, yes. A Pinkerton divorce detective on duty at Seabright would set the rumor mill grinding. I cannot guarantee that a threat of legal action—mine or yours or anybody's—would block a high voltage story in *Town Topics.*"

"But we all know that *Town Topics*—"

"—is the trash that Newport swallows and savors. We agreed on this at Seabright the day after Sylvia's funeral, am I right?" I nodded. Sam had promised strong words to the *Town Topics* publisher. So far, the weekly scandal sheet had refrained.

"Count on somebody in Newport to send a clipping to Dudley or write an anonymous letter," Sam continued. "Let's say the packet with *Town Topics* reaches Dudley Forster in the middle of the Pacific Ocean by the end of August. Just think of his state of mind when he opens the envelope and reads something like, 'Pinkerton Divorce Detective Scouts Seabright Cottage' and is helpless to act. Think of him brooding, filled with doubt...."

"Terrible," Roddy said. I shook my head in silence.

"I have a suggestion," Sam said. "May I have your promise of open minds?" Sam sounded like a schoolboy. We nodded. "I have given a good deal of thought to the problem. All of yesterday afternoon while Miss Sylvia's will was being read, I kept an eye on Cassandra and thought about her protection."

A moment passed, as if Sam needed to distill his thoughts. Almost shyly, he said, "You know that I serve on the board of Brush Industries?" We nodded. "I am always, however...reluctant to divulge my duties on the board."

"Surely it's something related to engineering," Roddy said.

I agreed. "Something mechanical."

"Not so. Nothing of the kind." Sam's smile was wan. He hesitated, and then gushed his words as if to be rid of them. "I chair the communications committee of Brush Industries."

Roddy and I exchanged glances once again. It sounded like a confession, but neither of us understood how this connected to Cassie, her husband, the children, or Seabright cottage. Or Sam Brush, for that matter. What was the communications committee?

"Is that about advertising?" I asked.

"No, nothing like that." Sam looked embarrassed. "I am overstaying my visit," he said. "I am intruding on your lunch hour."

"Not at all, Sam. Would you like a bite? We can—"

"No, thank you. Please let me explain." He swallowed. "There's a postscript to the Brush labor strike and why I chair the communications committee. It may provide useful in our concern for Cassandra's protection. If you're interested...?"

"By all means," Roddy said.

"Please..." I added.

Sam tugged his tie, although it was already loose. "I was about six years old when the woodworkers went on strike. My brother accused the reporters of socialism. The public turned against us. Brush sales were slumping, but there was something new called public relations that got favorable press coverage for corporations, and my brother hired a public relations firm to 'tell the Brush Industries story.'"

Sam slowed as if to recall a distant memory. "Part of the plan was to send me into the Maine and Wisconsin woods, a tiny goodwill ambassador to play with wood workers' children."

Sam's complexion flushed as he went on. "They dressed me in overalls and put me on a wagon loaded with logs and sent me into the lumber mill towns. A photographer came along to snap plenty of pictures for the newspapers. 'Wood King's Baby Brother Visits Sawmill.' I have a scrapbook of clippings. They gave photos to the mill kids too. Their families were thrilled, tacked them to their walls. Peace in the mill towns." He looked from Roddy to me. "End of story," he said. "Sales picked up, and I was called a public relations prince...the Brush Industries rabbit foot."

"Amazing," I managed to say. The word could have been "confused."

"And so, you are a member of the Brush board of directors," said Roddy,

"chairing the communications—?"

"—committee. I know, it's bizarre, Sam Brush the tinkerer, but he oversees public relations for the company. Harry was so pleased with the stunt that boosted sales that he told every manager my most important job at Brush Industries must be communications when I grew up." Sam shrugged, then smiled the good natured smile we knew so well. "I never thought public relations would be useful, but this is the moment. Ready?"

"We're on the edge of our seats," Sam," I said.

"So hear me out...." Sam batted his palm on the chair arm. "Because the 'public' in this case is the Newport community—our Newport. No Pinkertons, not one Pinkerton. But protection, yes! Everyone understands that Mrs. Dudley Forster is now an extraordinarily wealthy woman and that her husband is not in residence in this summer season. Everyone understands, therefore, that Cassandra Van Schylar Fox Forster's safety must be assured."

We nodded in unison. I sipped my bubbly water. Roddy folded his hands. "The servants at Seabright," Sam said, "form a second community of sorts.

Inside and out, the entire household must be inspected and made to understand their sacred duty to the wellbeing of Mrs. Forster and the children."

Roddy and I waited. So far, Sam had said nothing we did not already know, but his buoyant enthusiasm was infectious, perhaps the very tone he struck at Brush board meetings.

"Are you with me so far?" We nodded obediently. "A second group, we might say, is made up of tradesmen and shop clerks, the servers in the Village tearoom, the Casino employees." He spread his hands like wings. "The country club workers...even the caddies." He looked from Roddy to me. "You see my point?"

We tried to follow.

"So I urge this—that Cassandra be strongly advised to employ a squad of off-duty and recently retired Newport policemen, with the ex-chief Ronald Cherry to lead the men. They will be armed and wear uniforms, and they must be stationed at the front gate and at strategic locations, such as the seafront and gardens. In addition, a police detachment must accompany Cassandra to all outings and social events—and accompany her children when they are off the premises of the cottage."

Sam looked up to see our response, but quickly plunged on. "Their sheer presence will deter wrong-doers," he said. "Picture it—on patrol around-the-clock, the police detachment will be a visible protective wall to surround Cassandra and her children." He drank the last of his punch. "Fortunately, we of Newport—our own Newport—support the police force. I contribute annually to the benevolent fund and the Independence Day parade.

Perhaps you also are supporters?"

Of course, we were. Each Fourth of July, the modern brick police station on Market Street was festooned with red, white and blue bunting. Brass bands played, war veterans marched, children waved flags, officials gave speeches, and fireworks lit up the night sky. At the moment, Sam Brush presented his own fireworks. "So, friends, I am prepared to ride from Drumcliffe directly to Seabright to call upon Cassandra. If she accepts my proposal, I will drive to Market Street this afternoon to have a discussion with police officials." He added, "Of course, it is vitally important that Cassandra have your approval of this plan."

What could we say? If only Roddy and I could talk privately about the notion of armed, helmeted police everywhere at my friend's cottage...in her presence, and the children's. A stockade of policemen. So visible. As Roddy had warned, however, time must not be lost.

"If conditions were different," Sam said, "I would have wished to introduce the idea of police protection more slowly...in a lower gear, we might say. But the notion of Pinkertons in the floodlight of the last will and testament... it's nearly thrown me, I admit." Sam used his pocket handkerchief to pat away a milky upper lip "moustache."

"Also," he added, "I feel responsible as a member of the Brush and Van Schylar families. In Dudley's absence, like it or not, I am temporarily the head of the family."

The very point that Roddy had hammered a few days ago, that family matters were best handled by families. As for being the "head," Cassie's father, Robert, might object. Then again, Robert Fox was preoccupied with his divorce.

"You make a persuasive case, Sam," my husband said.

"Then I have your approval?" He looked my way. "Valentine—?"

"A worthwhile plan," I said at last.

"Please say 'worthwhile' when you speak to Mrs. Forster...Cassandra. I shall send a note to Seabright. I trust that you will keep us fully informed."

"Fully," Roddy said, his voice firm and insistent. We all rose and walked toward the entrance. The men's heels clicked on the marble hallway floor. We were now beyond the topic of my questions about the mother and daughter's deaths.

Sam Brush had offered a sensible plan. Whatever Roddy's or my reservations, we had both endorsed it. There were no objections at the moment, none that I could voice, though in a deeper, visceral gauge, the word I might use to describe my feelings might be "dread."

Chapter Thirteen

WE HAD GATHERED AT the end of Easton's Point, a rocky outcrop overlooking the sea and Easton Beach, which Society called the public or "common" beach that was dotted with its common bathers who frolicked in the surf, sunned themselves, or strolled fully dressed along the sand far below. How enviable, I thought, to enjoy the beach without the police protection against... against what? Coincidental death? Possibly homicide? The weather was warmer, but I shivered.

Around the Point, a half-dozen young men set out camp stools for each lady and gentleman. It was early August, time for the Newport Clambake Club's annual tribute to "New England's most famous feast," as *Town Topics* put it. That scandal sheet could not resist asking "whether the blue tunics of Newport's constabulary will once again be in evidence at the clambake, as they have been over the past week in the Village and at the Newport Country Club, or wherever else a certain fine lady has chosen to recreate."

The unnamed "fine lady" was indeed here at the clambake to "recreate" with fashionable Newport. My friend had ventured out bravely these past days to shop and golf and stroll, resisting the temptation to huddle inside the Seabright walls. She seemed comforted by the blue tunics everywhere in evidence around her. Chief Ronald Cherry was like an uncle, a barrel-chested figure with turquoise blue eyes and a swerving white moustache that looked like little birds taking flight. His eyes had narrowed as he oversaw the police escort who accompanied Cassie in her Victoria carriage from Seabright to this remote outpost. He had also ordered the strategic positioning of the eight—no, I counted nine—officers who were stationed around the clambake grounds where we would spend the greater part of this Monday pretending to be simple folk indulging in simple pleasures.

The police had staked out the park-like grounds, including the entrance, each officer with a thousand-yard stare in his eyes, each by turns fingering his nightstick and Colt service revolver as he scanned the scene. On this festive occasion, the police did not "see" us, nor do we "see" them, though all of Newport was aware of the men in blue who surrounded Cassandra Van Schylar Fox Forster, and why they were omnipresent in her orbit.

Sam's plan had made sense after all. The clambake was well protected, a special point of pride today because Sam Brush was a vice-president of the Clambake Club.

At the rock-encircled pit stood the elderly Jim Reeves, the legendary master of the clambake who procured every item of seafood and vegetables and cooked them in a pit of hottest stones. His "bake" had been underway since long before dawn, and his helpers were distributing three-legged canvas camp stools to one and all. Except, of course, the police.

Like every gentleman at Easton's Point today, my Roddy had dressed for his "simple pleasures" in white duck trousers with silk suspenders, a navy blazer, a white linen shirt, bow tie and straw skimmer hat. (A few bolder gentlemen, such as my friend Theo Bulkeley, and also Ed Glendorick, sported wide-striped blazers.) We ladies had flocked to the clambake wearing long white skirts of silk, tulle, and crepe that caught the breeze to convey what Cassie called insouciance. Our sun hats were trimmed with ostrich feathers that likewise fluttered in the breeze.

Odors of salt brine and seaweed vied with scents of *Eau de Lavande* and *Colonia Classica* and other new French perfumes favored by the ladies of Newport this season.

For me, the nuisance was the gloves. For cold weather or garden tasks or holding the reins, everyone needed gloves, but long kidskin gloves at a clambake in August? "Roddy, this is ridiculous," I said early this morning as we prepared to leave Drumcliffe for the long ride along Ocean Drive, Bellevue Avenue and Marine Avenue to Easton's Point. My white kidskin pair was clutched in a fist.

"Val, if you choose not to wear gloves, be assured that I care only for your full enjoyment of the day."

Translated, Roddy wouldn't mind if his wife were the only bare-handed lady at the clambake. Noland had waited at front entrance with our Victoria hitched to Apollo and Atlas, our midnight-black Hackneys. Off we had gone, the gloves lying in my lap until we neared the Point, when I decided to leave them in the carriage. At previous clambakes, I was subjected to jokes—they called it gentle "ribbing"—about the Westerner who must forego sourdough biscuits to master the lobster and corn on the cob. Maybe I'll appear in *Town Topics* as the "alleged lady" who apparently had lost her gloves, like one of the "three little kittens who lost their mittens." Conform or not, one paid a price.

"Val, my dear—" Roddy leaned close as we stood on the crushed oyster shells that carpeted the clambake grounds. "I will accept the next camp-stool and be seated over there where the good sea breeze is cleanest. I declined to make up a 'Clambake Club' punch and would rather not to be 'grilled' about cocktails I'm working on for a certain hotel for this autumn."

He pointed to a spot at the edge of the scene. "I'll be over there...protected by Chief Cherry and his armed squadron." Roddy scanned the scene as if he, too, were on guard duty.

"Let's try to relax," I said, "if possible." With the deaths of her auntie and her cousin hanging like a dark cloudbank over Cassie, we would try to appear at ease, comfortable in public and cheerful with one another...all the while avoiding **the** topic. We owed ourselves a pleasant day. (Truth to tell, steamed clams were luscious.)

Roddy squeezed my hand. A young man carried his stool. "I'll receive visitors, so come visit." He blew a little kiss and sauntered to the far side of the "bake" where servants were settling champagne in ice-filled tubs and setting out racks of crystal flutes.

Carriages were still arriving with all Newport that saw itself coming and going in these weeks of dinners, balls, yachting parties—and certain funerals. Here were the Whartons, Teddy and Edith who pled penury but was always a fashion plate. And the Edwin Glendoricks, the shipping mogul who could talk of nothing but Cuba, while his wife, Madeline, obsessed about their daughter Emily's possible nuptials to the British Earl. Then the Goulds of Old New York lineage, and the Dovedales who reminded one of the nursey rhyme about Jack Sprat who "could eat no fat," and his wife who "could eat no lean." Indeed, Florence Dovedale seemed ever stouter while Herbert shrank visibly.

Here, too, was Archibald Romberg, the would-be Casanova so vivid in his striped flannel suit, the newest fashion in men's summer leisure wear. And here came Robert and Rowena Fox, each receiving a peck on the cheek from Cassie before going separate ways, Robert to the nearest tray of drinks, Rowena as if in search of a particular friend, although whoever counted as her friend was a mystery at this point.

And now, here were the Philbricks, Victor and Gladys with the snow-white coiffure. Gladys, who had been present during her friend Georgina Brush's death throes. At this moment, I overheard Gladys Philbrick report that she and Victor were off to a house party in the Hudson Valley tomorrow morning and would be gone for at least a week.

Dare I speak with her today about Georgina's terrible death, a violation of basic good manners that would no doubt cast me as a pariah and an embarrassment to Roddy? Still, it was high time for my friend Cassie to know the details of what he and I knew, that Georgina's agonizing death closely mirrored Sylvia's. We had studiously avoided discussing the particulars with Cassie, especially since the inheritance had become a millstone. Undecided, I kept my distance from Gladys for the moment.

In this social hour, I spotted the banking heiress, Elizabeth Drexel Lehr with her husband, Harry, the witty court jester all the ladies adored for his charm, although their husbands, I noticed, disliked him. I also recognized two young servants uncorking champagne at the rustic "bar," the Irish country club caddies Michael and Rory who had banished the seagulls from the skies above the Newport Country Club. They poured and circulated with trays of champagne. Taking a flute from Michael, I believe he winked.

I started toward a group near the elegantly bewhiskered Colonel Twist and Florence Dovedale, but my heart sank as Ed Glendorick came close, his plate steaming. He leaned in close to the colonel, no doubt about to hector the man about his favorite topic.

"Cuba must be ours, Colonel. Don't you agree? As a military man, you see the situation clearly. If the Philippine Islands are ours, and the other island too...?

The colonel patted his side whiskers. "Puerto Rico?"

"Cuba! Whatever happened to the 'spoils of war'? We fought fair and square, and we own it. Everything depends on getting this right. Cuba and the Florida Keys are our island chain. A word from you to our fellow in Washington, I count on you."

I stepped away and picked up Harry Lehr's voice. "Just think," he said, "that in the Sandwich Islands the natives roast pigs in lava pits, while we of Society gather on the very spot where the Indians once gathered for councils and feast on raw clams."

"Some say the savages are feasting here to this very day, dear Harry...." I recognized Mamie Fish's voice and moved quickly away.

"Val, do join us." Sam waved. He and Evalina were chatting with the Whartons and a young man in a rumpled linen jacket who came with them. "Do meet Mr. Ogden Codman, the architect." Codman had been Wharton's co-author on *The Decoration of Houses*, the explosive grenade that the two had hurled at Society's home décor.

"Mr. Codman is redoing the Whartons' cottage, Lands End," said Evalina, her pink ostrich plumes nearly concealing her pixie-ish face. "And Mrs. Wharton tells us that Mr. Codman is undertaking the furnishings too. Imagine that!"

"Highly unusual for an architect to arrange furniture," said Teddy Wharton, "but Edith knows best."

Edith smiled a tight little smile and said, "Interior décor must be wrested from mere upholsterers."

Evalina's voice crooned in a sweet southern drawl. "Oh, Mr. Codman, I do wish you would persuade my husband that mechanical devices belong in a factory, not a home. I fear that our Stone Point is something that only Mr. Edison would admire."

We feigned amusement. Sam looked pained. Codman said that elevators were a great convenience, as were electrical sconces on certain walls. "But we all agree," he added, "that nothing takes the place of the warm glow of an open fire."

We all agreed. From the corner of my eye, I saw Ed Glendorick chatting with Gladys Philbrick. Perhaps I could introduce myself in the hope of having a conversation with her and Cassie after lunch, but Mamie Fish was cruising toward our group.

"Excuse me," I said, "but I owe Mr. Bulkeley a word."

"Oh, Valentine," Evalina gushed, "may I offer you a pair of gloves? I have an extra pair...clam juice so untidy."

"Thank you, but no," I said, fanning my fingers. "I'm going naked to the elbow all day, Evalina."

Her pink ostrich plumes danced. "I do believe that I see your husband on a lonely camp stool way over there," she said. We all looked as she pointed to the far side of the rock pit. "Sam was hoping your Roderick would mix us a magical punch today," Evalina cooed. "I'm afraid he's disappointed the Clambake Club."

"Maybe next year," I said, moving toward Theo but scanning the scene, as did Roddy from his outpost.

"Our first year for a clambake police detachment," Theo remarked. The policemen had changed duty stations around the grounds, doubtless on Chief Cherry's order. They all stood at attention, each looking outward, encircling the scene. "A precedent, but we'll become accustomed." He glanced toward Cassie. "Under guard," he said to me, "and so much for the liberation of the heiress."

I nodded. "Pleas for money are already pouring into the post office, Theo, and the newspapers couldn't be happier with their Brush Industries 'heiress' story. It's a good thing the police are nearby. A rotten drunk showed himself at the Seabright front gate at midnight, yelling and banging, but an officer on duty at the cottage had him arrested and jailed right away."

Theo cocked his head. "Do you hear that? I thought I heard something...like a growl?"

"I don't think so. Maybe you heard one of the horses?" We listened together. Other conversations briefly halted, then continued. Cassie was chatting with the Goulds. "Cassie's parents," I said to Theo, "are no help at all."

"Speaking of whom—" he said in his lowest voice, "turn around slowly and see what I see...."

I turned. "Rowena," I said. "It's Rowena and...Romberg. Rowena and Archibald...."

"Toasting one another...and Romberg is smiling."

Was "shock" too strong a word? I searched the crowd for Cassie, whom I saw just over Edith Gould's shoulder. She faced away from her mother.

"Listen…that growling sound…" Theo interrupted. "Did someone bring a dog?"

"I hear Evalina has a new French bulldog she adores. But I can't imagine she'd bring it here."

"No, it sounds like something big, bigger than my spaniels, like a very big, angry dog. It sounds hurt. Don't you hear it?"

"I do hear something…."

Conversations paused once again, then resumed with nervous laughter.

One policeman, I saw, fingered his holster.

"They're laughing together, Val. Those two, Rowena Fox and Archibald Romberg, sipping and laughing. Wonders never cease."

"Good heavens—"

A bell clanged, and Harry Lehr's voice rose. "Ladies and gentlemen, Mr. Reeves proclaims—or rather, *proclams*—that The Clambake Club bake of 1898 is ready to—"

He broke off. In that instant a huge black animal burst from the trees, its eyes glazed, its jaws open, its teeth bared and foam dripping from its muzzle. Wolfish, it hurled itself toward Cassie's group, its growl ungodly, nothing that ever before struck my ears.

"Rabid!" I heard someone cry. "Rabid wild dog!"

The next sound I heard was the crack of a bullet fired from a Colt revolver, then another, and another. The animal yowled, slumped, collapsed and was still. We all watched, frozen, as Chief Cherry and the officer with the smoking

Colt whispered together, then beckoned to another policeman who fetched something like a blanket—a canvas. The
animal was bundled off quickly. From the corner of my eye,
I saw Cassie lean heavily on George Gould's arm, averting
her gaze. At length, Chief Cherry turned to speak.

"Ladies and gentlemen, all danger has passed. The
Newport Police Department appreciates your patience.
We wish you a good afternoon."

He resumed his outlook over the squad as two officers
trundled off with the cargo, and the policeman who shot
the animal holstered his gun. No one spoke.

The quiet was unnerving, then oppressive.

"Ladies and gentlemen, hear ye, hear ye—" Like an
emcee at the "bake," Harry Lehr held a champagne bottle
aloft in each hand. "Hear ye! This moment calls for further
aperifs by *les monsieurs* Moet and Chandon. For those who
wish to restore their spirits with the effervescence that
precedes the feast, Mr. Reeves must pause while we pay
tribute to Bacchus à la bubbles."

Lehr began to waltz about, dispensing champagne with
both hands. "Applause, if you please—" More bottles were
no sooner opened than emptied. A nervous merriment took
over, though no one seemed truly relaxed.

Grateful for distraction, however, all welcomed the
bounty that came forth from a pit of hot stones and seaweed—clams and bright red lobsters, fish swathed in
cheesecloth. The young waiters cracked open the lobster
claws and piled hot steamer clams on our plates, along with

corn and potatoes. Some ladies had removed their gloves, others chose to ruin theirs. Theo and I received our plates. Society was served.

Roddy and his group remained seated on camp stools, and others were roaming, plates in hand. The police were once again "invisible." Rowena and Romberg, I noticed, dined à deux.

Cassie sat nearby with a group that now included Gladys Philbrick. She refused the proffered plates at least twice, I noted. Though she said something about a large breakfast, I doubted she had eaten anything today. Her face looked thinner. My friend was showing physical signs of strain.

"Dear Valentine and Theodore—" I turned to greet Madeline Glendorick, whose husky voice was nearly at a whisper. "I am having a quiet word with everyone who dined with us just weeks ago when we introduced our guest, the Earl of Cleave," she said. "So do expect our announcement. Edwin and I are soon to reveal what all Newport anticipates…?" Her voice rose as if to quiz us on the announcement.

Theo said, "…that Emily Glendorick will soon become the Countess of Cleave?" Madeline beamed. Theo and I offered our congratulations and promised not to spoil the "secret." Madeline moved off to whisper the good news elsewhere.

"The Glendoricks to be royalized at last," Theo said when she was out of earshot, then asked, "Is your friend well?" He gestured toward Cassie. "Is Cassandra on that vinegar and bread regimen?"

"Not to my knowledge." I was tempted, just then, to tell Theo my concerns about Georgina's agonizing death, but I ought to think carefully and consult Roddy first. So, once again I held back, filled with doubt.

A few guests had finished, their plates and shells and corncobs cleared, but the champagne still flowed. Cigarettes were lighted, and some of the gentlemen prepared to shoot clay pigeons in a far field. Others would play at baseball, using a tennis ball and a racquet as a bat. The police fanned out, but their vigilance was unrelenting. Nearer to the site of the "bake" a few gentlemen enjoyed second helpings. Some ladies too.

In the days ahead, Roddy and I searched our minds to recall the precise sequence of events that occurred in the next few minutes. It was difficult to recall exactly who was where and at what exact moment. What we both knew for certain was that Roddy left his camp stool and came toward me just as Michael, the caddy, brought a plate of food to Cassie and told her—as my friend afterwards recalled his words—that Mrs. Fox insisted that Mrs. Forster enjoy the clambake.

I saw the caddy proffer a full plate toward Cassie, who had already lighted a cigarette. As Cassie shook her head to refuse, Florence Dovedale stepped up to say that if Cassie didn't want it, she was happy to relieve the waiter of the plate.

Such succulent fare must not go for naught, Florence Dovedale said. I especially recalled that she kept her gloves on as she enjoyed a clam. Roddy and I disagreed on whether Florence ate any of the potatoes or yam or corn. What we knew for certain was that within an hour, as the shotguns fired at clay pigeons and the laughter echoed from the improvised baseball diamond, Florence Dovedale complained of lightheadedness and asked Albert to order their carriage.

They left the Point at once, leaving Roddy and me clouded with suspicion and fear that soon proved to be justified.

∽◈

"How is she today?"

"A bit better, I hear. They hope for the best."

"Dr. Bentley is still with her?"

"He is."

The rabid dog and Florence Dovedale's precarious health were the talk of the town. The much-respected Dr. Dennis James was summoned to the Dovedales' cottage on the evening of the clambake, and a telegram to Dr. William Bentley had brought Society's own physician from the city the following day.

Nurses were in round-the-clock attendance. There was talk of treating the patient at the Newport Hospital, but for now she was kept comfortable—whatever "comfortable" meant to someone wracked by nausea and treated by round-the-clock nurses, all graduates of the Newport Hospital School of Nursing.

"So, Florence has taken a turn for the better, yes?"

"It seems so. They're not sure. Another few days will tell."

Roddy and I were sitting together in an ivory-toned alcove just off the Drumcliffe reception room, a perfect space for private conversation. Three days after the clambake at which Florence Dovedale was taken ill, Roddy had just returned from Stone Point, where Sam reported the news that had set all Newport talking. Roddy excused the footman, and we kept our voices low.

"What else did Sam say?"

"—that Jim Reeves swears to the freshness of every clam and lobster at the bake. He claims his preparations were exactly as they have been for over twenty years and that Mr. Stuyvesant Fish and many other gentlemen will vouch for him." Roddy loosened his collar. "Reeves is both insulted and frightened. His livelihood depends on summer clambakes."

"So, suspicion of food poisoning would put him out of business."

"Completely. And of course, Sam feels responsible as a vice-president of the club, especially since he is a newcomer to Newport." He added, "Relatively speaking."

"Relatively" encompassed a number of summer residents, such as the younger brother of the wood king and the daughter of the silver mining magnate. To be specific, Sam Brush and Valentine Mackle DeVere were here by virtue of marriages into the Van Schylar and DeVere bloodlines. Our probation by Society might last our whole lifetimes, and Sam was expected to be grateful for election to office in the Clambake Club as well as membership-by-invitation in the Reading Club, the Rod and Gun Club, the Green End Club and whatever other congregations existed to exclude the unworthy.

Roddy drummed his fingers on the seat cushion. "Val, we better hope to heaven that Florence Dovedale ate a bad clam. Or a rotten potato."

A clock chimed five p.m. while I absorbed the meaning of my husband's words.

"This is not a knock on Reeves," Roddy said.

"I know."

Minutes pass, and neither of us stirred. "The police were at Easton's Point from the beginning," I said. "Nine of them, and Chief Cherry too. And then that mad dog...."

Roddy nodded. "Fortunate the police were with us."

"So fortunate."

Finally, I said, "Suppose it wasn't the clam...Just suppose it was...."

"I am thinking of nothing else."

"Then what should we do? That plate of food was meant for Cassie. Rowena specifically sent the plate over to her. Fortunately, Florence Dovedale is a very stout woman... but Cassie...I hadn't noticed how thin her face has become. Roddy, if she had eaten...."

"Stop, Val." He put his finger across my lips. "Let's not say what we both are thinking. Yes, we heard that Rowena intended the plate for her daughter. The caddy seemed clear about that, but we dare not jump to a conclusion based on hearsay or suspicion alone." He crossed his legs. "Let's back up a bit. I have an idea." I leaned closer. "Val, I am thinking once again about the Pinkerton agency."

My disappointment was barely contained.

"The police are vital," he said. "Don't misunderstand me on that point. We had proof of their usefulness at the clambake. Believe me, more than one gentleman will carry a concealed pistol to Easton's Point from now on." He paused. "Sam's idea is sound, and the police details ought to continue. They provide a necessary protection. But protection isn't the same as detection."

My impatience rose. "Cassie must not have 'divorce detectives' lurking around Seabright. We agreed on that."

"I am not thinking that way. I am thinking about undercover detection."

"You mean spies."

"Put crudely, yes. Detectives in disguise."

"In costumes? Theatrical wigs?"

"Val...." His hand was on my knee. "Please, let's be sensible. The police are fully capable of handling the common crimes, the burglaries, the assaults. They catch the raging drunk who bangs a hammer on Cassie's front gate at midnight. Or the thief who steals a horse that's recovered just before the poor animal is loaded on a barge bound for the city. Or the rabid animal. But undercover detectives are more suited for crimes that are, by nature, undercover."

I swallowed hard. "How would this work?"

He sat back, collecting his thoughts. "Secrecy is crucial. No Newport telegraph operator can be entrusted with the message. I will take the train to Providence myself and send a telegram to Robert Pinkerton in the New York office."

"Have you consulted Sam?"

"Not yet. He'd feel insulted at this point, as if I'd undercut him. He's worried enough, and life with Evalina seems rather…insistent."

I managed a smile and said, "The famous southern hospitality." Roddy smiled too. My next question was the most obvious. "What about Cassie?"

He did not hesitate. "She must agree. And she must keep the secret." The clock chimed the quarter hour. Roddy took both my hands in his. "She must keep the secret, Val, because we both know that her life might depend upon it."

Chapter Fourteen

CASSIE CAST A FRETFUL look at the shoreline where her children frolicked exactly at the place where sea and sand met. Their nanny, Cara, kept watch over them, as did other nannies with children on this midmorning here at Bailey's Beach. Society's playground, this beach was guarded by a gold-laced watchman who knew every carriage on sight and dispatched intruders who dared encroach upon the treasured crescent of sand that Mrs. Harry Lehr—Elizabeth—called "Newport's most exclusive club." Seashore sounds blended with the children's cries and horses' hooves on the roadway behind us, and always the pounding surf.

"I'm not sure that Cara is paying close enough attention, Val. It only takes seconds for a child to slip under the waves." We both stared unwaveringly at Bea and Charlie and their nanny, relieved when she guided the children back to the sand and the beach toys.

"Oh, look, Bea and Charlie are building a sandcastle together. Let's wave to them."

We waved to Cassie's children, both in their bathing costumes, Charlie bare-headed and Bea sporting a sun bonnet. They waved back and dashed about the children's section of the beach, filling sand pails that they quickly overturned, squealing with delight at the molded shapes. The tide was coming in.

Cassie and I sat on over-sized bath towels wearing similar bathing costumes, gray-tinted flannel "sacque" dresses with trousers underneath. And water shoes with socks. The "oilskin" caps protected our hair from the fierce sun. James Van Alyn was sunbathing nearby in his white straw skimmer hat and monocle and the widow Cushing in her black velvet bathing ensemble with a bath cloak and pearls.

Cassie resumed the conversation that had stopped just short of a debate. "It's no use, Val. I was never good at dramatics at school. Miss Pye took pity on me. I was 'Fairy Number Three.' Or 'Six.' I never had a speaking part."

"Cassie, it's not a role in a play. You are the mistress of Seabright and have decided to hire a new footman and a groundskeeper. You only have gardeners working this season, right?"

"Four gardeners. The groundskeeper quit last year over the huts and the grass plots. 'Weeds,' he called them." She meant the grasses and native species that Cassie's Dudley insisted upon at Seabright.

"So now," I said, "simply let it be known that you've decided the cottage needs a groundskeeper."

She looked dubious. "So late in the season?"

"Just say the grounds need attention, from the cottage to the stable and carriage house." I added, "And a cottage can always use another footman."

She traced a finger in the sand with a newly manicured finger. Cassie had been visited by Madame Riva, and I dreaded to hear about it.

"A footman whose duties are flexible," I said. "Day by day, hour by hour, he will be assigned to work throughout the cottage, including the kitchen." A footman normally had specific duties, such as serving or tending the curtains and draperies to adjust the light as the sun moved throughout the day. This subterfuge would require some adaptation. "He'll be like a man-of-all-work," I said.

"I suppose so."

"And you'll treat both of them as you treat servants and employees— respectfully but with authority."

"So, one of them will be on duty inside the cottage," she said, "and the other outside."

"Exactly."

"Detectives," she said, "snooping. It's eerie. I'll feel spied upon."

I gestured behind us toward the five policemen on duty at the low wall by the bathhouses. Uniformed in wool, they had to be sweating—or, as Newport preferred, perspiring. In my flannel bathing garb, I fully understood. In the West, we did not "bathe," but swam in knickers and a lightweight chemise at the most. "There's your morning police detail," I said. "Do they seem like spies to you?"

"Of course not. They're police."

I caught sight of little Bea charging toward the surf and tugged back by her nanny. "Think of the children too, Cassie. The three of you. And Dudley."

She cast a long, loving look toward her children. "Charlie says he wants to be a policeman when he grows up. And Bea calls Chief Cherry 'Grandpa.'"

"Sweet."

My friend suddenly turned to me, looked intently in my eyes, and asked the question point blank. "Val, do you believe that someone really wants to kill me?

That rabid dog, was it meant to attack me?"

"No, not the dog."

"It was a stray?"

"It was. The police are certain."

"Then I can rest at ease."

I held her gaze. Roddy and I had finally spoken to Cassie. We had told her about Georgina's lingering death, the light-headedness that turned into days of retching and agony. At once, Cassie drew the connection with Sylvia. Now I brushed away a sand fly and said, "That plate was meant for you, Cassie. If you had eaten it...if you had...."

Did I dare to finish the statement? To be brutally frank? Yes, I must. "If you had eaten, we might not be here on the beach." I pointed to the children. "And your Charlie and

Beatrice...." I paused to let my friend finish the thought. "Fortunate that Florence Dovedale is recovering at last," I said. The worst health crisis of her life."

"What am I to do?" Cassie cry rang plaintive against the crashing surf.

"The first thing," I said, "is to accept the Pinkerton detectives. You will pretend the new footman and groundskeeper have come from an employment agency with bone fide references. Your butler will supervise them as usual."

"Our Hayes," she said. "But the butler is not to know that the footman is really a—"

"Not a word." I shook my head. "The footman will lodge with the others, and the groundskeeper will sleep in the coach house loft. O'Boyle can help him settle in."

"But O'Boyle is not to know."

"No one is to know, Cassie. Not a servant, not a friend, not the police who guard you." I added, "Not even a family member."

"But Sam—"

"Not yet. Sam has business in the city next week and plans to see Mr. Frear to learn more about the cause of Sylvia's death, if he can. No, the two detectives must be completely undercover. Completely."

"But why—?" She searched the surf as if for answers. "Why would anyone want to kill Auntie Georgina? She was so full of life."

"She was also very competitive. Remember her nickname, the 'Wicked Witch of the Wicket.'"

"But people loved her."

"Someone, it seems, did not."

"—and Sylvia too. A mother, a daughter…a niece."

"Not 'a' mother or 'a' daughter," I said. "And not simply 'a' niece. All three are heirs of the Brush Industries fortune."

"It's all too much. It's already starting. My secretary sorts the morning mail, and it's taking hours. I gave her one of Dudley's file cabinets to help with the volume." Cassie looked at the sea and sighed. "Strangers' letters come addressed to 'Missus Brush, Newport,' but they're meant for me."

"Pleas for money?"

She nodded. "Even one in Spanish. You know I did not study Spanish. Only French, and German."

Yes, those were the languages used by Society. German aristocrats were sometimes guests at dinner, and Edith Wharton, I'd noticed, often slid into French at parties. Myself, I'd picked up a few words of Spanish from the gold and silver miners who'd come to Nevada from Mexico, and Papa was nearly fluent.

I said, "You are not obliged to read Spanish, Cassie. For your own peace of mind, let the pleas for money go into Dudley's file cabinet whatever language they're written in."

She seemed not to hear me. "The entreaties are never ending. They remind me of letters we found in Sylvia's bedroom," she said. "And a man is coming to talk about dog kennels."

"What man?"

"He was at Sylvia's funeral service. He wrote me a letter too."

"And you agreed to receive him? Here at Newport?"

"I must. It said so in Sylvia's will. The kennels were one of Auntie Georgina's favorite projects, and remember all those paintings of dogs in Sylvia's bedroom? I am meant to carry on the work...'in accordance and pursuant to the interests of my late mother.'"

"But the will did not say 'immediately,' did it?" Cassie shook her head no. "And what about your mother's threat to challenge the will?"

"She hasn't done it yet. Sometimes her fury does its damage, and then she finds something else to find fault with...or someone."

"But Sylvia's will has not been through the probate process, has it? No beneficiaries have received their...." I hesitated to say the forbidden word 'money,' "Their shares?"

"No, not yet.

I did not express the doubts I felt.

"And the suffragettes," said Cassie. "Like those two women at Sylvia's service at Trinity Church. They marched down the aisle like soldiers. Votes-for-women—"

"You've heard from them?"

"One left a card. Miss Somebody-or-other...Hastings? Hastly? I can't remember."

"Not Annie Flowers?"

"No. I'd have told you, Val. I'd have told you at once." Slightly exasperated, Cassie pulled off the oilskin cap, ran a hand through her glorious auburn hair, and tucked the cap back on. "Surely, no suffragette would be a guest at one of the cottages. I cannot imagine who would host such a person. We are fortunate that the Ocean House was never rebuilt."

Newport's one and only hotel, Ocean House, had burned to the ground a good many years ago, before my time. Today, a visitor came to Newport only as a guest or as a "day tripper" who departed on the last ferry or steamer. I said, "Cassie, if a suffragist writes or calls on you, promise to tell me right away."

"I will. I promise."

"And let's move the towels. The tide...the little waves are nearly at our feet." We rose, tugged the towels up the hot sand, put them down again. Around us, colorful umbrellas sprouted for shade.

"We should have brought an umbrella," Cassie said. "One more thing I've forgotten. I had to borrow a sun bonnet for Bea. And Charlie's little shoes are falling apart. I meant to take him for new ones." She bit her lip. "And the children... if anything happened to me...." She sniffled. "And to think people say they are being poorly raised."

"What 'people?'"

She gestured around the beach. "The other mothers. You don't see them here, only the nannies."

I looked about. She was right.

"I want my children near me," she said, "not raised by a nanny and nurses." She looked down the beach. "Oh, at times they are a trial, but I love the funny things they say. I love how they feel when we touch, how they smell, how they laugh. Bea asked me whether the moon is made of cream cheese. As heavy as he is, I can still pick Charlie up. And Bea sits at my dressing table in front of the mirror, and I style her hair and let her apply rouge to her cheeks...little cheeks with nature's rouge because she's four years old."

"That's lovely, Cassie."

"But it's not proper, not the way it's supposed to be done. And the other mothers let me know it. At every opportunity."

"Cassie," I said, "Who else says such a thing?"

Her eyes filled. "My mother, for one. You grew up in the West, the Wild West. If you and Roderick have a child, you'll hear it it soon enough." Sniffling, Cassie patted her bathing costume in vain for a handkerchief. I too uselessly patted the waistline of my "sacque."

"My mother would not neglect to bring handkerchiefs. She would have an umbrella."

"Cassie, stop. Do stop. Take a breath. Get a grip on yourself. Remember, 'delicate and resilient.' Let's put our feet into the water. Without our shoes," I said. "Let's feel the sand on our toes."

She nodded, and we took off our shoes and socks, my friend revealing carefully filed bright red toenails.

We walked to the water's edge and felt the wonderful cold current as our feet were lapped by frothy wavelets. Cassie's bright red toenails winked like jewels.

"Perfect nails, as always," I said. "I see Madame Riva has come to call,"

"She has, yes." Cassie took another step into the deeper water.

"Dare I ask whether she offered you a séance?"

We both faced the sea, speaking to one another in parallel. "Val, we've already had our conversation about Madame Riva. I see no point...." She paused as an incoming wave jolted us a bit.

"Let's wade in a little further," Cassie said. "The water feels so good." We took a few more steps. The spray soaked our trouser legs, midway up our calves. "You can swim, can't you?" Cassie asked.

"I can. We swam in the rivers in Colorado. Nevada too. The river currents are swift, so swimmers take care. And Lake Tahoe...the water like turquoise." The water was up to our "sacque" dresses, soaking the hems.

Cassie said, "Do you know how much a woman's bathing costume weighs when wet?" Her voice sounded oddly high. She stepped further into the surf. I was about to caution her that we must not get too close to the drop-off. "Do you have any idea?"

"No idea. Too heavy for swimming, that's for sure. Let's not go further."

"One of my mother's friends weighed her wet bathing costume. Hazard a guess?"

"Twenty-five pounds?"

"Forty."

That was her last word before a wave knocked us both over. Down we went, the cold thrill of sudden immersion in surf and sand, water up our nostrils, oilskin caps lost as we struggled to rise against the pull of the water and drag of wet flannel. I say "we" because it could not be otherwise, two women wading, falling, righting themselves in the shallows of Bailey's Beach.

Except that Cassie was no longer with me.

Upright, my eyes burning from salt, I saw my friend flail as the ocean pulled her away. The undertow—Bailey's Beach was notorious for rip currents. The tide was surging in, but Cassie fought uselessly against the current. Her head appeared, disappeared, her arms.... In vain, I looked for a strong swimmer in these waters. No one. My drenched clothing clung to every inch of skin, but I pulled the "sacque" over my head, kicked off the trousers, and swam.

The drowning person, it is said, endangers her life by clutching at the rescuer in panic. Cassie clung to me in a stranglehold that nearly lost us both in the ocean. When caught in a current in a river back home, we swam sideways, and so I did. It seemed like the struggle took hours. In truth it must have been minutes, just time enough for a staring crowd to gather on the beach—children, nannies, elders who had left their chairs on the club veranda to view the spectacle, the coughing and gagging woman and her nude companion who was immediately enfolded in the widow Cushing's beach cloak.

In days to come, Cassie and I would refer to "that day at the beach," but at this moment, as our coachmen and Cassie's policemen helped us into our separate carriages, Cassie said to me, "It's 'yes' to the new employees at Seabright, Val." She added, "Madame Riva says there's a Borgia in the sphere."

Chapter Fifteen

"*MERMAID COMES ASHORE AT Bailey's Beach,*" blared the *Town Talk* headline.

Roddy read further. "'King Neptune's own aquatic *créature* was observed demonstrating the pescatarian arts one recent midmorning....'"

"What does 'pescatarian' mean?" I asked.

"'Like a fish,'" said Roddy. My husband and I sat together on an oak bench in Touro Park near the ancient stone tower whose origin was a complete mystery, Newport's own Stonehenge. We had come to this public place for the privacy that was not guaranteed in our fully staffed cottage, whose kitchen—like all Newport cottage kitchens—was the headquarters for servants' gossip. Nor could we trust the Casino where the veranda had "ears." Noland had driven us here and would return in two hours. We'd have time to talk, first privately, and then with the caddy, Michael, who had agreed to meet us here.

Roddy had brought the latest *Town Talk* at my insistence. The episode on Bailey's Beach was certain to be featured, and ignorance was not bliss. The articles were unsigned, but someone (or some ones) who had witnessed the scene had tattled to the scandal sheet that in turn had baked this raw dough into a vile loaf. Cassie's near-drowning and my emergence in-the-buff from the waves was titillation for all Newport.

He read on. "'The men in blue, Newport's Finest, leered as a certain *belle dame* of our social world found herself out of her depth in the briny deep and'... shall I continue?"

"No. The 'mermaid' jibe is quite enough. We're grist for the gossip mill once again."

So disappointing. If Cassie had drowned while I wrung my hands, all respectability would be intact, her demise understood to be the result of a tragic accident. If I, too, had drowned while attempting to help her while handi-capped by forty pounds of wet wool, the response would be respectful pity for my failed efforts and condolences for Roddy and his parents.

As it was, the rescuer's nudity was thought scandalous enough to sully the DeVere family reputation. First, my offensive ride on the grocer's wagon, and now, except for the widow Cushing's beach cloak, I would be known as the "burlesque" or "stripper" queen from the Wild West whom Roderick Windham DeVere might deservedly divorce.

Roddy, for his part, had been sympathetic and kind, even amused. He applauded my courage but, as always, feared for my safety.

"Val, I should have told you, if you want to swim, you should try Third Beach."

On this, my third summer in Newport, Roddy still offered "should haves," often followed by "everyone knows" that left me in arrears every time. "I didn't actually plan to swim," I said with forced calm. "But where is Third Beach?"

"At the Sakonnet River. It's tidal, and it's warmer. No violent breakers. Noland can drive you. He knows the way."

"I'll keep it in mind."

Roddy glanced at his gold pocket watch. "You do have the photograph?"

"Of Cassie?"

A small sepia photograph of Cassie and Dudley was tucked in the side pocket of my dress, the only one I could find at Drumcliffe, a tiny image from a box camera. "Yes, of course."

"Good. Michael will be here before we know it. So let's talk—"

He broke off as a boy walking a large brown dog on a leash crossed in front of us. We all smiled and wished one another a good day. The brown dog wagged its tail.

"About Cassie's new footman and a groundskeeper," I said when the boy and dog were out of earshot. "She hopes they will blend in at Seabright. She hopes they find nothing out of the ordinary."

Roddy shifted on the bench. "Robert Pinkerton had quite a time finding the right men. He had to get them from the office that his brother William manages in Chicago."

"A thousand miles to find two undercover detectives? There's so much crime in New York that the supply of detectives has run low? I suppose this is what political economists call the law of demand and supply?"

Roddy laughed. "Most private detectives are assigned to impersonate business executives, not servants. The new 'groundskeeper' is a man who knows a thing or two about gardens in the Chicago area, but finding a lawman willing to wear a footman's garb was a challenge."

I knew nothing about hiring detectives, but perhaps I should have. The Mackle fortune could make me a target too. One never knew. "Can Cassie count on them?"

"I'm sure Cassandra can trust their work." He paused. "Of course, she'll pay substantially more for the footman."

"The humbler the disguise, the costlier the detective?"

"In a word, Yes. You've heard Harry Lehr calls the servants 'our footstools?' One must be paid to put up with that." He crossed his legs. "Shall we talk about toxins? And can we start with the theory that two similar deaths—and a third that was narrowly avoided—are not coincidental?"

I sighed. What did I know about murder? The West had its share of killings, most from guns or knife fights, many from temper flare-ups fueled by whisky. Not cocktails, but shots and swigs. Some were revenge killings over mining claims. I had read about such things in the *Gold Hill News* but was never tempted to view the gallows in Virginia City or Gold Hill. Not that Papa or teachers at the Fourth Ward School would permit such a thing.

As for poisons, my papa had talked about the numbing hands and feet of workers who handled the quicksilver that helped to turn crushed ore into silver bars. The men's muscles weakened, and they smeared creams on skin rashes that felt like hornet stings. The foremen didn't know what else to do but pay the men extra and coax them to pray. I'm not sure the problem had been solved to this very day.

"So start with poison," I said. As if to ward off the horror, I chirped, "Perhaps the one used to murder Hamlet's father? Or consumed by the doomed Emma Bovary in the French novel?"

"Val...."

"Sorry, Roddy. It's so awful." I dabbed my forehead with a handkerchief. The sun was already hot, and my morning dress too snug.

"I've done some reading," Roddy said. "I believe we can rule out strychnine." He paused, waiting for "why?" but I stayed silent. "It's very fast-acting, two or three hours."

"I don't need the details."

"Then let's talk about cyanide and arsenic, especially arsenic. It's the more likely culprit. Arsenic, let me mention, is measurable in marine life."

"So, perhaps the clams that Florence Dovedale ate...? And a seafood dish at Mrs. Astor's ball? Suppose Sylvia ate some fish she'd purchased from a pushcart on the Lower East Side.... Could these three be accidental."

Roddy gently squeezed my hand. "Slow down, Val. It's not possible, even if all three ate seafood. The amounts are too tiny."

In the quiet moment, two dragonflies circled each other, buzzed and flew off. "So," I said, "we're back to Georgina and Sylvia, both stricken and dead in just days. And Florence Dovedale's close call. And perhaps arsenic in dosages high enough to be...fatal."

"All the symptoms closely match," Roddy said. "There's headache and drowsiness—"

"Lightheadedness," I added.

Roddy nodded. "Followed by acute symptoms—vomiting, convulsions. The cardiovascular system...."

"The heart. 'Convolutions of the heart,' that's what the quack doctor said about Sylvia." The memory of her starved body in that tenement apartment came surging like an ocean wave, and I abruptly stood to walk.

My shadow in front of me on the path, and Roddy's shadow too. A gentleman, of course, must not sit on a bench when his lady was on her feet. He was at my elbow. "Let me have a moment, Roddy, please."

"Where are you going?"

"I don't quite know. Just give me a few minutes by myself on the grass, on the path...anywhere besides this fatal landscape of mind and memory.

Mere steps took me to the stone tower, ringed by six tall arches with keystones and strong supporting columns. The whole thing reminded me somehow of the mines at Virginia City, the work of hands and brains that knew how strength was built into structures. And finally turned imaginations into the forms of durable things.

Slowly I returned to the bench where my husband waited. Little birds pecked in the grass. "Black-capped chickadees," Roddy said.

I knew swifts and coots from the Colorado mountains and beautiful evening grosbeaks in Virginia City. The birds of this place were a mystery. One more mystery. "So, how is it possible to acquire enough arsenic to kill a human being?"

"It's easy, Val. Arsenic is the main ingredient in insecticides. Cyanide is also an insecticide, but arsenic is preferred. Gardeners rely on it to keep bugs down, and cooks use it when ants and flies get into the sugar or the flour. Its technical name is chromated copper arsenate."

So, apparently, the Newport cottagers' gardeners were pushing poison around in wheelbarrows. I had mistaken it for fertilizer. And in our kitchens too…. I couldn't bear the thoughts. "Roddy, what does arsenic taste like? And cyanide?"

"Cyanide is said to taste like almonds. Arsenic is tasteless."

"So, it could contaminate…anything on a plate, or in a bowl or glass."

He nodded, then glanced toward Mill Street where a young man approached in a youthful stride. Roddy waved to beckon him. "I believe your caddy is here, Val."

"Michael," I said. "Michael Keefe."

"Ma'am...Sir." I introduced him to Roddy...to Mr. DeVere. He was taller than I recalled, his smile quick but guarded. He took off a cap with the letter "C" above the visor, then squatted on his hams, declining to join us on the bench. Instead of his caddy uniform with the necktie and coat, he wore knee-length stockings, knickers that appeared to be padded, and a short-sleeved shirt that was loose at the shoulders with letters spelling "C-O-V-E-L-L" across the front. He carried a very thick leather glove.

"You play baseball," Roddy said.

"I do, sir. I am an infielder on the Covell team.

"Covell Hardware," Roddy said. "Excellent."

"It's my day off. We have a game this noon. The Pawtucket team thinks they'll beat us, but we don't agree." He seemed to relax a bit at the small talk.

"Michael," I said, "I have told Mr. DeVere about our misadventure on the golf course....and your suggestion that we might rid the golf course of seagulls with your falcons."

"Did you wish to speak of that today, ma'am?" His Irish voice rose in a musical lilt, and he looked so eager that I regretted disappointing him.

"I'm afraid not, Michael. We have asked you here for a different reason."

"A private matter," Roddy added. "A matter to be held in strict confidence." Apprehension clouded the young man's eyes. He shifted his footing, a bit wary.

"We won't detain you long, Michael," Roddy said. Then pointedly, "Last Monday at the clambake...."

"At Easton's Point."

"Yes, that's right. You served a plate—"

"—mostly beverages, sir. Champagne for the guests. All the bottles are accounted for, sir...ma'am. Every last one."

He wet his lips, and I guessed he felt suspected of theft of beverages. "Michael," I said, "this is not about the Champagne."

"I do honest work. I caddy at the country club all summer. In the winter I work the coal wagons at Pinniger and Manchester Coal. You can inquire of Mr. Pinniger."

Roddy sat forward and leaned down just inches from the young man's face. "Michael, this is not about your work. We thank you for helping Mrs. DeVere and her friend, Mrs. Forster, on the golf course. Those gulls are a nuisance, and I hope we can soon consider your falconry for assistance. Mrs. DeVere and her friend were very upset when the birds flew over...you remember?"

"That I do, sir."

"And do you remember Mrs. DeVere's friend, Mrs. Forster?"

"The lady that needs a good many strokes to reach the greens? Yes, I do recall...no disrespect, sir. A ball that's no bigger than a parrot's egg makes for a difficult game."

"Indeed, it does." Roddy smiled and paused to let the young man's thoughts settle on the memory of Cassie. "And Mrs. Forster was a guest at the clambake last Monday. We were there too, Mrs. DeVere and myself."

"Yes, sir."

"Perhaps you recall Mrs. Forster at the clambake?"

Michael paused. "The ladies mostly all wore white dresses and wide hats, I do believe. So forgive me if I cannot say for certain."

"Mrs. DeVere has a photograph."

From the pocket meant for smelling salts, I took out the photo with its sepia tints, penciled on the back, "Mr. and Mrs. Dudley Forster, New York, 1897." It showed Cassie with Dudley in Central Park, two tiny figures in a tiny photograph. We waited while Michael held the image close to his face. Better pictures of Cassie were pasted into our photograph albums in the city, and I could send for them if necessary. If there was time? Was there?

Michael shook his head. "Very sorry, ma'am...sir. I'm a sad boyo on this account. I don't recognize the lady."

He squinted again at the tiny photo. I had taken the picture with the new point-and-shoot Kodak camera. ("You press the button, we do the rest.... The only camera that requires no instruction.") I could have used instruction. The image was slightly blurry.

"The gentleman, though.... He looks like a gentleman I remember at the clambake, Mr. Dyer. He fancies himself a lobster chef, he does." At his cottage, The Rocks, Elisah

Dyer was famous for serving a dish of his own creation, lobster *a l'Americaine*, to his guests. He was not our man. Inwardly, I groaned.

Michael handed the photograph back to me. "The gentleman in the carriage resembles Mr. Dyer a bit."

"Michael," said Roddy, "the gentleman in the photograph is not Mr. Dyer. He is Mr. Forster, who was not at the clambake."

"Very sorry, sir." He began to rise. "And I'm afraid I must soon crack on. I mean, get going."

"One more thought," I said. "Some ladies lighted cigarettes at the clambake. When you offered Mrs. Forster a plate, she was smoking a cigarette, and she refused it. Do you remember?"

"Ah..." His face lighted. "An infield fly ball on that," he said. "Yes, I do recall.

And the other lady, a bit on the wide side, she took it instead."

"That she did."

"Our question, Michael, is about the person who fixed that plate—who put the food on it?"

He fairly bounced on his thighs. "The mother sent it her way," he said. "It was the lady with all the jewels. Every finger with rings a-glitter."

That would be Rowena. "And did she prepare the plate?" I asked. "The clams? The vegetables?"

"Lordy, ma'am...." He scratched an ear. "As to that, I cannot say for sure. I do remember the gentleman that stood by."

"Gentleman?"

"Beside the lady with the rings, the gentleman all in stripes, coat and trousers both."

"That would be Mr. Romberg. The two were together? The lady with the jeweled rings and the gentleman in the striped suit?"

"Best I can recall," Michael replied. "The striped gentleman also favors a ring on his finger." Roddy and I gave him a moment.

"A wedding ring, perhaps?" Roddy asked at last. Michael scratched his head.

"Or a school ring? Perhaps a club signet?" This odd line of questions was doubtless my husband's effort to focus the young man's thoughts.

"A big bright stone, it was," Michael said. "So green I thought of the Emerald Isle."

"Your own Ireland."

Michael nodded.

"But you are not certain of who—exactly who—put the food on the plate?"

"It would be a lie, sir. Mr. Jim Reeves pulls out of the "bake" first, but after that, different ones have a hand in it."

"But as clearly as you recall, the plate was handed to you by the lady with jeweled rings—?" Michael nodded. "And you were directed to tell Mrs. Forster that her mother wanted her to have this particular plate."

"That I can say for sure. You are bang on. Swear to God." He stood. We stood.

"Michael, you have been most helpful. For the time being, we would prefer that this conversation be kept among ourselves," Roddy said.

"Cross my heart," Michael said, his hand tracing a cross over the name of the hardware store.

"And Mr. Romberg…" Roddy said, "the gentleman in the striped suit. He was standing close to her? Next to her?"

The young man paused, seeming to search for the perfect words. At length he looked both of us in the eye and then spoke to Roddy. "As close as you are, sir, to Mrs. DeVere on that bench."

Chapter Sixteen

WEARING FORMAL EVENING DRESS, Roddy and I were seated on the Louis XV rococo settee in Cassie's "Blue" drawing room. She was upstairs putting the children to bed before we all headed to an evening lecture at the Casino. Our early arrival at Seabright had allowed us to meet with the two new members of the Forster household staff, all in the guise of "helpful" advice about their work in this cottage. The word "homicide" was not to be spoken, we had decided, much less "poison" or "murder."

Cassie had given her butler, Hayes, the night off, lest that maven of manners scuttle this interview. No butler worthy of the name would approve of Mrs. Forster's friends meeting her new servants in a drawing room. Nor did the maid approve, seeing us into the "Blue" room upon the presentation of our calling card *("Mr. and Mrs. Roderick W. DeVere")*, then ushering the twosome in with pursed-mouth disapproval.

At the sight of the undercover private detectives, my heart sank. First impressions can be deceiving, but these two looked like a sad pair.

"We understand that Mrs. Forster has given her butler the evening off," said the taller one in a thin voice. "That would be Mr. Hayes?"

"Yes, Hayes," said Roddy to the new "groundskeeper" who introduced himself as Dennis Erbson. A clean shaven, pale, balding man of medium height, he looked to be in his later thirties, with broad nose, wide-set dark eyes and the beginnings of a double chin. His soft, sloping shoulders may be the reason for the extra padding in his obviously new denim jacket. His carefully filed, spotless fingernails prompted questions of why, from his thumbs to his pinkies, a groundskeeper would take such personal care of his hands. Or why a man at work outdoors in the daytime would be so pale. Had the Pinkerton manager given these matters a thought when he arranged to send the Chicago-based Detective Dennis Erbson to Newport?

"I understand that we will meet Mr. Hayes first thing in the morning," said the new "footman," Harvey Dunlap, who was shorter and thinner than his companion, a wiry figure with a thin face, tight lips and a nose as narrow as a thorn. This "footman" looked tightly coiled and ready for a boxing ring, not to spar but to win by a knockout. "Is Hayes to be called 'Mister Hayes?'" he asked in a rusty voice.

"Yes, a footman addresses the household butler as 'Mister,'" I said. "And the housekeeper as 'Missus.' That would be Mrs. Frayer, who oversees the maids."

Both men nodded. "'Mister Hayes and Mrs. Frayer,'" repeated groundskeeper Erbson. At least they were careful to stand at a respectful few feet before us.

Roddy and I paused in this awkward moment. Both detectives Erbson and Dunlap knew that Mr. Roderick DeVere was to be their Newport liaison, since he was the gentleman who had initiated the active Pinkerton file on behalf of Mrs. Forster. They were to report their findings to him as well as to the New York office. For the time being, the Newport police were not to be informed of the Pinkerton agents' presence at Seabright. For a fact, these two looked nothing like the Newport policemen who were on duty outdoors.

"You both arrived late this afternoon?" Roddy asked.

"We did," said Erbson, the groundskeeper.

"By the Fall River steamer," said footman Dunlop. "We were met and driven here by O'Boyle—or is it 'Mister O'Boyle?'"

Was his tone slightly sarcastic? For Cassie's sake, I hoped not. "Simply say O'Boyle," I said, adding, "I trust you were taken to the service entrance. The front entrance is solely for the family, their friends, and invited guests." Just to be sure, I repeated, "…invited guests only."

"You were shown your lodgings?" Roddy asked. "And given supper?"

"And introduced to the servants?"

They nodded. "Five servants, including the cook. We took supper in the downstairs," said footman Dunlap. "They served us well." His hazel eyes scanned the room like search-lights, registering every item of bric-a-brac (Cassie called them "*bibelots*"). This was a hopeful sign of vigilance. "We are to meet with Mrs. Forster in the morning," he said. "She will discuss our duties."

The awkward moment continued as we all played our assigned roles, the detectives as groundskeeper and foot-man, the DeVeres solely as family friends of the Forsters here for a visit in a typical Newport summer season. The unspoken topic—homicide—underlay every glance, every syllable, but there would be no conspiratorial winks among us, no whispered phrases, no secret notes. In the days ahead, Roddy might stroll the Seabright gardens with groundskeeper Erbson, seeming to consult about plantings at our Drumcliffe cottage. Inside Seabright, my husband might request that footman Dunlap, who just happened to be nearby, undertake a task that required a brief vocal exchange.

According to the Pinkerton contract, it was Mr. Roderick W. DeVere who, in the absence of Mr. Dudley Forster, rep-resented the interests of Mrs. Forster and their children, Charles and Beatrice. As for informing Mrs. Forster of the detectives' work, the contract was deliberately vague. Roddy emphasized to Robert Pinkerton that Mrs. Forster's sensitive nature required communication with utmost care. Mr. Pinkerton inquired about a possible clergyman as confidante, but Roddy explained that Anglican ministers took rotating turns all summer. Mr. Pinkerton then asked whether a gentleman in the Brush or Van Schylar families might not keep Mrs. Forster informed in tactful terms—perhaps her father or a cousin?

Again, Roddy was persuasive. He said that Mrs. Forster's father, Robert Fox, was occupied with personal legal matters that took him regularly into the city and proved distracting. As for Sam— Samuel D. Brush—he recalled the phrase that Cassie once used to describe her cousin: "so-near-yet-so-far." He was ever ready to help out, but as a newly married man, his bachelor days not far behind, he could be excused for seeming awkward and brusque. Roddy had pointed out to Robert Pinkerton that Sam's penchant for urging mechanical devices as the solution to every problem was itself a problem. "He might advise Mrs. Forster to install some sort of electrical invention or motorized gadgetry." It was settled. The liaison would be Mr. Roderick DeVere.

"You will find Mrs. Forster to be a lady who is appreciative of her household staff...including her gardeners," I said to the men in Cassie's drawing room. "She takes great care with scheduling so that her servants' might be permitted time for their needs and recreation."

"Such as Hayes's evening off tonight," said the new groundskeeper. "Mister Hayes," corrected footman Dunlap.

The two eyed one another, and I guessed their first acquaintance was this very day. Partners who had never before worked together? How many problems would this create? I glanced at my husband, who surely shared my concern.

"While Mrs. Forster attends to the children's bedtime," Roddy said, "we wish to take the opportunity to offer this advice. For instance, you might take notice of the detachment of Newport police who patrol this property day and night."

"None of our affair," said the new footman.

"Agreed," said the groundskeeper. Both had clearly been advised on this matter. "And Mr. Forster," asked groundskeeper Erbson, "is he expected to return to Newport soon—?"

"Not this season," said Roddy.

"He is away on extended...." Foolishly, I had begun to explain Dudley's absence. His extended what? His calling? His fossil hunt? "Business," I said.

"International?" asked Dunlap.

Are those godforsaken rocks where he digs a nation? "Yes," I said, "he was called abroad."

"And may I ask, as a footman, whether Mr. Forster travels by yacht? You see, sir...and ma'am... I get seasick and would not wish to be assigned to serve aboard a yacht. So if Mr. Dudley is a yachtsman...."

"He is not," Roddy said.

This seemed an odd topic for Dunlop to pursue, until I realized that he was prodding about the Forsters' marital status. Was Dudley Forster gallivanting on a yacht to keep his distance from an estranged spouse? Or, worse, with a mistress? Was a marital split and the division of property looming? I suspected that Harvey Dunlap, the new footman, was asking whether his true assignment for Pinkerton might be as an undercover divorce detective and if he might potentially be called as a witness in a courtroom.

Roddy quashed the matter. "Mr. Forster is deeply concerned about the wellbeing of Mrs. Forster and their children." His firmest voice was coupled with his steely stare. "He will return as soon as is possible. He will expect to find that his wife has been under the best protection and care." The two detectives seemed to shrink into their shirt collars. Was this part of their act? I couldn't tell, though when necessary, Roddy could be intimidating with servants, tradesmen, and certain gentlemen of Society.

"And we wish to emphasize," I said, "that Mrs. Forster is a lady of delicate temperament and must be treated accordingly. We are sure you understand?" They nodded. I pushed on. "She takes great care of her young children—as you see this very evening. They are lovely children, Beatrice and Charles, and they, too, merit respect and care. You understand?" Again, nodding.

"And you might observe us...Mrs. DeVere and myself," said Roddy, "as frequent guests here at Seabright." A warning that the new footman and groundskeeper would be monitored and that Robert Pinkerton would be kept informed as needed. "Frequent guests in the daytime and evenings as well," Roddy said.

The same purse-mouthed maid reappeared at the door. "Pardon," she said, "but Mrs. Forster wishes to say that she is ready for the evening." She frowned at the footman and groundskeeper, seeming satisfied that they stood the required number of feet from the gentry on the Louis XV settee. Had they been seated, she would have been scandalized. So many servants, I noticed, were more rigidly formal than their employers.

Roddy and I rose and were escorted to the entrance where Cassie awaited us. Our escort was a footman posted just outside the "Blue" drawing room who might have heard every word of our conversation. Neither Roddy nor I glanced backward but could picture the maid dispatching the new footman and groundskeeper to their proper places, where they belonged.

The Casino butler, Mr. Ives, seemed to be everywhere at once. He patrolled the tennis courts and measured the water level in the courtyard fountain. He counted the balls and cues in the billiard room and adjusted the armchairs in the Reading and Conversation room on the second floor. No one knew where he came from, nor his age, but if a member or guest needed assistance, count on Mr. Ives, who was unfailingly courteous, respectful, and helpful day or night.

We had no reason to ridicule this man, except for his height and his hair. Barely five feet tall from foot to crown, Mr. Ives added inches with a wavy salt- and-pepper pompadour that glistened with oil. Defying wind and gravity, the hair never moved. Some believed it a wig, others thought it stiffened with wax.

Hypocrisy soaked our snide remarks, for every lady in Society cared deeply about her coiffeur, and the men's whiskers were marvels of skilled razoring. All the same, the name "Mr. Ives," prompted snickers and eye rolls, though Roddy told me that every member of the Casino had been saved from embarrassment or privately informed of a crucial matter at one time or another by Mr. Ives. "He never divulges his sources," Roddy said, "but his facts are rock solid, and his intuition is uncanny."

Ives would never think to interrupt a card game, billiards, or a social gathering on the porch or veranda. (Mamie Fish had called him the Casino's Cheshire Cat.) He did not, therefore, interrupt my tennis lesson—which was going well, my serves inbound and fast, my forehands hit with satisfying "thwocks." Instructor Dickie Thatford's rare compliment was music to my ears. ("It's your day, Mrs. DeVere. Have your racquet restrung, and you'll be a player yet.") Lesson concluded, I arranged for new catgut racquet strings, changed into a white cotton duck suit and deerskin walking shoes, and strolled toward a favorite remote shady spot on the veranda for a lemonade.

Suddenly, Mr. Ives was at my shoulder. "Pardon, Mrs. DeVere, but might we have a word?"

His voice so confidential, I paused at once. Mr. Ives never claimed a member's attention for a trivial matter. Gauging emotional temperatures was his genius, and he often eased tensions between rival Society "queens" who vied for a porch chair as if it were the last seat on a Cunard liner lifeboat.

"Yes, Mr. Ives?"

The pompadour nodded in the direction of the wicker chair and table that I had selected.

"In the past fortnights," said the Casino butler, "Mr. Glendorick has preferred that particular table, and we expect him momentarily."

"Oh? So, that's now Mr. Glendorick's table?" So many places and spaces excluded us women here in the East, and the one and only ladies tennis court at the Casino was supposedly a gesture of equality. "Reserved for Mr. Glendorick?" My voice was rimed with frost.

"Please do not misunderstand, Mrs. DeVere. Every Casino member is entitled to our facilities."

At this point, I simply thirsted for a lemonade, never mind the location on the veranda. "Thank you, Mr. Ives, I'll just sit over there."

Again, the pompadour signaled disapproval. "For your comfort, Mrs. DeVere, I suggest that you might prefer the Horseshoe Piazza." He meant the curved porch at least fifty yards away. "You see," he said, "there is a certain man who meets Mr. Glendorick here."

"A man?" I echoed deliberately. "Not a gentleman?"

"Not to my knowledge. He is neither a member nor a guest of a member.

On several occasions, however, he has occupied a certain table with Mr. Glendorick." Mr. Ives hesitated, then added, "Both this season and last. I believe the two conduct affairs."

"Business? At the Newport Casino?" What was Mr. Ives trying to say? The Casino was strictly recreational, and Newport entirely social. To conduct business was to violate etiquette, which meant everything to Society. It was breeched, of course, on a sliding scale of offence. The misuse of tableware at a dinner, for instance selecting an oyster fork for a salad (my frequent *faux pas* before Cassie took charge), gave Society a droll anecdote about a newcomer's crudity. But a stock-holding member of the Newport Casino using the site for business? Out of the question. With the Glendoricks' daughter soon to be married off to a British aristocrat, it was unimaginable. The offence was volcanic.

"May I be clear, Mrs. DeVere?"

"Please, Mr. Ives."

"The man who meets with Mr. Glendorick... I believe he speaks English with a foreign language accent...if I am not mistaken, Spanish."

"I see." What else but Spanish, given Edwin Glendorick's fixation on Cuba. Specifically, his demand that the U.S. take possession of the island.

Mr. Ives's expression said something far more troubling than a social gaffe was at stake. He had subtly informed me that a Casino member conducted forbidden business on this veranda. My duty was to let it be known to someone— or some ones—who could put a stop to the offensive behavior.

Avoiding Edwin Glendorick and his companion, I pivoted to the Horseshoe Piazza to sip my lemonade. I did not set eyes on the offending Casino member that afternoon but caught sight of the man Ives had recognized—a man about six feet tall wearing a heavy navy blue jacket and a neck scarf, his jaw set square, his goatee and moustache black. He looked as if he searched the scene for incoming storms.

I recognized him at once. He was the man I had seen in the Trinity Church pew at Sylvia's funeral, the man with the stone-cold eyes. His appearance was chilling then. And chilling now.

Chapter Seventeen

THE TIDE WAS CHANGING, but the water was calm when Roddy and I set out in a dinghy from the yacht club landing. It was midmorning, and the sun shone behind fleecy clouds. The air was crisp. Once again, we sought the absolute privacy that ruled out the cottage where the walls had ears, and the Casino, Bailey's Beach, the village, or a public park. "I am no oarsman, my dear," Roddy said. "But I can row us out far enough."

"You're sure?"

Shushed with a look, I helped us push off from the pebbly shore, then clambered aboard to sit facing the bow while Roddy took up the oars and began to stroke. His shoes and trouser legs were soaked from launching the little dinghy, and he pulled hard to get us moving straight.

If the weather stayed calm this afternoon, these waters would come alive with catboats sailed by youngsters, but now we had the inner harbor to ourselves. Neither wind nor rainstorms were forecast, though Roddy reminded me that weather prediction was a throw of the dice. The moon was almost full, and the tides, as he mentioned, were both very high and low.

At last, far from shore, he rested the oars and left us with the soft gurgle of water against the hull. We faced one another on the board seats, both of us in lightweight clothing and hats.

"About those two detectives—" I began.

"Not quite what you expected? Not exactly Sherlock Holmes?"

"Seriously, Roddy. They look like misfits for the jobs. Erbson looks nothing like a groundskeeper. Not one callous on his hands, not a speck of soil under his fingernails. And that brand-new denim jacket—"

"And Dunlap?"

"—like an escapee from a prize fighting gym. One thing I learned from your parents, every footman must enhance the household. Your mother was dead set on this point. 'They must be visually appealing,' she said to me. The footmen at Seabright all fit the bill, every last one handsome in his uniform. But skinny Dunlap looks like he's ready to don boxing gloves. I'm sure Cassie's servants will have plenty to say when they gossip in the kitchen."

"Anything else?" I felt my husband was waiting me out. "We can't judge yet, Val. We must give them a chance. Pinkerton and his Chicago office recommended them highly."

"Chicago is not Newport!" My exclamation literally rocked our boat. "Sorry, Roddy."

"We'll be sorry if we lose our lunch." He meant it. We had brought a little knapsack with a canteen of water, apples, and cheese with crackers.

"Chicago must be a very different kind of place," I said. "I imagine Chicago as a western town. Cattle, cowboys, the frontier...." In truth, I had never visited Chicago.

"Let's agree," said Roddy, "we owe Cassandra and her children—and ourselves—the benefit of the doubt. Pinkerton told me that Dunlap exposed a counterfeiter who is now serving a prison sentence, and Erbson caught the vice- president of a bank embezzling. These two have solid records. Let's see what they can do. Let's also remember that police are on duty."

I faced my husband, his eyes shaded by the brim of his Panama hat. "The police were no help when Florence Dovedale ate the clams that were intended for Cassie."

Roddy gazed toward the shore, then back to me. "So, we now confront the puzzle."

"Deadly puzzle. Murderous puzzle."

"Val, we must try to keep our emotions in check. Let's leave melodramas for the Casino theater."

Mention of the Casino rankled. "I'm furious at myself for not seeing the obvious about Glendorick," I said. "His obsession with Cuba was staring us right in the face. He's adamant about US possession. But 'Freedom for Cuba' was one of Georgina's greatest causes. Cassie swears she was passionate about it. And Sylvia…" I paused, recalling the items that Cassie and I had fingered in Sylvia's bedroom at Tuxedo Park. "We found a record of a donation of one hundred…. No, it was one hundred fifty dollars for *Liberacion de Cuba.* It was dated last spring." A little wave lapped against the boat. "And there was some kind of flag…."

"What flag?"

"On a stand. We thought it might be for a yacht club. It was red, white and blue—and with one large star. One star."

Roddy studied an oarlock. "It sounds like the flag for the Cuban revolutionary uprising in the late Sixties. If I'm not mistaken, 1868. Cespedes's flag."

"Who?"

"It was soon after our Civil War. Perhaps Cespedes was inspired. He freed all the slaves on his sugar mill and declared a revolution against Spain. They call him the 'Father' of Cuba."

My husband, a virtual *Encyclopedia Britannica.* He looked rueful.

"I've mostly known about Cuba from rum bottle labels, Val. Bacardi rum makes splendid cocktails. Let's not talk about that now. Let's think of why Georgina, in all innocence, put her life at risk promoting Cuban independence. She's never visited the Caribbean?"

"As far as I know."

"Did she speak Spanish?"

"Cassie said no."

"Then let's think about her husband, Sylvia's father."

"Harry Brush, the wood king...could Harry have wanted to expand his timber business there?"

Roddy laughed. "The royal palm is elegant, Val, but useless in practical terms...all the more reason the Caribbean might be a good market for wood, maybe an independent Cuba at the center of it. Wasn't his slogan 'Wood for the Whole Wide World?'"

I nodded.

"So," Roddy said, "Harry Brush might have encouraged Georgina to promote Cuban independence, to make it one of her causes."

"I doubt that 'encourage' is the right word, from what we know about Harry Brush."

Roddy chuckled. "So, he bribed her, or bullied her, or struck a business deal with his wife. It was Brush money for everything *de luxe* if Georgina promoted her husband's interests, including a free and independent Cuba to open up markets for Harry's empire of wood. I'd guess that Brush money paid for weapons for the revolutionaries, and maybe Georgina became a true partisan. Maybe she was really passionate about the revolution. We'll never know. What we do know is that Edwin Glendorick will oppose Cuban independence with his last breath."

"So his ships can anchor there?"

"So he can dominate shipping in the entire Caribbean, monopolize it, beat back all competition. Glendorick will pounce—that's the prize.

"But only if the US owns Cuba."

"So he thinks."

The memory of yesterday at the Casino sent shivers through my summer dress. "That man with the cold eyes... Roddy, he could not possibly have been a guest at Mrs. Astor's ball when Georgina fell ill. But Edwin and Madeline Glendorick probably attended. If they did, maybe their names appeared in newspaper coverage. Hearst, Pulitzer... all of them."

Roddy reached for the canteen in our knapsack. "Who catered the Astor dinner?"

"The ball?" I said, "well, it would have been Demonico's or Sherry. I think it was Louis Sherry this year. Why does it matter?"

"Perhaps your evil-eyed man could be linked to someone in the catering staff who served Georgina at her table."

A horrible thought. "Which means that a waiter could have poisoned Georgina...on Glendorick's order."

"And Glendorick might have watched it all from his table at the ball." The dinghy rocked as the water grew choppy. Gulls wheeled in the distance.

I paused while Roddy unscrewed the canteen and offered me water.

Instinctively I hesitated.

"Val, I filled the canteen myself."

"But if arsenic *were* put into the canteen—?"

"Tasteless," he said. A silent minute passed. "Fear and suspicion are contagious, aren't they? But we must not surrender our judgment." He winked at me. "Cool heads, yes?"

"Cool heads," I repeated, though feebly. Our dinghy was rocking as the tide shifted and the breeze freshened. I never got seasick when we shot the rapids in western rivers but felt the slightest queasiness just now. The sky had turned a pale gray, and I tugged at my sun hat as a light gust blew.

"And Sylvia?" I asked. "What do we know about her?"

"Not nearly enough," Roddy admitted. "She was seen shopping in your Ladies Mile, wasn't she?"

He pronounced 'Ladies Mile' as if it were on the moon. "And suppose she were to get hungry or thirsty? Where do the ladies go for tea? Or to eat?"

"For a woman alone in public," I said, "there's only Maillard's." Roddy looked blank, typical for a gentleman on this topic. "Maillard's Luncheon Restaurant and Bonbon Store," I said, "and there's also a soda fountain at Macy's." I noticed a dark gray cloud on the horizon. Roddy put the canteen back in the knapsack and took out an apple.

"The waiters at Maillard's and the Macy's countermen," I said, "they can't earn much of a living doing day work."

"No. Many of them 'moonlight' at special events."

"...meaning that extra waiters might have been hired for Mrs. Astor's ball," I said. "One of them could have served at the ball where he poisoned Georgina, and then also put arsenic in Sylvia's luncheon sandwich, or her cup of cocoa."

Roddy began to cut the apple. "And he would recognize Sylvia from the many 'Brush Heiress' photographs in the news accounts after Georgina died...or took note of her name when she charged the cost to her account."

"He could have waited," I said, "and watched. And fulfilled his 'contract' with Glendorick and the man I saw at the Casino."

Roddy offered me the first apple slice. "Here's another possibility, Val."

"I'm listening."

"Suppose Sylvia took a lunch with her on her excursions from Tuxedo Park? Perhaps the housekeeper prepared something for her."

"Maude Gowdy," I said.

"Just in case Miss Sylvia Brush felt a bit hungry?" Roddy cocked an eyebrow. "Isn't it possible that the housekeeper might have poisoned Sylvia? Or hastened her death?" He cut another apple slice. "Didn't Sylvia's will leave the housekeeper five thousand dollars for an…'enterprise,' wasn't it?"

"For her silver polish formula."

"But only upon Sylvia's death. We remember Sam noting that stipulation. Maybe Sam knows something about Maude Gowdy that we don't know." Roddy sighed. "I wish he could help, but Sam's mind runs on one track. If the problem cannot be solved with gears, girders, or electrical power, he is not interested. If it could be motorized, silver polish might interest him."

My husband's laugh was soft and bitter. "It's irritating, Val. Since the clambake, everyone has been saluting Sam for hiring the police that shot the rabid dog. It has gone to his head, as if he alone shielded the Clambake Club from a wild beast. He'll be club president next year, and Evalina is delighted with her hero-husband."

"Vanity," I murmured. We both took deep breaths. My queasiness rose as the boat rocked.

"Suppose Sylvia took a lunch with her from Tuxedo Park," my husband said again. "Where would she eat it? Might she sit on a public park bench and unpack her lunch?"

I paused. A dark gray cloud caught my eye. "From what we heard from Annie Flowers, I'd say yes, especially on a warm spring day."

The cloud seemed to be moving toward the dinghy. At the oars, Roddy's back was turned, but I faced it. I would keep watch on the darkening sky. "Or perhaps Sylvia would eat her lunch on a mezzanine balcony in one of the department stores," I said. "They have chairs for shoppers to rest."

I pictured Sylvia—the Sylvia in the coffin in Trinity Church—on a mezzanine nibbling Maude Gowdy's Irish soda bread and butter. Mixed with arsenic. I shuddered, both at the effigy in the coffin and the thought of Sylvia Brush embalmed with arsenic.

Roddy flung the apple core overboard. We watched it toss in the waves. "We haven't quite finished with these events, Val."

The apple core disappeared. "I know." I waited for him to speak.

"The clambake."

"The clambake." It felt wearying to say the word.

"Rowena Fox," said Roddy.

"Cassie's own mother."

"Her estranged mother...."

"I know," I said. "Her temper runs hot and cold, and she raged when her late sister's will cut her out. I can see her smashing a vase...vases." And always, I thought, that dark frown smoldering between the eyes. I could repeat Cassie's lament, how Rowena's eyes sparkled at the sight of jewels but never at her own daughter, how she appraised herself before every mirror, but never spared a smile for her grandchildren.

"It doesn't make her a murderer," Roddy said. "It makes her a suspect."

"And let's not forget Romberg, my dear."

I nodded. The dandy in the striped outing suit at the clambake. Archibald Romberg, the heir to a failed milling business and a loser at croquet—but a killer?

"Romberg..." I said. "You're serious?"

"Very."

"Because he lost money betting against Georgina at croquet?" The notion of revenge killing over a croquet match was ludicrous.

"There's something else, Val." Roddy leaned toward me as if to confide in a small space. "Romberg's bankrupt. He needs money, and his best bet is marriage—so he thinks. Consider this...suppose he tried to court Georgina when Harry Brush died. The croquet rivalry might have been a flirtation. But wagering put him in deep debt, and the widow Brush rebuffed him."

I nodded, absorbing the idea. The boat rocked. "So... if Georgina were no longer in the picture...then her heir... the heiress, Sylvia."

"Precisely," Roddy said. "So, Romberg decided to visit Tuxedo Park to try at romance again."

"But failed…because the reclusive Sylvia wouldn't see her visitors…she ordered Maude Gowdy to send them away." I shifted as a little wave broke. "But with Sylvia gone," I said, "another possibility could open up for Romberg. Cassie's mother will soon be divorced and free to remarry. That's your thought, isn't it?"

The clambake scene appeared before me, and Theo snickering at the sight of Romberg and Rowena laughing together. And the caddy, Michael Keefe, swearing that he saw the two stand so very close, shoulder to shoulder, when the toxic plate was dispatched to Cassie.

"Roddy…." Just then, salty spray splashed into the boat, and I choked on my own, sudden thoughts. "The Brush fortune, Roddy," I said, "It's Cassie's fortune now…but if something happened to Cassie, her mother could claim it. Rowena could….."

I gripped the sides of the dinghy. "Could Rowena act alone? Or join with Romberg? Would she dare? Would those two be so greedy…murderously greedy?"

The dinghy rocked. I felt dizzy, gripping the gunwales at the sides of the boat. All at sea, I felt all at sea, but also feared that my husband's and my imagination had run wild.

"Roddy," I said, "this might be a good theory…but how could they have done it? Can we really imagine that Romberg would reach into the coat pocket of his flashy new striped suit for a deadly dose of arsenic…and not be seen doing it?

Or Rowena… fumbling in her long kidskin gloves at a skirt pocket to get hold of a vial of arsenic to sprinkle on the plate?" Or had she taken her gloves off? I couldn't remember.

My husband did not answer immediately. The wind was up, the water choppier, and he struggled to maneuver the boat. "I wish it wasn't possible, Val. I wish my thoughts were beyond a reasonable doubt. But consider their jewelry, both hers and his…."

"Rowena's? Her brooches and necklaces, the gold and every gemstone, bracelets…. Roddy, what are you saying?"

"Her rings, Val. Her antique rings."

Rowena's antique jewelry was her calling card. One aigrette had adorned the tresses of Marie Antoinette. "Rings, of course," I said. "She always wore antique rings."

Roddy's laugh was soft, yet ominous. "Rings from the Italian Renaissance," he said, "were sometimes fashioned with a hollow compartment that was hinged like tiny jewel box beneath the stone. Do you know about them?"

"Vaguely." The queasiness increased.

He pressed on. "The cavities could be packed with poison, concealed by the shiny gems. At a touch, the hinge was opened, and the poison released."

"Onto food…."

"Or into a goblet or chalice. A flick of the wrist would do it, and the gem would be back in place." He flicked his wrist to demonstrate. "The Italians used a special arsenic blend they called 'cantarella.'"

I swallowed hard. "And Romberg...." The huge emerald ring that Michael had described that day in the park, comparing the gemstone to his own beloved Emerald Isle. My thoughts spun. "Madame Riva," I blurted.

"Who?"

"A gypsy woman who manicures ladies' nails...and holds séances. She said something to Cassie about the Borgias. They were Italian, weren't they?"

"They ruled at the height of the Italian Renaissance, very nasty bunch."

"Before I could ask more details about the poison, I looked at the sky.

"Roddy, there's a dark cloud behind you."

"We better start back." He took up the oars and pulled. The tide was going out fast. "We've stayed too long," he said, "and the current is against us." He fell silent, all energy at the oars as the slate-gray cloud bank drove toward us, the tide sucking the little dinghy outward. I sat helpless as he rowed.

Lightning gashed the cloud, and the flash came with a roar. It was suddenly cold. At my back, wind pushed us shoreward, and the rain fell like needles. My hat flew off. Roddy's Panama was pulled tight over his forehead. Eyes closed tight, he rowed, his chest heaving. Rainwater sloshed in the dinghy, and I tried to scoop with my palms. A futile gesture. The horizon was a flat gray.

Suddenly, I felt stones strike us both—at my back, my bare head, Roddy's face and chest and legs. White stones shot into the dinghy.... "Hail," Roddy called. "It's hail." The hailstones pelted us, mixed with cold rain and shrieking wind. I could barely see. Then there was a grinding sound, and the dinghy lurched to a stop, pitching me forward into my husband's arms.

"The shore," Roddy said with relief.

Shivering, soaking wet, I trembled at all that had assaulted both body and mind.

Chapter Eighteen

THE TWO OF US, pickled in brine, soaked to the bone, dripping wet, clothing ruined, distraught—faced our butler Sands as if nothing was amiss when he ushered Mr. and Mrs. DeVere into the Drumcliffe front entrance. The hailstones had ceased and the storm moved to the east. We left puddles on the Italian marble tiles of the foyer, and Calista assumed my brooding was due solely to the unforeseen weather on our boating excursion. Silently, she helped me change and asked no questions. Roddy's valet, Norbert, assisted as if nothing were out of the ordinary.

How we wished it were so.

The storm of suspicions continued, and today was another day. We planned an afternoon visit to Cassie and the children at Seabright, hoping to hear something useful from the new "groundskeeper" and "footman" as we sought to shore Cassie up. Also, I hoped to propose an idea to her—something hatched in the nighttime hours of my insomnia, something I wanted to put before Roddy first thing this morning.

"A gig, Val? Are you sure?"

"I am." We rarely ordered the simple cart pulled by a single horse and favored for short errands, usually by a servant. Comfort would be out of the question, and a rough ride a certainty.

Roddy objected. "Why not the cabriolet? Or one of the dog-carts? Something with a cushion."

I shook my head. "Not today. Have another slice of toast?" We breakfasted quickly in the small oak-paneled side room midway between our bedroom suites. "Let's dress down this morning and drive a gig along Thames or Spring Street." I added, "So we won't be noticed. I have an idea, and we need privacy."

Roddy dipped his toast into his usual two poached eggs, and I ate a last bite of bacon-and-beans hash, a reminder of campfire breakfasts in the West. From nostalgia or habit, it was often my morning fare.

"And we'll take Clover. I think?"

"Yes," I said, "slow and steady."

Within the hour we boarded the gig pulled by the old dapple gray. Having hitched the old horse, our coachman Noland handed Roddy the reins with a look of disapproval and puzzlement. We were wearing the plainest of clothing, Roddy in a twill overshirt and a derby or "plug" hat, and me in a brown flannel skirt and a shirtwaist with a cambric vest.

I had twisted my diamond wedding ring so the platinum band alone was visible and easily taken for silver. We were seated side by side—hip to hip—on the narrow hard wood seat. Clover's hooves sounded softly on the Drumcliffe drive and on the roadway of packed clay, then sharpened as her iron horseshoes struck the cobblestones of Thames Street, along Newport's commercial hub.

"Not exactly what I'd call 'privacy,'" Roddy said. He called out the business names as we slowly passed. "Dry goods," he said. "Western Union, George Hermann's jewelry store, Ladies and Gents Fine Footwear...." He turned to me on the narrow seat. "Val, are we here to view the merchandise?"

"We are hiding in plain sight," I said. For proof, I pointed out that horse-drawn vehicles passed without taking any notice of the couple in the gig.

"So, what brings us to Thames Street, in camouflage? What's your idea?'"

"Are you ready?" I asked.

"Ready." The reins were loose in his fingers, the horse plodding.

"Here it is." I wet my lips and took a deep breath. "I propose that we take Cassie and children and go away. And do it right away."

Roddy's fingers tightened on the reins. The horse slowed. "Are you joking?"

"For their protection, scoop them up and take them to safety in the West. We can order our rail car brought here to Newport and depart together from the train depot." Since our marriage, the car was newly christened *Louisa* in honor of my deceased mother, the mother I never met.

"Here's a plan," I spoke. "We order the *Louisa*, reserve the rail lines west, and we—all of us—get aboard and go. There's plenty of room, bed chambers for everyone. The children's nanny could come too."

We had had the rail car completely refurnished and outfitted with onyx washstands, silver fixtures, and a nine-foot bathtub encased in mahogany—never once used. "We could go to Virginia City...where we met."

The horse slowed. Roddy squeezed my hand and turned to face me. "My dear, you need not remind me of the place where we met. I treasure it." Despite Roddy's kind words, his jawline signaled reluctance. He snapped the reins, and we moved.

"It's for their safety," I said. "We'll rent a house in Virginia City...two houses. We can stay until we know that Cassie is safe from harm." Roddy's jawline did not soften.

"The children will love it," I said. "The mountain, Mount Davidson, and the real West. It's better than the Buffalo Bill show. And Cassie can rest at ease."

"Val, I don't think...."

"Or we could all go to Denver. We could take suites at the Brown Palace. We'd have every comfort a hotel can offer." I paused, saw his set jaw tighter, and went on. "And Newport is full of railroad men to help with arrangements. What's the line that Mr. Fish owns?"

"Stuyvesant Fish is president of the Illinois Central."

"And the Vanderbilt—?"

"Willie K… William Vanderbilt is president of the New York Central."

"Men we see socially, Roddy. It would be easy. You can call upon your railroad friends for help making the arrangements. They do this all the time." Still, that rock-firm jaw. "Why not?"

He nudged the horse. "Val, it's a lovely idea, but it sounds rather like some adventure in an old-fashioned novel."

"Novel? What novel?" My own jaw tightened. "This isn't fiction, Roddy."

He turned toward me. "No, it's not fiction. I wish it were."

"Then why not go West?" Stamping my foot on the dashboard, I felt like a schoolgirl.

A wagon load of barrels passed us. "How many weeks are left in the season, about three, yes?" I counted. "It's August…so there's Tennis Week and the Newport Horse Show, and it's over. Then we'll all go back to the city."

"But not right away," he said. "There are sojourns at country houses. Some cottagers go yachting. The social season doesn't start until October…really, November."

"Roddy, I know the calendar." I almost said, 'Your calendar, not mine.' "How long would you imagine us remaining in the West?" he asked.

I hadn't imagined. "Until Cassie is safe…and the children."

"And their whereabouts supposedly unknown all that time? And ours? Realistically, Val, could we all simply vanish into Nevada? Or Denver?"

"Well, not really…. Close friends would know, of course, and some servants. Cassie's father…." I said a bit more shrilly than I intended, "What is your point?" But I knew his point.

"Must I go on?"

Quietly, I said no. Awake in the wee hours, I had thought about the escape itself, not the problem of disappearing…a vastly different matter. "You think Cassie could be hunted down in the West?"

"A Pullman car can carry trouble to any depot." He paused. "But there's something else."

"I'm listening."

"Simply this—" He made a clicking sound to encourage the horse. "Both deaths occurred in the city, yes? Georgina and Sylvia—"

"But in two different worlds, from Mrs. Astor's ballroom to the Lower East Side."

"By way of Tuxedo Park?"

"We don't know that for certain," I said.

"True, we don't, Val. But suppose it seemed more efficient to strike in the city?"

"Not at Newport?"

My husband shifted the reins. "Crime detection," he said, "involves seeking out patterns. The deaths of both Brush heiresses took place in Manhattan. The murder that was attempted here in Newport failed. It targeted Cassie and hit Florence Dovedale, who survives, so suspicion falls on spoiled seafood. The next plan for homicide could very well be in the city."

"So, Cassie is safer here for the time being, is that it? Until it's time for us to close up the cottages and go? Which gives us less than a month to figure out who wants to murder my closest friend."

Hearing my voice rise, I waited for Roddy to remind me that Seabright was under guard day and night, and the new "footman" and "groundskeeper" were on duty inside the property. Which he did. "So, we accept the status quo?"

"For right now. Remember, my dear, we're keeping cool heads. Yesterday in the dinghy—"

"—we might have drowned...."

"Val, look at me." Roddy's eyes were steadfast. "We had an important talk yesterday. We'll go forward. We must also live our lives." He tugged gently at the reins. "Old Clover has earned her oats," he said, "and I see a tobacconist on that corner. I'll stop for newspapers. Yes, copies await in our breakfast room at Drumcliffe, but for two cents it will amuse us for a little while. You can read me what's going on in the world while Clover takes us home."

He handed me the reins, stepped down, and returned momentarily with a morning paper. "A bit of distraction will do us both good, Val." We swapped reins and the newspaper. "The *Herald* headlines, if you please, Mrs. DeVere."

The distraction was indeed welcome. With the paper on my lap, I read, "*Peace Protocol Signed by President McKinley and Spanish Ambassador.*"

"That's good."

"Here's another one. '*Heavy Verdict Against Life Insurance Company*.'" Then the headline that all but leaped at me. "'*Fracas in Ladies Mile*.'"

"What 'fracas?'"

"Suffragettes," I said. "'A remarkable incident... coterie of suffragettes at the fountain in the Siegal-Cooper Department Store...ruckus and rioting women...'Votes-for-Women' banners raised and trampled... hurdy-gurdy smashed.' Roddy, listen to this, '...Miss Annie Flowers arrested.'"

He turned. "The woman from the Lower East Side."

"It must be her. 'Public nuisance,' it says, and 'resisting arrest.' She is 'being held' at the Tombs. Is that a jail?"

"Yes."

"A terrible name."

"Officially,' Roddy said, "it's the Halls of Justice and House of Detention, but it's called it the Tombs because it looks like an Egyptian tomb."

"But it's a prison for women?" From her slum apartment to a jail called the Tombs...how cruel. Did a young woman turning a crank on a hurdy-gurdy deserve imprisonment as a "public nuisance?"

Roddy nodded. "Yes, a women's prison. Are other women named in the *Herald*?"

I reread. "No. It's a short article, no illustrations. Let's see what the *World* and *Journal* say."

"As soon as we get home."

Chapter Nineteen

THE RIDE HOME COULD not have seemed slower, the old horse pokier, even when she expected her stall, hay, and comfort, though little comfort awaited the two of us at Drumcliffe. A quick bite, and we sped to our suites to "metamorphose" (as I termed it) for the afternoon version of ourselves. In the rush to freshen up and change, not one minute could be spared for today's New York newspapers, though Roddy instructed Sands to set them all aside for later.

To appear at Seabright wearing our morning's apparel was impossible. Cassie had taught me much about Society, and I owed her the proof of her tutelage, especially in this time of extreme stress. If we had all fled West, maybe she would have seen my point of view, but now Calista hooked me into an afternoon walking dress of sky-blue serge with salmon piping at the cuffs and neckline. Fashion-wise, my maid knew the score.

She held up two brooches. "Must I?"

"To complete the dress, ma'am."

"Then the carnelian—"

"I believe that is Thai garnet, ma'am."

The real gem was Calista from years working on those coastal steamers as a stewardess. She fastened the brooch.

"And ma'am, remember you and Mr. DeVere plan to attend a musical performance this evening. Shall I select a gown?"

I had forgotten we were due for the operatic arias at the Casino theater tonight, sung by the great soprano Adelina Patti. Roddy had been looking forward to it.

"Yes, please, a gown." I slipped on my pumps. "And Calista," I said, "would you do an errand for me this afternoon?" She nodded. "Mr. DeVere and I are members of the Redwood Library on Bellevue Avenue," I said, "so you will represent us."

"Yes, ma'am."

"Noland will have a liveryman drive you, but not behind poor old Clover. Please ask the librarian to show you the New York newspaper accounts of Mrs. Astor's ball last January on the thirty-first, the last Monday in the month. You can find the papers in the reading room. They'll be yellowed but readable."

"Yes, ma'am." Calista kept a neutral expression.

"I want you to look at the New York *World*, *Journal*, and *Herald*." Fastening one final hook, my maid began to look

puzzled. "Quite simply," I said, "I will need your advice."
Calista nodded.

"We must prepare," I said, "for the wedding of Mrs. and Mrs. Glendorick's daughter, Emily, to a member of the British royal court. Mr. DeVere and I expect an invitation." Calista nodded. "And I must not in the least diminish the splendor of the mother of the bride."

"Surely not."

"So, if you will, look for descriptions of Mrs. Glendorick at Mrs. Astor's ball, so I can get a good sense of her style, to avoid seeming to outdo her."

"Yes, ma'am. I can do it this afternoon."

I put the question about Annie Flowers and the Tombs to Roddy as we drove to Seabright in the cabriolet, Roddy wearing a light gray corduroy suit with a silk neck scarf and cordovan boots. Our chestnut mare clipped along smartly.

"The choice of the Ladies Mile for the rally probably put the suffragettes at higher risk," I said, "even in the summer when ladies of Society were not in the city.

"What store was it that they rioted?" Roddy asked.

"Siegel-Cooper," I replied. My husband was not expected to know the palatial emporiums built for ladies, but the six-story beauty of French design (Cassie says "*beaux-arts*") with sky-lighted courts and an indoor marble fountain was so alluring that ladies simply said, without further explanation, 'Meet me at the fountain.'

I asked, "Do you think Annie Flowers would be in jail if she played her hurdy-gurdy somewhere else? Broadway?" I asked flippantly. "The Bowery? How about Wall Street?" One of Roddy's "looks" answered my taunts, and we drove in silence on a very hot, sunny afternoon.

"Auntie Val! Come and see! Come to the garden where we can play hide- and-seek!" Little Beatrice tugged at her nanny Cara's arm and reached for my hand. Such dear children. "And Uncle Roderick, you come too. There's a surprise!"

At the Seabright entrance we saw another carriage, a four-wheeled chaise drawn by two matched white ponies. Other visitors would crimp our conversation, perhaps make it impossible, but the afternoon call must go on.

O'Boyle and a groom took charge of both vehicles, and Cassie's butler, Hayes, took our calling card and ushered us down the hallways, past receiving rooms and drawing rooms. We glanced right and left for a sign of the "footman," Harvey Dunlap, but saw only maids before arriving at the terrace that overlooked garden plots and faced the sea with its blessedly cool inshore breeze.

Cassie swept forward. "Good afternoon, Val, Roderick. How delightful to see good friends." To my ear, her voice sounded shrill. "We're all here, are we not? And we have a surprise visit from Mr. and Mrs. Brush."

"All present and accounted for—including my bride!" Sam bellowed. Evalina was a vision in voluminous hot pink taffeta and box-pleats with lace appliqué. Her tiny hat straw hat overflowed with flowers.

"Now Beatrice, go find your brother. He must greet our guests, so please find him. Cara will help you. Let's do sit here on the terrace." Cassie's pallor was troubling, doubly so against the lemon yellow afternoon dress with a sapphire necklace that she adored, a birthday gift from her Dudley. Her face looked thinner than ever.

"On the terrace?" Evalina seemed troubled. "Oh, Cassandra, if only I thought to bring a sun bonnet. In the South we are always so careful. An hour in the sunlight, we could be mistaken for farmers."

We all flashed dutiful smiles. "I'll have a footman lower the awnings," Cassie said. "Hayes, if you will…. And our refreshments…."

The butler withdrew, two footmen appeared, and the awnings were lowered. Neither of the footmen was Harvey Dunlap, and there was no sign of Dennis Erbson, the groundskeeper. As we sat, Cara came forward with little Beatrice and her brother Charlie in tow—and a leashed, dark, pointy-eared dog trotting at his side.

"That's the surprise, Auntie Val! Her name is Velvet. She is a… what kind of dog is she, Mrs. Brush?"

"A French bulldog, dear." The children nodded. Bea curtsied, and Charlie bowed.

"And I came by Seabright this morning to make certain our canine guest would be welcome this afternoon," said Sam. "I nominate Cassandra as the most generous hostess of Newport."

"First-class passengers on the Cunard line bring their dogs all the time now," Evalina said. "Her breed is officially registered in the American Kennel Club this year,"

Velvet wriggled and licked at our shoes and boots, completely indifferent to pedigree or a potential ocean voyage. Three footmen and two maids wheeled a refreshment cart to the terrace, poured tea and set out an array of little cakes under a screened "dome" to block flies. Evalina reminded Cassie that tea was drunk with ice in the summer in her native South Carolina.

"Tea with ice?" The moment was needlessly awkward. Cassie ordered ice and glasses from a footman, and Sam's bride now waxed nostalgic about the flora of her home state. "Oh, the oleander flowers," she swooned, "the dearest oleander shades of pink…. And the jasmine, heavenly, divine jasmine….

Cassandra, if your new groundskeeper…what is his name?"

"Mr. Erbson," said Cassie.

We all scanned the gardens. No sign of Erbson.

"If he knows a trick to make jasmine and oleander grow here at Seabright, promise you'll share the secret," said Evalina. Cassie promised. "At Stone Point, my oleander plants wither and die. I believe they are homesick."

"We hear that you plan to start a kennel at Stone Point," Roddy said.

Velvet licked his fingers.

"Just as soon as my husband completes his plans for their water and mechanical feeding." Her hot pink taffeta arm and slender fingers gestured at the blue sky. "I do believe the summer will end before the Brush machine-age kennel comes to Stone Point."

Sam's smile looked forced. "They're not like cats, you know. Dogs don't look after themselves. Anyway, a good many demands on my time these days...gearing up for meetings in the city, patents to file. As president-elect of the Clambake Club, there's much to do...safety assured for next season." He sat very straight, poised over the imaginary wrestlers' mat before him. "We'll insist on the police detail, of course. A committee will have to decide whether Jim Reeves continues the 'bake.'"

"Excuse me, sir...."

I turned to see a footman at Roddy's elbow. Dunlap's wiry frame looked gangly in his uniform.

"Sir, a message for you on the telephone. If you will...?"

Roddy excused himself and followed Harvey Dunlap inside. Smoothing my skirt, I wanted to go with them.

"The telephone," said Sam, "a marquee invention of our time." He raised his teacup. "I hereby toast Mr. Alexander Graham Bell."

"I find it unnerving to talk to a box on the wall," Cassie said.

"You will feel differently when you hear your husband Dudley's voice from that box telling you he's landed in San Francisco on his way home to you, Cassandra," said Sam.

Cassie's eyes filled at the mention of her husband's name and his return. She thanked Sam for the sentiment. Silence fell, and flies buzzed at the screened- in cakes. Roddy's reappearance was welcomed by all.

"Everything smooth sailing?" Sam asked.

"A business detail," Roddy said. "Nothing interesting." His eyes, however, said much more than a "detail" had entered my husband's mind. Whatever it was—on the telephone or something from Dunlap—it was not to be revealed here and now on the terrace of Seabright cottage.

Our light chit-chat continued as the sun cleared the trees and began its descent into the sea. I tried to catch Cassie's eye to ask, silently, about her state of mind, but her glances darted like a frightened bird. The afternoon visiting hour expired, and we all rose. The children reluctantly returned Velvet to her "parents," and Cassie saw us to the door. The chaise with white ponies was waiting, as was our cabriolet, and we all bid adieu. Neither Cassie nor Mr. and Mrs. Samuel Brush planned to hear the operatic arias tonight at the Casino, but all wished us a delightful evening. Sam helped Evalina into her seat, and Roddy assisted me as etiquette demanded.

All the way back to Drumcliffe my husband looked preoccupied with private thoughts. Perhaps he was called to represent a city tavern that was suddenly shuttered by the police. Or had a club begged him to concoct a drink to honor a high profile guest? He did not share what had transpired when he had attended the "telephone." His facial features, however, said it was important—and worrisome. I would hear it in due course.

Chapter Twenty

THE LARGE ENVELOPE MARKED "Mrs. DeVere" rested on my dressing table at Drumcliffe when we returned. Shoes off, I tore it open to find Calista's neat handwriting on my monogrammed stationary and her lines copied from newspaper accounts of Mrs. Astor's ball of last January.

Hearst's *Journal* touted "...one of the most largely attended private functions of the year looked forward to by society, the climax of the season...." And under the headline "Some Handsome Gowns," a rapt account of "Mrs. Edwin Glendorick's magnificent gown of white satin embroidered in ruby and pearls...cascades of ruby rose chiffon falling from the waist to the skirt...corsage a combination of rose and white and with it was worn a sash of scarlet." Mrs. Glendorick, the *Journal* reported, "wore around her neck a superb riviere of diamonds. The corsage of her gown was covered with the same precious stones and a large diadem of brilliants crowned her head."

Bulls-eye. I hastened to Roddy's suite with the new evidence.

"Mr. DeVere is indisposed," his valet Norbert informed me at the door. "I believe he is bathing, Mrs. DeVere. Would you wish to confer with him?"

Confer? With my own husband?

"Or might you prefer to wait until he has dressed for the evening?"

An indirect critique of my bare toes and the afternoon dress I had not yet shed. "I wish to see him at once."

The valet stood aside, opened the door, and I stepped into the steamy bathroom to find Roddy stretched out in the deep marble tub filled to the brim, while clouds scented of lemon and lime from bath oils wafted to the very ceiling.

"Roddy—"

"Val, what a surprise…will you join me?" He opened his arms, then saw my face close-up. "What is it?"

The paper dampened in my fingers as I perched on the edge of the tub. "The Glendoricks," I said, "were at Mrs. Astor's ball. Calista found the description of Madeline's gown and jewels…all in the *Journal*. So, Glendorick could have seen Georgina collapse…. Now, won't you tell me what you learned when the 'footman,' Dunlap, summoned you to the telephone?"

"Not yet."

"Was it about cocktails? Or a court appearance in the city?" He reached for the soap. "Or something closer…to Cassie? We're in this together," I said.

"I must think a bit further."

"How much further? Is it something to do with Glendorick and Cuba?" He reached for a back brush.

"Or Rowena? Romberg? Just tell me this: was it a real telephone call?" A slight pause, then, "No, it wasn't."

"Something Dunlap said?"

Roddy nodded, soaping his back. "Don't ask me anything more just now. Let's get ready for the evening. To hear Patti sing the arias? I wouldn't miss her."

"Roddy, there's something else on my mind…."

"My dear?" He held the brush over one shoulder.

"It's the suffragette locked up in prison."

"The hurdy-gurdy girl?"

"Not a girl, Roddy. Annie Flowers misbehaved, but she shouldn't be imprisoned."

"I don't disagree."

"Might we help?"

He began to rise. "I can have our attorney see about her case."

"That's so…impersonal."

"My towel, dear?"

I reached for the snowy Turkish towel, vast as a blanket. "Roddy, "I think we can do better…. I can do better."

The bathwater draining, my husband stood like Neptune rising from the sea. Swathed in the enormous towel, he leaned close, kissed me, and said, "Please tell me that you are not pondering a visit to the Tombs."

We kissed again. "How about this?" I said. "A day trip into the city tomorrow?"

"How about this?" he rejoined. "Let's both of us prepare for a delightful evening at the Casino...and then a delightful time later...in your boudoir?"

The Casino theater was a godsend. All summer long its auditorium offered plays, music, vaudeville acts, and lectures that lent variety to the relentless balls and parties at the cottages. Society fully deserved Oscar Wilde's tart quip that, at Newport, "Idleness ranks among the virtues."

This evening the famed operatic soprano, Adelina Patti, would perform a selection of arias from Mozart and Verdi, who had said she was the best singer who had ever lived. Newport had easily met her fee of five thousand dollars, as had Virginia City, Nevada, where Piper's Opera House also featured the world's celebrated performers. I closed my eyes and saw it up the hill on North "B" Street. How I wished we were at Piper's this evening, Roddy and me, Cassie and the children, where we would be safe and snug.

Arriving early, Roddy and I faced the stage. Calista had suggested a cerulean gown with lace at the collar and cuffs, and a royal blue shawl, plus a blue evening fan. She did her best with my hair. Roddy's mother's rope of pearls "went" with this ensemble, Calista insisted, and whenever Cassie was not on hand to consult, I trusted my maid's judgment. The pearls pleased my husband.

The room was filling. I glanced left and right to see Mrs. Astor take her seat with Harry and Elizabeth Lehr in the third row, and Stuyvesant and Mamie Fish took seats behind them. George Vanderbilt had arrived with his new bride, Edith, and both sat at the end of our row. We all smiled and nodded to one another. The balcony was quickly filling with townspeople, who were entitled to enjoy the concert for twenty-five cents per person. I recognized Tisdall, the grocer whose wagon taxied me from tennis to Drumcliffe and amused Mamie Fish. I stood and waved to him. He caught my eye. As Mamie Fish stared, I blew Mr. Tisdall a kiss.

Roddy was studying his program. My mind darkened with thoughts about who was behind us, Madeline and Edwin Glendorick and their daughter? Would they come to hear Mme. Patti? Miss Emily Glendorick would soon become the Countess of Cleave. Suppose her father was a killer? Suppose...suppose....

Suddenly, hot electric chills ran up my arms and back at the sight of a twosome at the edge of my vision. "Roddy, look...no, over there." I pointed with my fan. "Look...."

"Ah, well..." he said, "If it isn't Archibald Romberg—

"With Rowena Fox on his arm. That man with them... with the slicked-back hair. Who is he?"

"No idea. Val, don't stare."

"He looks familiar...sort of shiny."

"I don't know...but there's your Theo."

I waved my fan, and Theo Bulkeley saluted with his program. Roddy managed a wan smile of greeting. "He's not 'my' Theo," I said.

"I can be a bit jealous, can't I?"

"If you must. Be assured, my dear, that Theodore Bulkeley is a confirmed bachelor. Understood?"

A second too long, Roddy murmured, "Understood."

In moments the house lights dimmed, Mme. Patti took the stage with her accompanist, applause thundered, and we were plunged into the arias promised on the program, *"Don mi dir"* from Mozart's *Don Giovanni*, followed by *"Oh, patria mia" and "Ritorna vincitor!"* from Verdi's *Aïda*, and *"Caro nome"* from *Rigoletto.*

Intermission, and everyone rose to socialize. Roddy preferred to stay in place, as did I, all the while scanning the hall in dread. That whey-faced young woman standing by the wall sconce was Emily Glendorick. She had apparently come with an older couple I did not recognize—her grandparents? Parents of the vile Edwin Glendorick, the possible murderer? And where were Romberg and Rowena?

"Val—?" Roddy touched my arm. "Are you cold?" He smoothed the shawl over my shoulder.

"Dark thoughts," I said.

"Not dark thoughts at this time of year, I hope." Here came Theo, cheerful, tall and slender, his slightly nasal voice the hallmark of his native Boston. He shook hands with Roddy and took my hand with a slight bow. "Roderick," he said, "Isn't Patti the best? Verdi calls her 'stupendous.'"

"Worth her weight in gold," said Roddy.

"From you, Roderick, a true tribute." Theo gestured around the theater. "Sadly, Newport gauges Madame Patti's voice with ears tuned to the Wall Street tickertape. For many, she's a bull market."

We chuckled. "I trust you've seen Rowena Fox and Mr. Romberg here tonight," I said.

"Indeed, I have. Quite the spicy item, just when the season was growing stale." Theo lowered his voice. "And fortunate that Cassandra is not here this evening to see her mother...nor Robert either...salt in an open wound."

"Did you see the man with them?" I asked. "Who is he?" Theo's smile was coy. "That's Arnold Creesey."

"He looks familiar."

"Surprised you haven't seen him in the Village. You might remember his appearance. Some wickedly dub him 'Greasy Creesey.'"

I remembered him now, the dandy at Sylvia's funeral with the patent leather boots and satin vest. And diamond rings. "That's the man I compared to a riverboat gambler, Roddy. Remember?" Roddy nodded. "Who is he?"

"A jewelry merchant," Theo said. "But don't dare call him a dealer. 'Connoisseur' is the word he uses. He specializes in antique pieces."

"Like rings?" I looked at Roddy. "Rings?"

"Centuries-old rings, lavaliers, stomachers...whatever you fair damsels desire. And he dabbles in alchemy."

"Alchemy?" I echoed.

"So to speak. He mixes metal powders and claims they have ancient provenance. It's part of his mystique."

"And men? Do men buy his rings?" I held Roddy's gaze.

"Some, I suppose," Theo said. "Most of us prefer a simple signet ring, but a few enjoy a stone of many carats and gleaming facets." He smiled. Theo paused. "Are you DeVeres enjoying the evening? Isn't Madame Patti beyond divine?"

"Divine, Theodore. And I'll feel even better if you can dissuade my wife from her wish to go into the city tomorrow to visit the Tombs."

Theo looked startled. "The prison? What on earth for?" I didn't answer immediately.

"Not another slum tour, Valentine." Theo's voice scolded. "Surely once was enough on the Lower East Side."

The two men began to talk as if I were an absent third party. "My dear wife is smitten with sympathy for a suffragette who was arrested playing a hurdy- gurdy in a department store."

Theo grinned. "I read all about it this morning."

"You did?"

"Pulitzer's *World* put it on the first page. Did you miss it? The headline said something like 'Votes-for-Women Doused in Fountain,' a big spread, pictures of women soaking wet. Bedraggled, every one."

"Don't say any more, Theodore. Mrs. DeVere will be all the more determined to visit the suffragette in the Tombs." Roddy's eye had a devilish gleam. "Any additional word you utter on the topic will be held against you, Theodore Bulkeley." The house lights were dimming as the bell rang to call everyone to their seats.

"Time for Mozart's *The Magic Flute*," said Theo. "She's doing the aria for the Queen of the Night." He pronounced it in the German language that he and Roddy had been taught from boyhood. *"Der Hölle Rache kocht in meinem Herzen."* The two men exchanged knowledgeable glances.

I knew the translation—"Hell's vengeance boils in my heart."

Chapter Twenty-one

HOW IT CAME TO pass that Theo Bulkeley sat beside me on the Fall River steamer to the city can be reduced to a few essential facts. The men's back-and- forth at the Casino had indeed set my resolve to visit Annie Flowers in the Tombs. I insisted on going alone without delay, hinting that a Waldorf-Astoria hotel room awaited me if I missed the last steamer back to Newport.

Roddy would not hear of it. No lady in the DeVere family must ever ruin (in his word, "besmirch") the reputation of the DeVere lineage by staying alone in a hotel...etc. etc.

Theo had stepped in. With Roddy's assent, gentleman-to-gentleman, he promised to call for me in the earliest a.m. for travel into the city. Theo advised me of a surprising prison custom, that a visitor was expected to bring foodstuffs and reading materials to the prisoner. "Decent" food, he said, magazines and books too. And perhaps clothing."

On the steamer this morning, Theo peered at the basket in my lap as we journeyed to the city. "What's under the cloth, Valentine?"

"An invention of the Earl of Sandwich," I said. At dawn, tiptoeing into the Drumcliffe kitchen and alarming our cook, I had guessed that whatever New York City's prison fare, the heavenly fresh bread just out of the Drumcliffe oven would be as welcome as an Escoffier dish at the finest table. I now held a bundled fresh loaf split and buttered and stuffed with ham, cheese, and roast beef. And apples and three peaches, all in a basket covered with a checkered cloth. Theo said it reminded him of Little Red Riding Hood's picnic. I did not bring items of clothing. Annie Flowers already had my cloak.

We barely spoke on the journey. I paused at a newsstand, where I snatched copies of *The Overland Monthly.* "There's a new writer, Jack London," I said. "His stories about the Klondike gold rush are thrilling, and a welcome diversion." Theo paid for the magazines.

A hansom cab took us to Centre, Franklin, and Elm Streets, then to the entrance to the women's prison on Leonard Street, a forbidding granite hulk. An American flag with its forty-five stars drooped from a towering pole, its red-white-and-blue faded and tattered. It was after eleven-thirty on a dreary, overcast morning. A horsecar with few passengers passed by, and two policemen twirling their nightsticks chatted on the walkway. They nodded, and Theo touched the brim of his bowler hat in response. He held the thick steel-sheathed door, murmured, "Ladies first," and we entered the women's prison of the Hall of Justice and House of Detention.

The odors assaulted us—of a swamp that had been over-spread with lye. Theo clapped a handkerchief to his nose. My eyes burned, and the gloom was nearly impenetrable, with thin rays of light seeping in from the small, barred windows above.

"Yes?"

The challenge of a woman's voice, punctuated by the sound of clanking metal. Were the cell doors banging open? No, it was her keys.

"Yes?" she repeated.

The matron could have stepped directly, in character, from a stage play.

Her ash gray Mother Hubbard dress was sealed tightly at her neck and wrists but otherwise covered an outsized figure that moved with ponderous steps on feet encased in thick black oxfords that were laced, oddly, with bright pink ribbons.

Her coal-black hair was tucked in a tight bun, her eyes little dark beads in a broad face with a tight, narrow mouth. Her gaze quickly shifted from Theo to my skirt and jacket, suitable for a ramble in the woods, and new shoes that had already pinched and probably had raised a blister.

Her first words were, "Visiting hours are afternoons, two to four p.m."

A glance at Theo told me he was not going to help. He clutched the magazines tightly and held the handkerchief to his face.

"Two to four," she repeated.

"We have come from…." Never mind Newport. I cleared my throat, also burning from the acrid air. "I trust you are the matron in charge."

"I am."

"We are…. That is, I am here to visit a prisoner, Annie Flowers." Theo had made it clear that he would not accompany me into Annie Flowers's cell. Just as well. "Perhaps you can verify that she is here, Miss—?"

"Mary Quirt." Arms folded across her chest, she cocked her head, either to listen or deny my appeal. I said my name.

"Miss Flowers once helped a very sick family member," I said. "I have brought her some food. Could I possibly…?"

"Possibly?" She seemed to spit the word. "Over and again, could we 'possibly?' Fifty women's cells, and let's break rules every time for a thief, a pick- pocket, swindler too. Or a killer."

"Miss Flowers is not a criminal."

Mary Quirt's scoff echoed from the granite walls, as if I had cracked a joke. "The newspapers say she broke a law against…peaceful assembly," I said. "She is a suffragette."

Another scoff. "Suffer? It's the crime victims that suffer."

Should I try to explain that 'suffrage' meant votes? My gaze fell upon Mary Quirt's pink shoelaces, and I tried one last gambit. "Miss Quirt," I said, "I would gladly return this afternoon, but every step in these shoes is torment. They are brand new. I should have thought about the long walk."

We both looked at my feet. I slipped off the left sharp-toed shoe to display a sizable blister. "The other one is starting to hurt too," I said.

The matron softened around the mouth and chin. "Nothing worse than sore feet." I had hit my mark. She gestured at my basket. "We can see she gets it."

A silent moment was broken by a metallic echo and the sound of dripping water. "It's mostly family that comes," she said.

I kept my eyes down and head lowered. And waited. Time seemed stopped and endless. Then, from Mary Quirt, "Keeper—" Keys clinked. A short, heavyset man with a ring of brass keys appeared from the gloom. "Keeper, show Mrs. DeVere to cell number thirty-eight."

She added, "Twenty minutes," gestured to Theo and pointed at a bench. "You, mister,' she said, "over there."

Magazines and basket in hand, I followed the Keeper down the slimy cement corridor to a barred cell door. "Visitor," he called, turning the lock. I entered, heard the door slam behind me, and I was locked inside the dank cell with a young woman I had last seen at Sylvia's funeral.

"Hello, Miss Flowers."

She sat ramrod straight on the plank of a bed, her shoddy tweed suit shaped around her shoulders and hips, as if it had been washed and dried while on her body. Her hair hung lank to the shoulders, and her eyes barely concealed disappointment as she rose. I recognized her ruined shoes, the very shoes that once belonged to Sylvia Brush. "You're Mrs. Forster—"

"DeVere," I said. "Mrs. DeVere."

"The other one," she said.

"I brought you food...a lunch." She nodded. "And something to read. I have twenty minutes."

"Then sit down?" She gestured to the plank. Neatly folded at one end was a thin, coarse blanket. A covered bucket stood in the corner.

I pulled back the cloth that covered the contents in the basket. "Ripe peaches and apples," I chirped, as if a picnic lunch could brighten the dismal scene. "And a sandwich too."

"Charity," said Annie Flowers, biting into a peach. She sounded dismissive.

Did I expect gratitude? Somewhere in the cellblock a woman moaned. "The newspapers reported your arrest," I said. "I'm terribly sorry. You'll have to appear in court, yes?

Her bitter laughter echoed in the cell. "I will plead 'innocent,' and the judge will declare me 'guilty.' The reporters will give the newspapers a column or two."

"And your sentence...."

"A fine. Dollars that I do not have, so I will 'pay' the fine by serving my sentence here. The city of New York will get its justice by confining me to a jail cell and feeding enough fatty soup so none of us die of starvation."

She gestured at the cell block, bit the peach again, and sat up straighter. "There will be setbacks, Mrs. DeVere, but suffragists will win out." Her posture so erect, but peach juice ran down her fingers to her wrist. The handkerchief I offered was taken with resignation and resentment.

"Do keep it," I said.

"Little girls launder your handkerchiefs," she said, "and your petticoats too. All your lingerie. Do you know that?" She mopped her fingers. I shook my head. "All for ten cents per hour. They toil in steam laundries. Votes for women will change that. Girls belong in school."

I nodded.

"Our cause is righteous. Scripture says, 'God is in the midst of her, she will not be moved.' Psalm Forty-six." I remembered the cross on Annie Flowers's wall in the Lower East Side.

"I'm sorry about your hurdy-gurdy," I said, and watched her open the sandwich and pluck at a morsel of bread and a sliver of ham. She ate with delicate eagerness.

"The hurdy-gurdy was Miss Sylvia's idea," she said.

"Oh?"

"We planned to take turns." She took a thin slice of roast beef and another bit of bread. "Of course, Miss Sylvia paid for it. And the drum too."

"You had a drum?"

"A suffrage sister beat the drum, a big bass drum, but it was ruined. The police smashed it too. They pushed us into the fountain."

"At the Siegel-Cooper department store—?"

"The police had a good laugh, and ladies laughed too. But time will change that." She picked at a slice of cheese.

"Quality food," she said. "Like the dinners Sylvia gave us."
She looked directly at me. "Miss Sylvia was our sister and
our patron."

"Patron…" I repeated.

"Suffrage sisters need a patron—a woman of means who
understands our movement. Sylvia sent us to the seashore
to lift our spirits for the long campaign."

"Atlantic City?"

"New Jersey," she nodded. "We bathed in the Atlantic
Ocean and strolled on the boardwalk and stayed in a hotel
as guests." She paused. "But a gentleman did help us too.
Like Sylvia's friend."

What friend? "A minister at Tuxedo Park?" I asked.

"No. It was somebody that invents machines."

"Machines? Are you certain?"

"She did not give us a name. We thought perhaps a
gentleman was courting her, someone from the city."

"Not where she lived in Tuxedo Park?"

"We thought the city. Sometimes they met in the city."
She fingered the peach pit. "I tried to learn his name when
she got so sick."

"And—?"

"And it was too late. She was too sick. It happened
so fast."

A bellowing voice interrupted us. "Time's up! Time's
up!" Keys clanked in the lock, and the cell door squealed
open on its hinges. The Keeper readied to escort me out.

"The basket," said Annie Flowers. "You have to take the basket." She held a palm full of bread and cheese and an apple. "You have to take the rest. Because of the rats. At night, the Tombs belong to the rats."

Chapter Twenty-two

"MACHINES, RODDY. 'SOMEBODY THAT invents machines' were Annie Flowers's exact words. Who else could it be?" We sat on a sofa in the music room across from the harp and piano. "Don't remind me that inventors are everywhere because this is the modern Machine Age."

"But they are. Just guess the number of patents the Steinway Company—?"

"This is not about pianos." We were both irritable. Our housekeeper scheduled a piano tuner who worked all morning on our Steinway grand, which neither of us played. The notes echoed through the cottage for hours, a musical torment. We'd have escaped outdoors, but it was pouring rain.

"It's Sam Brush," I said. "'Sylvia's friend' who invents machines has to be Sam. Can't not agree on that probability?"

Roddy looked toward the windows, rain streaking every pane. "Suppose it's true," he said. "What, then?"

274 A GILDED DEATH

"...then Sam has lied about feeling guilty for neglecting Sylvia... so pious at her funeral, and here at Drumcliffe too. 'I barely knew her,' that's what he told us. Was it an act for our benefit?"

"That's harsh, Val."

"Harsh? The Tombs prison is harsh...a dungeon. Annie Flowers doesn't deserve another day behind bars."

With his hand up, Roddy quieted me. "Our lawyer is on her case."

"When?"

"Now. This morning."

"I don't understand."

My husband's patience was annoying. "Before you came to breakfast," he said, "I sent a footman to the Western Union office with a telegram instructing attorney Matthew Harding, Esquire, to take all appropriate action on behalf of Miss Flowers. As we agreed to do last night when Theo brought you—"

"Theo didn't 'bring' me."

"Escorted you home."

A moment passed. "It's going to rain all day," I said.

"It's a squall. It will pass."

"Why would Sam lie?"

Sheets of rain slammed against the windows, and the wind wailed. "Maybe he genuinely feels that he failed to understand Sylvia." Roddy rubbed his ear. "Are your ears ringing?"

"From the tuning? A little."

"Remind me," Roddy said, "of Miss Flowers's exact words about Sylvia's mysterious 'someone.'"

I felt grilled. How much did I remember? "The jail cell was horrid, Roddy, so dank and fetid I could hardly think. Annie Flowers remembers knowing about 'somebody' who invents machines. Sylvia met him in the city, and he 'helped' the suffrage women."

"Doubtful that it's Romberg. He had no part in the machinery of the Romberg Mills."

"And it's unlikely to be the 'man' that met Glendorick at the Casino... the one with ice-cold eyes and a Spanish-sounding accent...."

"Probably not. What about the antique jewelry dealer?" Roddy asked. "Theo knew a good deal about him...Creesey?"

"Greasy Creesey? If he's the man I saw at the funeral, he might have gone to Tuxedo Park. The housekeeper remembers a winter visitor with diamond rings and unseasonable footwear."

"Unseasonable?" Roddy scoffed. "That's definitely not Romberg. Archie dresses in season, not a day early or later than the solstice or equinox. But we know that Romberg went to Tuxedo Park."

"But Maude Gowdy said no visitors were received. At most, they got a snack and hot drink and were sent on their way. But Annie Flowers said the 'somebody' who met with Sylvia invents machines. We are back to 'machines,' where we started."

Roddy stood, went to the window and said the sky was lightening.

I joined him. The distant cloudbank was a chalky gray. I felt my wedding ring, a wonderful emerald-cut diamond from Cartier, a feast for the eyes. To imagine gems that could release to eject poison...and the human minds that contrived such a thing.

Beside me, Roddy took my hand and said, "So, we are back to Sam."

"We are."

"Let's walk outside."

"Roddy, it's still raining."

"Good warm rain," he said, "and it's almost over. Let's go."

We "sneaked" outside, meaning no footman opened the door for Mr. and Mrs. DeVere, whose casual clothing was not meant for a social scene. Roddy's corduroy trousers lacked a belt or suspenders, and his shirt, open at the neck, was minus its collar. I tucked a shirtwaist into culottes, which I preferred for straddling the saddle, a western saddle with a deep seat and a saddle horn for a lariat to rope a calf, which all Newport thought was like the circus.

The rain had slowed to a drizzle, but the trees dripped, the tall copper beeches that were so favored in Newport.

"We could use a rain umbrella," I said. "Too late."

"But my hair...."

Roddy gave me his chiding look. "Valentine Louise Mackle from Virginia City, Nevada, fussing about her hair?"

"When transported to New York and Newport? Yes, sir, indeed she is." We kissed, then stepped onto the garden paths arm-in-arm, ignoring the puddles.

Roddy reminded me that we were expected at Stone Point for dinner.

"Sam and Evalina," I said. "Mr. and Mrs. Samuel D. Brush...their first dinner party of the Newport season." Evalina had doubtless been consumed with preparations. To give a perfect dinner was the supreme accomplishment of a hostess, insisted the etiquette manuals.

"Roddy," I said, skipping over a puddle, "I just had a new thought about Sam...." My husband took my arm. "Samuel David Brush," I said, "is a very modern man married to a woman steeped in tradition...."

"Steeped," Roddy repeated.

"...but a man who might, in secret," I said, "support Sylvia's campaign for suffrage...he could advise her, steer her away from charlatans. He would take pride as her counselor, meet her in the city. What do you think? We could ask Sam in a roundabout way...."

Roddy did not give an answer.

"Or I, myself, could ask him in little hints." A rose thorn snagged my sleeve as the path curved. Roddy tightened his grip on my arm. He looked grim.

"Shall we continue our walk, Val, because I need to tell you about that telephone call at Seabright when the new 'footman' called me to the phone."

"Only, there was no telephone call."

"No."

"You told me that much."

"I did."

"Roddy, don't tease. Tell me what Dunlap had to say."

My husband grew quiet as we strolled. The sky was clearing, with blue patches and tattered clouds. In the distance, the ocean heaved in metallic grays.

"It's true, there was no call, but Dunlap wanted me to know something that might or might not be meaningful, which is why I have delayed...."

"Until now."

He nodded. "And it might mean nothing at all, merely incidental."

"Understood." We walked on.

"The afternoon at Seabright," he began, "when Sam told us he had stopped to see Cassie that morning—"

"To make certain that the little dog would be welcome for an afternoon visit. Yes, I remember."

Roddy peered into the distance at a ship slipping below the horizon. "Sam did something else that morning at Seabright. Dunlap told me he inspected the kitchen."

"Cassie's kitchen? Whatever for?"

Roddy pushed away an overhanging branch. "Sam said he plans new devices to regulate the temperature of stoves and ovens."

"More inventions—?"

"That's a question, Val.... Why more inventions right now when Sam has so many devices underway? And so many claims on his time? Dunlap said that he led 'Mr. Brush' to the kitchen, as was proper for a footman. And he stayed downstairs, to lead the way up after inspection of the Seabright kitchen equipment."

"Cassie didn't go along?"

"No."

"I'd be surprised if she did." Many ladies, Cassie included, never set foot in their kitchens. So far, however, nothing sounded noteworthy. "And this, my dear Roddy, is the big exposé from our Pinkerton detective—that Sam Brush looked at the fifteen-foot cooking stove surface in the Seabright kitchen and opened oven doors?" My left foot landed flat in a puddle. So much for the deerskin shoe.

My husband looked grave. "It's a bit complicated."

"What do you mean?"

"It seems Sam paid very little attention to the Seabright kitchen equipment. Dunlap said he asked the cook a question or two about the stove and ovens, but his main interest was the spices and herbs."

"Spices? Which herbs?"

"I can't make sense of it. Dunlap said he was quite pleasant with the cook. He moved from one container to the next and asked about each one. Dunlap tried to listen, but a footman must stand back. The cook was evidently flattered by Mr. Brush and spent an hour with him. Dunlap timed him."

"Maybe he was scouting for Evalina...." I broke off. How absurd. The southern "Belle" gave us all gift cookbooks but would never cook a dish herself. I doubt she has once toured her Stone Point kitchen.

"Roddy, do you suppose Sam is planning a dish for our dinner?—something to rival Elisha Dyer's lobster à l'Americaine?" I searched for the shadow of a smile on Roddy's face. "Suppose Sam wants the applause we give Elisha when he presents his annual lobster. Maybe something like seabass à la Samuel Brush?" I paused. "You're not smiling."

"I have a bad feeling about this."

"Suspicious?"

"I'm not sure. Dunlap was concerned."

"I doubt Harvey Dunlap knows a spice from an herb."

Roddy scanned the flower beds. No gardener was near a shrub or tree. "Dunlap reported that Sam charmed the sculleries and the cook, and the pastry chef. He asked very specific questions about the spices and the herbs. Tins and jars were opened for him, and he wet a finger and tasted several."

"Such as—?"

"He seemed especially interested in the cocoa powder."

"Why?"

"I can't guess."

I pictured the little tins in our kitchen shelf here at Drumcliffe—Bee Brand pepper, Coleman mustard, Hershey's cocoa powder. The herbs were lined up in glass jars, the spices in tins. Sprigs, dried leaves, and colorful tins.

"And Dunlap thought he heard Sam ask which ones were Cassandra's favorites."

"Perhaps to honor her with a special dish? Something with chocolate?"

"Let's hope so."

Roddy released the overhanging branch, which dashed us with rainwater. "I don't know what to think, Val. Maybe Brush Industries is venturing into clove trees." He glanced my way. "You didn't know cloves grow on trees?"

My right foot struck a puddle. Both shoes soaked. "No, I didn't know. Let's turn back. Calista will need extra time with my hair. I wouldn't want to look like a Wild West 'gal' with wild hair when Evalina greets Roderick and Valentine.

Our turn on the Drumcliffe garden paths was complete. Roddy stopped and took a breath. "The rain has cleansed the air," he said, "but on other matters the air is rank. And reeking."

Chapter Twenty-three

OUR CARRIAGE ARRIVED AT Stone Point by seven-thirty o'clock that evening. Evalina was poised in a gown of pearl-gray chiffon, embroidered in silver with strands of pearls as shoulder "straps." The bust, draped in white chiffon, hinted at an empire line—the line that often suggests a baby on the way. (Cassie prefers the discreet *enceinte*.) The possibility that Sam and Evalina were expecting would be noticed by every female guest. So would the likelihood that Evalina had deliberately sent this tantalizing signal of maternity.

"Heavenly ensemble, my dear," murmured Florence Dovedale as she eyed our hostess's gown at the entrance. "Splendid to see your health restored," replied Evalina to Florence, whose husband, Albert, simply smiled. No further word on the clambake incident need be spoken.

The Dovedales moved on, and the smooth southern voice of our hostess welcomed us. "Valentine and Roderick, so delightful to have you at Stone Point. The evening is assured by your presence."

Roddy handed his ebony walking stick and top hat to a footman, and Evalina's maid touched up my hair in the standard ritual at dinner parties. We offered appropriate greetings and moved into the reception area and, as usual, admired one another's silks and velvets, satins and tulles. And of course, the diamonds and sapphires, rubies and pearls. Among others, the Mitchells were here, and the Alderbachs, Colonel and Mrs. Twist, The Chanlers, Edith and Teddy Wharton...Edith exquisitely stylish as usual. Cassie arrived with the Livingstons, and we smiled at one another. Theo appeared, escorting Roberta Webster, the Bellevue Avenue dowager. The ceiling fans spun lazily, and a slight floral scent hovered.

Jasmine?

The Stone Point reception room was newly paneled in cut velvet with floral medallions—Evalina's idea—but the tapestry of the forester with his shiny silver axe against a field of stumps still covered an entire wall. Sam's shrine to his beloved brother had not yet been removed by his bride, though Evalina doubtless counted the days before she could banish the gaudy forester forever. Just under the tapestry hung a framed artwork I had never noticed. New? Something of Evalina's? I stepped close. The wildly ornate frame was more compelling than the art, if it was art. Gold glittered over multiple inset layers of delicately carved pine boughs and leaves of oak and maple. Others appeared to be different hardwoods. The jasmine aroma seemed more intense. Someone's perfume?

"Splendid, is it not?" Sam was at my elbow, smiling. "It's just up today. We had a certain friction about it. My bride is a dynamo, but I held on like a steel cable on the Brooklyn Bridge. Evalina huddled with the artist to design a beautiful frame, and a goldsmith did the rest."

"What is it, Samuel?" Albert Dovedale approached. "My eyesight isn't what it used to be." He peered at the glass. "Help me out."

"You are looking at one of the first shares of our stock ever offered to the public," said Sam. "It belongs here with the tapestry that honors my brother, the Brush Industries founding father."

"A share of stock…why, of course it is." Dovedale pulled a monocle from his vest pocket. "If you don't mind, Samuel… my failing eyes."

"Help yourself." Sam's chest swelled.

"Engraving perfect…" said Dovedale. Thought it might be a diploma. Yale's forestry school, you know."

Sam's mouth tightened. "Harry Brush had a sixth-grade education, Albert. He succeeded in spite of it."

"Of course." The monocle moved in for closer inspection. "Shame, it looks like a corner is missing."

"A small tear," Sam said. "Can't be helped…the years, relocations. Thrilled to have it. You see the company name, year of incorporation, the seal." He pointed to the lettering.

"...'according to the laws of the state of Oregon.' And my brother's signature."

Albert Dovedale nodded, pocketed his monocle and moved away, murmuring, "my health," as someone sneezed nearby.

"Impressive," I said, my eyes fixed on the torn corner that was not a diploma.

More sneezing, and the gentlemen began offering handkerchiefs to ladies.

Roddy, I noticed, had moved toward a far window that was slightly open. The floral scent was stronger. My throat was tickling, but the torn corner drew me like a magnet.

Sam was watching me. "It's worth a hundred times more today," he said. "Two hundred...three." He stepped between me and the frame, blocking my view of the stock certificate. "A torn corner," he said, "don't give it a thought."

I looked for Cassie. She must see this, but she was across the room, and we would all vacate this reception room in minutes, the opportunity lost. Sam's eyes narrowed, and he did not smile. "I mean it," he repeated, "don't give it a thought." He seemed rooted in place, a wrestler in formal wear. He began to speak, but the guests' sneezing became coughing, then sounds of choking. Sam stood at my shoulder.

A strong alto voice was heard to say, "Evalina, my dear, we seem to be under the spell of jasmine this evening." It was Roberta Webster, dowager of Bellevue Avenue.

"Dearest dears," Mamie Fish's inimitable voice, "is that a scent? Or a fumigation?" In the instant, a swish of Evalina's gown as she claimed her husband and murmured inaudible but urgent words. Her neck and shoulders had tensed, and her fingers clutched his sleeve.

At Sam's signal, the ceiling fans stopped their rotation, and footmen sped to open windows. "...Sam Brush at it again," I overheard. "Whatever this time...?"

"Has our host chosen this evening to try a new invention?" It was Theo's Bostonian voice at my ear.

"What invention?" I asked.

"A system of ventilation. Scented air. We're inhaling Evalina's favorite jasmine because Sam attached vials of the stuff to the ceiling fans."

"So the whole reception room smells like....?"

"Every cubic foot." We felt the evening breeze begin to circulate. "Evalina looks near tears...tears of rage."

"Who can blame her, Theo? A hostess bears the brunt of any misstep. I should know."

The Brush butler, Sollers, saved the moment. "Dinner," he proclaimed, "is served."

My dinner partner, the banker Evan Doolittle, took my arm. "Mrs. DeVere, shall we go in?" And we marched slowly in twos through a short corridor toward the dining room, past artwork on the corridor walls featuring small paintings of fanciful animals, a nest of kittens, a basket of bunnies. Then I saw a small painting of a dog. It could be Evalina's own Velvet, a French bulldog with pointy ears.

The banker nudged my arm. We were slowing others down.

"Mrs. DeVere—?" He tugged me forward, but I drew us closer to the painting.

"Mrs. DeVere, if you please...."

At the moment of banker Doolittle's exasperation, I stood close enough to see brush strokes that brightened the dog's eyes and shined its fur. Close enough, what's more, to see the artist's signature, the same signature Cassie and I had seen on Sylvia's bedroom walls: R. Rupp.

Dinner was upon us. Courses came and went, nothing remotely like seabass à la Samuel Brush nor a chocolate dessert he could claim as his own. I thought of nothing but the painting while my voice made polite conversation ("The Newport Horse Show...so looking forward to it....").

Cassie was not in sight, but I managed correct utensils. Bouillon spoon and oyster fork, yes indeed. But the painting of the dog by R. Rupp was blazoned in my brain. And the torn corner.

The bronze dining room chairs became the next crisis of the evening. Two footmen were needed to move each one, so seating was slowed, as was our departure from the table. As the men headed off for their after-dinner cigars, I waylaid Theo.

"You belong to the Century Club, yes?"

"Yes." He fingered his Cohiba.

"Are there many artists in membership?"

He nodded. "Artists, writers...."

"Theo, do you know a painter named Rupp?"

"Ralph Rupp...the portrait painter. Planning to sit for a portrait, Val?"

Eager to escape and light up, the men were on their way. "The gentlemen's hour...join us, Bulkeley?"

I tugged Theo's coat sleeve. "Ask whether Mr. Rupp painted pictures of dogs, Theo. Don't ask why. Please do it as soon as possible."

Chapter Twenty-four

BY TEN A.M. HOUR the next morning, no word had come from Theo about the portrait painter, but Sands had been alerted to expect a message from Mr. Theodore Bulkeley, either a telegram or note from a messenger. I was to be informed immediately.

Forced patience felt useless, but I was reminded of Papa's advice from years-long prospecting in Colorado and Nevada: "patience always, and vigilance too." He also said, "A hunch can pay off, so trust your gut."

Calista appeared upstairs as I toyed with bric-a-brac for a charity donation. "Ma'am? Sorry to disturb you, but a footman has come to the front door. He seems distressed and insists on seeing you."

I sped downstairs, where a footman stood with scuffed boots, a misbuttoned coat, and a streak of shaving soap on one cheek. "From Mrs. Forster, ma'am."

Cassie? Not from Theo? His quivering fingers held no envelope. Flanking me at our entrance, Sands and Calista stood like guardians.

"Mrs. Forster wishes you to come at once. And Mr. DeVere too."

Mr. DeVere, as Sands whispered to me, had gone on horseback into the Village to The Reading Room. My thoughts raced, confused.

"There has been an accident," said the footman.

"Accident?" I repeated. "What accident?"

"If you might come along, ma'am. Mrs. Forster's groom is waiting to drive you. She requests you might come at once."

"Yes, of course."

"Would you wish a hat, ma'am? A cloak?"

"Cloak, Calista." In moments I was seated in a dog-cart and headed toward Seabright, so I thought. But no, the groom drove up a hill to the Newport Hospital, where a familiar coachman tended a carriage at the front entrance. Cassie's O'Boyle appeared agitated but tipped his hat as I went inside.

A nurse in starched whites met me at the door, said that Mrs. Forster expected me, and led the way down a corridor into a sterile room of white tiles and gleaming steel, trays, cabinets, and fearsome instruments. An antiseptic odor wafted, and a distraught Cassie sat with little Bea on a bench while Charlie lay prone on a table as a man in a suit bent over him. The doctor.

"Oh, Val...."

I rushed to hug her and patted Bea's head. "My dear... what...?"

A nurse shushed me, helped the doctor out of his coat, and presented a sequence of bandages, splints, and a mix that smelled like plaster. Cassie sniffled, Charlie was silent, and Bea sucked her thumb until the boy was helped to sit up with his left arm in a cast and a sling, the side of his face bruised and bandaged with gauze pads. His empty shirt sleeve was as poignant a sight as his wan young face.

The doctor rolled down his shirtsleeves while the nurse held his suit coat.

Buttoned up, he turned to us and said, "Charles's x-ray shows a clean break of the humerus bone in the distal region...near the elbow. The outlook is favorable, but we will watch for adequate blood supply and nerve function." He added, "Very little chance of scarring at his age. We'll see him again in two weeks."

He lifted Charlie to the floor. "You're a very fortunate little fellow. Be brave, young man, and be careful."

Outdoors, arms around her children, Cassie looked frail. "Come to Seabright with us, won't you, Val?"

"Yes, Auntie Val. And ride with us." Little Bea pointed to the carriage where O'Boyle held the reins and opened the door for all of us.

We reached Seabright by lunchtime. Cassie's footman had been sent to the Village to the Reading Room to request that Mr. DeVere to join us promptly at Seabright.

The uniformed Newport police stood guard at the gate and the entrance, as usual. We had not spoken.

What did the doctor mean by "fortunate fellow?" What had happened?

Cassie ordered clear soup and crackers for Charlie and ordered bedrest all afternoon. Nanny Cara would take care of Bea.

Auntie Val fibbed that she had already eaten lunch. By 1:00 p.m. Cassie led me outdoors beyond the terrace.

"Where are we going?"

"To the carriage house."

"I don't understand."

"You will."

Newport's Carriage houses and stables sit far enough enough from the cottages to insure freedom from odors. Cassie sped nervously, but why the carriage house? A lady seldom, if ever, visited that gentleman's domain. We walked quickly and silently, Cassie leading us off the path to cut across grass. One policeman, I saw, took notice. Good. The new "groundskeeper," Erbson, stood in a flower bed, a round-shouldered figure in a denim jacket. He looked up without expression. Hardly encouraging.

Pleasant aromas of leather, saddle soap, and brass polish offset the dim light of the barn-like building. Why were we here? Before I could ask her, Cassie called, "O'Boyle? O'Boyle?"

"Right here, ma'am." His fingers opened and closed into fists. He seemed to expect us.

"Let's show Mrs. DeVere the Ralli-car, O'Boyle."

"Yes, ma'am. I'll lead the way, if you please."

The coachman guided us through a labyrinth of dog-carts, broughams, buggies, Victorias, four-in-hands— the whole dizzying lot. We finally stopped at a vehicle that was obviously new, resembling a dog-cart but far more elegant, lower to the ground with side panels that curved gracefully over the two wheels.

"If you'll step to the other side, ma'am?"

Circling, I caught my breath at the sight. The far side was a horror— smashed and splintered wood, the second wheel bent, its spokes mangled. The damaged body of the car was propped up on wood blocks. "Little Charlie..." I said.

"Exactly." Arms on her hips, Cassie repeated, "Exactly. My son is alive by the grace of God. He could have been...."

"But he wasn't," I said. "His arm will heal. His face...." I took Cassie's hand in mine. "He will be fine. You needn't talk about it now, Cassie."

"But I must...we must." She stood straight, braced. "O'Boyle, if you will... please tell Mrs. DeVere what you found."

"Sure, ma'am." He cleared his throat. "I checked this Ralli-car this morning. You see, it hitches like the dog-cart, but the shafts run under the body. The model is new this year, and the grooms all took a good look. The policeman here at the carriage house was also interested." He looked directly at Cassie. "I saw to the hitching myself, Mrs. Forster. I chose the little mare, Pumpkin."

"And then—?"

"Then I took myself off for a morning bite, and the new order was given to take Master Charles to visit his grandfather. No more than a quarter mile on the road, and we smashed." He wet his lips. "It was the bellyband, ma'am. Keeps the shafts in place. Cannot drive without a good bellyband." He paused. "It was almost cut through."

"You're sure?" I asked.

"See for yourself, ma'am." He reached for a leather strap under the wreckage. "Sliced nearly through," he said. We three stared at the sabotaged leather band. At length Cassie asked, "Once again, O'Boyle...you're certain no groom or stable hand here at Seabright would have...?"

"Cross my heart, Mrs. Forster. Swear to God."

Cassie touched the band as if it were an open wound. She seemed unsteady. I took her arm. "O'Boyle," I said, "I will accompany Mrs. Forster to the cottage. We expect Mr. DeVere here soon, and if you would please show him the Ralli-car and the damaged band...?"

"That I will, ma'am." He looked at me. "God bless young Master Charles, but the thing of it is...the thing is, and Mrs. Forster knows this..." He whispered. "No adult passenger could have lived through that smash-up."

The next hour became a blur. Cassie looked in on Charlie, who was sleeping, then made certain that Bea's dress was buttoned up before seeing her off with nanny Cara. I insisted on a bowl of soup and toast for my friend and prescribed an afternoon of bed rest. I stayed at her side, coaxed every spoonful of soup and bite of toast, plumped her pillows, lowered the shades, and hinted that eyes closed promoted sleep. She accepted a quarter-grain of a sleeping powder and managed at last to nod off, but not before confessing a terrifying truth. The Ralli-car this morning, she said, had not at first been ordered for her son, Charlie.

"Charlie rode the Ralli-car at the last minute, Val. The sabotaged car was meant for me. Someone wants me dead."

Chapter Twentyfive

"WHAT ELSE DID O'BOYLE tell you?" Roddy put down his fork. We sat over beef stew in the nook where we often had a bite together. It was late afternoon at Drumcliffe. The footman had just closed the draperies.

"He suspects the bellyband was deliberately cut to time the failure to a quarter mile."

"What do you mean?"

Roddy leaned forward, his voice low. "If the strap were to fail at a certain point on the roadway, an adult passenger would be thrown head-first onto granite rock."

"Cassie...but not a child? Not Charlie or Bea?"

"No, not a child. A child, being shorter and lighter, would fall and strike gravel. Cuts and bruises, perhaps an injury."

"So, Charlie's broken arm," I said slowly, "but not Cassie's fractured skull." I paused. "But O'Boyle jumped clear."

"He did, luckily. He carried Charlie back to the stables in his arms. The stable hands hauled the damaged car to Seabright while O'Boyle took Cassandra and the children to the hospital in a carriage."

Roddy buttered a roll. "Eat up, Val. This *boeuf bourguignon* is—"

"Stew," I hissed. "It's leftover beef stew. And it needs salt." I reached for the tiny salt cellar and promptly oversalted my stew. "Sorry, Roddy. It's so upsetting. Cassie is terrified.

"With good reason."

"And you're certain O'Boyle knew that Cassie was meant to be his passenger?"

"He said exactly that. Charlie was excited for his grandfather to see the new Ralli-car, and Cassandra ordered the change so her father could see it. She hoped Charlie and the Ralli-car would cheer him up. The style is new this year, and every carriage house is certain to have one soon. O'Boyle ordered it himself, and he feels terrible. He apologized in terms of old Irish ways. 'It's the evil leprechauns' doings,' he said."

"Irish folklore," I said. "My papa wouldn't hear of it."

"But the myths are powerful. O'Boyle told me certain leprechauns are said to pull a wagon, and wherever the wagon stops, someone is scheduled to die. He fears the leprechauns are at work."

I speared a bite of potato. "Leprechauns in the carriage house, and superstition in the cottage. Cassie wants to consult Madame Riva about Charlie's X-ray. She's afraid of a machine that sees through the body." I sipped my water. "The timing seems odd, Roddy. The Forsters' carriage house was unoccupied this morning for…an hour? How long for sabotage?

"Boyle estimates no more than forty-five minutes. He went for a quick breakfast with the servants at 8:15 and was back by 9:00 to fetch Charlie at the cottage."

"But the police? Was a policeman stationed at the carriage house all that time?'

"O'Boyle says yes."

"Roddy, you don't suppose a police officer—?"

"We can't rule it out."

"Someone bribed a policeman to cut that strap?"

A long moment passed. A clock chimed somewhere in the cottage. I abandoned the salty stew and reached again for water. A footman appeared, removed our dishes, and asked about a sweet. "Rice pudding is just ready downstairs, ma'am…sir."

Roddy nodded and waited until we were alone again. "About the new 'groundskeeper,'" he said, "Erbson lodges in the carriage house loft, so if he wasn't already outside in the gardens this morning, he might have heard someone… seen someone. First thing in the morning, I'll visit Seabright to 'consult' about next year's plantings here at Drumcliffe."

"And I will look in on Cassie and see about Charlie. Little Bea too. I'll take them presents. And I'll talk to Cassie about something else…the scrap of engraved paper that she took from Sylvia's cottage."

"From the bathroom niche…."

"Stuck to the envelope. Roddy. I'm almost certain it's the torn corner of the stock certificate. Cassie has it, and I want to see it. Sam blocked my view, but I got a good look at the framed certificate. Albert Dovedale's monocle magnified it.

And that oil painting of the little dog…."

"Let's not leap to…"

"To the thought we both share at this moment? The suspicion too hideous to name? The name that starts with 'S?'"

We broke off when Sands appeared with a small envelope. "As you requested, Mrs. DeVere," he said.

"Thank you, Sands." The handwriting was familiar. "Roddy, it's from Theo.

Listen to this: 'Ralph Rudd confirms three months' spent on portraits of canines…service to Georgina Van Schylar Brush…believes canine 'pack' migrated to Tuxedo …prefers portraits of people, requests this info be 'kenneled' so no 'ribbing' at the Club.'"

"Will there be a reply, ma'am?" asked Sands. "No, Sands. This is all for now."

Chapter Twenty-six

THE MORNING DAWNED MISTY and gray, and breakfast was over without fanfare. We both dressed, and Roddy was eager to be off.

"Val, are you ready? I can drive us to Seabright in a dog-cart. I want to catch Erbson early...."

"You go ahead, Roddy" I said, "Noland can drive me. I want to wrap these trinkets for Bea and Charlie." My husband left, and I went to my boudoir windows to see the morning's marine mist beginning to burn away to give Newport a sunny day. Calista had gone in search of wrappings and ribbon for the children's little gifts. A clock chimed eight a.m.

"Here we are, ma'am, paper and pretty ribbons. Sorry it took a few minutes. And shall I ask Mr. Sands to phone for your carriage?"

"Yes...no, on second thought," I said, "I will bicycle." My white duck bicycling suit became the clear choice. Calista soon put the little gifts in the wicker basket over the handlebars. The morning was fresh, not a leaf stirring.

"Your gloves, ma'am."

Bicycling gloves, as the outfit required. On went the kidskin, and I was off and through the Seabright gate within the hour. The uniformed policeman saluted, and the front door opened as I pedaled and dismounted.

"Good morning, Mrs. DeVere."

"Good morning, Hayes."

"May I see to your wheel, Mrs. DeVere?"

"Yes, please do." I plucked the little gifts from the basket.

"Mrs. Forster hopes you will first look in on the children." The butler pushed my bicycle out of sight, and a maid led me down a hallway to the nursery. A medal was pinned to Charlie's pajama top. "An eagle and a star and a flag," he said. "It's grandfather's medal. He is a veteran. He visited last night and rewarded me for my arm."

"Excellent, Charlie, well deserved."

Wrapping papers rustled, and Charlie fingered a painted nutcracker, while his sister rubbed her little ivory elephant. "Mama doesn't feel good," she said, her little voice solemn.

"Then I should try to make her feel better, yes?"

They nodded. Nanny Cara rose from her seat armed with *The Blue Fairy Book*. A maid led me to Cassie's suite.

My friend lay in bed with the covers up to her chin. "Cassie...."

"Val...."

The maid pushed a boudoir chair to the bedside and withdrew as I sat. "So dear of Father to visit last evening. He has so much on his mind…. And now this," she said, her tone low with defeat.

"Bea tells me that 'Mama doesn't feel good.'"

"No, she doesn't." Cassie looked baleful. "What's the use, Val? Guarded outside the cottage and inside too, and still the …attack. The Brush money is cursed. I want none of it."

"Cassie, we're going to get to the bottom of this."

"After me, the children…all of us. Dudley will visit our graves."

"Absolutely not. Remember, we agreed, 'delicate and resilient.'" I put a hand on her shoulder. "Cassie, you cannot surrender. You must not lie in bed. The children need you. Dudley needs you. Sit up, please."

I helped plump pillows against the headboard. A breakfast tray lay nearby. "Here, have a sip of this juice." I held the glass. "And Cassie, I need a favor." Her gaze was more alert. "The envelope you took from Tuxedo Park…I need to see it."

"The postal card from Atlantic City?"

"No, the envelope."

"But it was empty."

"Please, I need to see it."

She struggled out of the covers, my friend so very thin from stress. I thought of Sylvia.

"It's in this drawer, Val, under some handkerchiefs." She pulled the large yellowed envelope from a bureau drawer.

I planned to keep a calm face no matter what I saw. Cassie must not be disturbed again. The envelope in hand, I deliberately removed the colorful postal card, glanced at the Atlantic City boardwalk and surf, then peered at the envelope flap. Stuck to the glue, there it was—the torn corner with little curlicues that I first mistook for a diploma.

"What do you see?" Cassie asked.

I pretended to look again. "Nothing more. Empty, just as we thought. But I'd like to take this with me, if I may?"

"A souvenir of Tuxedo Park? Val, I can do better. Any of my boudoir bibelots, take your pick." Her voice sounded more like the old Cassie.

"Bea and Charlie," I replied, "now have two of my mother-in-law's castoff *objets*, a nutcracker and an ivory elephant. "Isn't that the word you taught me for Society—*objet* instead of souvenir?"

Her smile was heartening. "I'll dress and see about the day," she said. "And I might well return for an afternoon visit. And one more thing...."

"Which is—?"

"Kitchen spices," I said. "Do the children like particular flavors? And if so, which ones?"

She laughed. "Val, young children won't go near anything spicy. Our cook bakes gingerbread men without ginger. The eyes are raisins because cloves are too pungent. But they do love chocolate. Candy or cake, as long as it's chocolate. And for me, a generous slice when a chocolate cake appears." She reached for a pair of slippers. "Why do you ask?"

"No special reason," I said.

A quick hug, and I snugged the envelope under my left arm. We left it at that. A maid and footman saw me downstairs and outside to the garden, where Roddy was chatting with Erbson beside a plot of wild grasses near the South Seas hut.

The "groundskeeper" bowed awkwardly to me and muttered, "Mrs. DeVere, ma'am," as if this were an amateur theatrical. He toed the ground in the arctic snow boots he probably brought from Chicago. No Newport gardener ever wore such footwear. With the envelope held loosely under my arm, I glanced about for my bicycle. No sign of it.

"Erbson is conferring about topiary trees," Roddy said. "I told him we're thinking of topiaries for next year."

"Topiary," I said, "how interesting...." Just then, we heard hoof beats, the snorting of a horse, voices, and footsteps pounding the pathways toward us.

Dismounting from a bay mare, here came Sam Brush.

"Morning, DeVeres" he called to Roddy and me. "It is still morning, I do believe." He was wearing lightweight tweeds and held a riding crop. "Just stopping by on my way back from the Village." He gestured to Erbson without actually looking at him. "If you'll excuse us...."

The "groundskeeper" disappeared into the farthest flower beds. "Valentine and Roderick," he said, "just the friends I hoped to see." He wiped his face with a handkerchief. "Why, I must ask, was I not informed about the terrible accident yesterday? All day long at Stone Point, I knew nothing about that carriage wreck. The Village talks of nothing else."

"It happened so fast..." I began.

"Those new Rolli-cars...if someone had asked me...far too much novelty, that's for certain. A car invented by a Greek—"

"What Greek?" Roddy looked puzzled.

"A Mediterranean shipper, Pandia Ralli, and what could he possibly know about horse-drawn turn-outs? I have my doubts. It was O'Boyle, acting on his own. I have spoken with him."

"You were at the carriage house?"

"To see for myself. The cut bellyband, what can we say? Leather is weak material. It rots, it decays. A fine steel mesh, that's what a modern bellyband ought to be."

We had nothing to say. "I trust you're here to see Cassandra and look in on Charlie," I said.

"Just to leave a card," he said, "so Cassandra knows that Evalina and I are at her service. Recuperation is the order of the day." His gaze fell to the envelope under my left arm and lingered there. "Going to the Post Office, Valentine?"

"Perhaps."

"May I assist?"

"I'll take it myself, but thanks." His eye focused on the envelope. "We western women, you know...."

"...Newport's Annie Oakley, isn't that it?" We smiled, our smiles like glass.

Sam looked around. "Gardeners hiding anywhere in this high grass?" he asked. "Dudley does insist on the exotic, so let's take advantage. Let's us three stand in the shade by the children's hut for a few minutes."

Somehow Roddy and I were backed against the side of the Polynesian playhouse while Sam faced us.

"Something is on my mind, from our dinner," Sam said. "I would have loved to begin with a famous punch by Roderick DeVere, but my Evalina took charge of every detail. And apologies to you both for the jasmine vapors. I hope you'll forgive my misjudgment."

"No need to apologize, Sam," Roddy said. "No need," I echoed.

"And something I have been meaning to tell you both, and Cassandra too." He halted, wet his lips, stared again at the envelope. "Something I have not meant to conceal, but something until now confidential."

Recalling Evalina's empire gown, perhaps a hint about a forthcoming new member of the Brush family?

"I have been awaiting an opportune moment…perhaps a ball at Stone Point when the orchestra pauses and we can toast with champagne, but…." He peered at my left arm that secured the envelope against my side. The riding crop flicked against his calf, but Sam's focus did not leave the envelope. As if he might snatch it, I clamped it tighter. Beads of sweat bloomed at his temples.

"We're in no rush, Sam."

"None at all."

He wiped his forehead and temples. "The fact of the matter,' he said, "is that I once visited Tuxedo Park. I did. I visited Sylvia…God rest her soul. I swore the housekeeper to secrecy." He paused for a reverential moment, his eyes pleading, the riding crop lightly whipping his leg. "I should have told you," he said. "And to make a full confession, I'll admit to meeting Sylvia in the city. Poor dear, I tried my best...."

"Your best...?" Roddy prompted.

"For her health. I had my doubts about the Irish housekeeper at the cottage. As for those radical women in the city...."

"The suffragists?" I asked.

"It's too much nervous excitement for a well-bred lady. Altogether too much." His boot heel dug into the path as if spurring a horse. "But there was another, very special reason for visiting Sylvia and meeting her in the city. Something I am prepared to tell you here and now."

"Please...."

"Please do...."

"You might recall my promise of a charity to honor my beloved sister-in-law."

"Georgina," I said.

"Georgina Van Schylar Brush." Sam nodded and licked his lips. "And I sought Sylvia's approval. In fact, I hoped she might become involved. A charity is a lady's proper pursuit, not street parades for women's votes."

"And did Sylvia agree?"

He overlooked my question. "I proposed to her," he said, "to name the charity both for Georgina and Sylvia, mother and daughter."

"Very thoughtful," Roddy said. The morning sunlight flashed over the children's playhouse roof, and Sam squinted but stood in place.

He stood at attention, squinting in the glare. "You are well aware of my devotion to progress, and progress must include charity for the unfortunate ones in our midst."

The riding crop flicked in rhythm. "Too many young children are crippled by accidents or other misfortunes, and many are orphans. I have been at work on devices that help these children move about, mechanical sleds with gears that let the children climb stairs." He paused, as if a drum roll might sound. "I propose an orphanage devoted to these very children—The Georgina and Sylvia Van Schylar Brush Memorial Home for Crippled Orphans of the Storm."

"Storm—?"

"The storm of life," Sam said, "a figure of speech."

"A true service," Roddy said. I nodded.

"And Evalina is more than enthusiastic. We have discussed the matter, and she agrees that we must begin this fall, once we are back in residence in the city. My bride looks forward to helping. She thought up the words on 'Orphans of the Storm' and she quotes Mrs. Astor on our responsibility to the poor."

Shading his eyes with a free hand, Sam said, "So, that's the whole of it, Valentine, Roderick...the whole story. Yes, I did visit Sylvia in the city and at Tuxedo Park too. I tried my best to enlist her in my plan. Would she have agreed? We'll never know. She was gone before I got an answer." He wiped his face again. "And now I must see about Cassandra and the children." He winked. "And let Mr. and Mrs. DeVere be about their day."

"My bicycle is somewhere," I said. "I'll ask Hayes."

"You needn't trouble the butler," Sam said. "If I know Seabright, I'm quite certain your bicycle is propped by the gardeners' tool shed near the kitchen entrance." He bowed and winked again. "I have kept you this morning in the hot sun, sorry to say. Valentine, give me a moment to retrieve your velocipede."

We all smiled at the old-fashioned name for a bicycle. Roddy went off for the dog-cart, and the sun neared its zenith when Sam brought the bicycle and joked about his temptation to ride it. "You ladies with your speedy bicycles," he said as I took my seat. "You can give a good horse a race for the money."

"Pedal power," I called. "And we'll soon vote too."

I long remembered afterward that the ocean waves crashed and the air was pungent with salt as I started for Drumcliffe. The gulls and terns flew overheard in the bright blue sky, and there was no wind. From Seabright to Ocean Drive, I pedaled comfortably, sitting straight, arms out and my coaster brake was surely reliable. For sure, the envelope was carefully secured in my basket.

How the next moments passed, I was never quite sure. Rounding a curve, leaning in, I felt the pedals stall, the frame begin to give way under me. Time slowed as my body and bicycle became like a sequence flickering in a Nickelodeon. Not a second let me jump free, for the steel frame and chain and arms and legs were all one—until we shuddered to the pavement and I felt my ankle crunch and go numb. The first sight when I woke was this: the smashed wicker basket, and the envelope nowhere in sight.

Chapter Twenty-seven

"I'M SURE IT BLEW away."

"There was no wind, Roddy. Not a breath. Don't you remember?"

"How could I? The sight of my wife sprawled on the roadway when I rounded the Ocean Drive curve in the dog-cart.... I feared the worst. The very worst."

I dimly recalled that Roddy kicked the bicycle aside, lifted me into the dog- cart, and drove very fast to Washington Square to the medical office of Dr. Norman Hubbard, M.D., who pronounced my left ankle seriously sprained and wrote a prescription for pain. Ordered to keep the ankle raised and iced, I was pronounced bruised, told how fortunate that my injuries were not more severe, and scolded. ("You ladies ride your bicycles too, too fast.")

Headache pounding, I lay on a paisley button-back sofa in a drawing room at Drumcliffe, my stockinged left leg propped high on pillows, the swollen ankle a sight to behold.

The late afternoon sun cast shadows over the carpet while Roddy stabbed at a block of ice in a galvanized pail. He wrapped the chunks in a linen tea towel and pressed the cold pack against my ankle. I had taken a pain medicine, something new called aspirin.

"The envelope, Roddy," I said, "it can't have blown away."

"Val, it's the least of my concerns. You could have been… the sight of you lying there…." He jabbed at the ice block. "If I hadn't lingered at Seabright to have another word with O'Boyle—"

"About the leprechauns?"

"No joke, Val. O'Boyle is consumed with his mistake about the Ralli-car, praying to the saints for forgiveness. I heard him out once again. How's your head?"

"A little better."

We were alone in the drawing room. "Roddy," I said, "listen to me, please. There has been no wind to speak of all day long. No wind. And the envelope that Cassie gave me was secured in my bicycle basket. When I opened my eyes, it was gone."

"I see."

"And something else."

He leaned close on a lightweight chair with spindly legs. "Tell me."

"My bicycle…" I said. "It's a good one, sturdy, dependable."

"An Overman," Roddy said, "the best." He squeezed my hand. Roddy had surprised me with the bicycle three years ago, our first summer in Newport. "Whatever happened," he said, "we'll get it repaired, repainted, good as new. Or we'll replace it. One accident will not stop you—"

"Roddy," I said, "it was no accident." Somewhere a case clock ticked. "No accident," I repeated. "The chain failed, and I couldn't pedal. The frame... the whole bicycle gave way underneath. I think a bolt was loosened. I think the chain was tampered with."

Roddy sat very still.

"After you left this morning," I said, "I cycled the whole way to Seabright, and everything just fine. Hayes took over at the entrance, and then Sam brought the bicycle from the Seabright garden tool shed...rakes, wrenches, screwdrivers... everything necessary for...."

Roddy frowned. "Sabotage..." he murmured. "We must examine the bicycle. I'll send Noland for it right away. He can take a groom to help him." He went to the window. "The days are a bit shorter, but the light will hold." Roddy stepped into the hall to telephone the coach house. "On the Ocean Drive curve," he said, "immediately."

"This morning feels like ages ago," I said.

"Another century, Val...and let me tell you the groundskeeper, Erbson, was helpful. He remembers some-one in the carriage house while O'Boyle was at breakfast. He doubts that it was a policeman."

"He saw someone?"

"He heard grunting sounds, like a workman prying or lifting."

"Or slicing stiff leather."

We gave ourselves a moment, neither speaking. Roddy put a new cold pack against my ankle. The melting ice block dripped in the tub. "It is time," Roddy said, "to say his name. It is not Romberg. It is not Glendorick. Nor is it Rowena Fox." He took a very deep breath. "Let us say his name."

"Sam," I said softly. "Samuel David Brush."

The name hung between us. "Who would believe us?" I asked. "Georgina Brush was in her late sixties, and Sylvia's health was fragile. Both deaths were due to 'natural' causes."

"The police ..." I began but went no further. Sam had hired them to protect Cassie at Seabright. They were Sam's police.

"Suppose the Pinkertons..." I said, but stopped. Whatever their suspicions, the "footman" and the "groundskeeper" could do nothing without evidence.

"And the Clambake Club plate meant for Cassie," I said, "...a sad case of spoiled seafood that sickened Mrs. Dovedale. So, Roddy, where are we? Back in the dinghy while a storm blows our way?"

He rubbed one cheek and paused. "So far, Val, no one is suspicious, but where did Sam get the arsenic? To kill a person quickly, the killer needs a small amount, highly concentrated."

I shifted on the sofa. "The antique jewelry dealer, Creesey," I said, "suppose he has old rings with the poison still in them. Is it possible?"

Roddy frowned. "Perhaps. Or an apothecary could compound lethal dosages."

"A druggist in the city, in league with Sam?"

"Possible. But right now, in Newport, the tactic has changed. The attempt on Cassandra's life by a violent accident...and your bad spill this morning." He kissed my forehead. "Pure luck that I was on the way."

The shadows deepened on the carpet. "Like a hunter spotting prey," I said. "And he knows that Cassie and I visited Tuxedo Park. I'm certain the stock certificate was inside the secret bathroom niche."

"I'll say this, Val...from the size of that envelope, I suspect other documents were hidden inside."

"More stock certificates?"

He nodded. "And other legal papers...binding agreements, contracts...papers the heiress would have in possession." He added, "Papers that ought to be in a bank vault."

"Unless the heiress mistrusted banks." I shifted on the sofa. "The question, Roddy, is why? Why would Sam do this? He's wealthy, his wife is wealthy. It can't be about money.... Or can it?"

Roddy's laugh was bitter. "Val, my dear, you are living in the land ruled by Wall Street. In this land, it's never enough."

A moment passed. The West, the East, and now the compass needle pointed South. "Evalina's family," I said, "what about them? Could Evalina be Sam's partner in this... this horror? The Sherwoods' wealth came from plantations, didn't it? Cotton? Rice?"

"All before the war," Roddy said. He crossed his legs.

"So, we have no idea about Evalina's involvement." Roddy shook his head no.

We sat. A footman asked permission to close the draperies for the evening, just as Noland swept past the butler to enter the room.

"Orders from you, sir...and we looked everywhere, Mr. DeVere. Myself and Holloway searched every foot of Ocean Drive between your Drumcliffe and the Seabright cottage and back again."

"And...?"

"Nothing, sir. The soil was a bit rutted at the curve, but no bicycle. There was no bicycle."

"You're certain?"

"Every foot, sir, especially the curve. We did find these—" He held out his palm. "A nut, sir, and a shaft with an 'O' stamped on it."

"'O' for Overman," said Roddy. Noland looked puzzled. "The Overman Wheel Company," said Roddy, "the premier manufacturer of the famous safety bicycle."

The coachman was thanked and withdrew, and a footman inquired about our preference for dinner. And would we care for an aperitif?

"Roddy," I said, "mix us something good...something pleasant and soothing...something that feels far away."

"At your service, my dear." He called for his wheeled bar cart, turned back his shirt cuffs, and soon dropped ice into two tall glasses, peeled the skin of two oranges that he cut and prepared to squeeze, then plied the bottles until the sounds of pouring, fizzing, and stirring gave us drinks that took us into a remote space of our own when we sipped.

"Delicious, Roddy...what is it called?"

"You requested something 'far away,' my dear, and we are sipping Hawaii cocktails.... Let's enjoy them. I fear this moment is the calm before a storm.

Hawaii cocktail

Ingredients
- 1 ½ ounces whiskey
- Juice of 1 orange
- Peel of entire orange
- Ginger ale
- Ice

Directions:
1. Put ice and orange peel in tall Collins glass.
2. Add whiskey.
3. Add juice.
4. Stir.
5. Top with ginger ale, stir gently, and serve.

It was morning. The drawing room was rearranged for the nights I'll spend in this Newport "encampment" (Roddy's quip) in honor of my ankle. A velvet sofa with goosedown cushions had replaced the button-back, and a bedside table was at my elbow. A new block of ice and fresh towels were on hand. Roddy's walking sticks let me hobble about our ground floor.

"Suppose we pay a visit to Stone Point when Sam is not at home...sometime today."

"And—?"

"And I chat with Evalina about the little dogs while you ask the servants about my bicycle?"

"Your ankle, Val—"

"I'll use your walking sticks. The ebony is strong."

A clock chimed, and Roddy looked at my ankle. "Your notion of a visit to Stone Point, Val...it's a good idea, but you need a good walking cane with a handle grip. Or a crutch. Or both. I want to make sure it's right. I'll go myself."

I did not expect the morning to go as it did, not by a long shot. Out West, a turned ankle meant a forked tree branch fashioned into a home-made crutch or sawed into a cane with a handle. For certain, Newport merchants would proffer the latest in stylish rattan and bamboo walking canes with handles sculpted into animal heads.

Calista had pinned up my hair and got me dressed for the day in a comfortable skirt and shirtwaist, and settled me onto the sofa when a maid entered with a card on a silver tray. "A caller, ma'am. I said you might not be at home this morning. But the card, if you please...."

She bent from the knees as I took the card and stifled my surprise: "Mrs. Samuel D. Brush."

"Please show Mrs. Brush in." I sat up and smoothed my skirt as the aroma of jasmine announced her presence. "Evalina, welcome," I said. "What a nice surprise."

"Dear Valentine...what in the world has happened to you?" She waltzed forward while untying a fuchsia cloak that she flung into the waiting arms of our maid. "What in the world—?" She clasped my hand while a footman brought up a tufted chair. A second maid carried a bouquet of pink flowers that Evalina had brought and thrust into our servant's arms.

"What beautiful flowers to brighten this space and my mood." I looked to the maid. "A vase, if you please, and fresh water." I smiled at my unexpected guest. Had she been sent by her husband to interrogate me? "Evalina, may I offer refreshment? Tea?"

"Iced tea, please," she said. "I have just come from Seabright with Punch and Judy puppets for the children and a bouquet of oleander for Cassandra, who does not look at all well. But how could she? Her son's arm must worry her to death." Evalina saw my stunned face. "A southern expression, Valentine, nothing about mortality. I shan't stay long, but do tell...?" She tugged off her gloves.

"A cycling accident," I said, "on my return from Seabright yesterday."

"Oh, bicycles, so tempting and so treacherous." She frowned. "I must take lessons in the city this autumn so that Sam and I together...Mr. and Mrs. Samuel D. Brush can join the cycling parties in the autumn in Central Park." But that ankle of yours, how did it happen?"

The question seemed innocent. If Evalina had conspired with her husband in the deaths of Georgina and Sylvia, I saw no hint of complicity. She seemed guileless, and I matched her word for word. "How it happened," I said, "I lost my balance. Simple as that."

Her tsk-tsk sounded sincere. "Such a shame to lose these precious closing days of the Newport season...."

"Evalina, I am determined to go outdoors. Roddy just went to buy me a sturdy walking cane."

"Oh, if we had known. I am certain my ingenious husband would make you a clever mechanical device to improve on a stick of wood." Again, Evalina's voice carried no hint of irony.

"I would guess Sam is busy designing devices for the crippled orphans," I said.

She looked puzzled. "Crippled orphans?"

"Amputees?"

She adjusted several gold bangle bracelets. "Sam is so busy with mechanical things, I can hardly keep up."

"For the orphanage," I said, "to honor the late Georgina and Sylvia...." She looked perplexed. "'Orphans of the storm,'" I quoted, "...'storms of life?'"

"Well, life can be stormy, as we all know."

A soft knock on the drawing room door, and I desperately hoped to see Roddy. "The flowers, ma'am, if I may...?" The maid entered at my nod and put the crystal vaseful of delicate pink flowers with their backdrop of green leaves on my mother-in-law's favorite Queen Anne candle stand. "Oleander," I said, "so beautiful."

"We southerners love them so," she said, "and my Sam is liking them better and better. At first he wasn't sure...."

"About the flowers?"

"The flowers, the South, many things...but Newport is God's country for Sam Brush. He is thriving."

"Very healthy," I managed. "Everyone appreciates Sam Brush."

Her tone turned pensive. "Everyone except Sam."

"I don't understand...."

"Oh, Valentine, I can say something now that Sam is rising in society, but his sadness was hidden for so long... deeply hidden."

"Sadness?" I tried to make the two syllables sound like an opening. "I had no idea."

"Oh yes, going way back to when he was a little boy. How he tried to get his brother to pay attention...his one-and-only brother, Harry."

"Sam worships him," I said. "The tapestry in Stone Point—"

She laughed. "Its days are numbered, Valentine. I'll have it rolled up for good at the first opportunity. Harry Brush had it woven in Switzerland, and Sam tries to pay tribute, so it hangs in Newport for the season, and then it will go into a reception room in the city for the winter. Such an embarrassment."

Her sigh was overcast with reproof. "I'll tell you this—without Sam, the famous older brother might never have got out of the woods. If it wasn't for my Sam, that brother would have wasted his whole life chopping down trees with an axe in Oregon."

"I don't understand. The difference in their ages is… twenty years?"

"Almost that much, but Sam's mechanical things showed up very early. He drew pictures all the time. There's a Brush machine…it lifts logs."

I remembered Theo's description. "The Brush Log Lifter," I said.

"It lifts logs onto railroad cars. It's patented." She arched her back. "It lifted up Harry Brush, I can tell you that."

"So, all's well," I said.

"No, it's not all well. The patent for the log lifter went to Harry and the company, but Sam invented it."

"What?"

"He drew the picture, and his brother…the truth is, Harry snatched it away and got the patent."

The room went silent. "Sam didn't get credit?"

"Not for the patent. He got whatever his brother gave him. Harry treated Sam like a hired boy." She fingered her bracelets, as if deciding to go on.

I tried to seem pleasant and receptive, open to a confidence. "I understand that Sam is head of communications at the Brush company," I said. "He told us a charming story about boyhood adventures in logging camps. Charming…."

Evalina's bracelets chimed. "Harry Brush," she said, "put Sam into overalls and sent him to logging camps to play marbles with the children of loggers." She wet her lips. "I sympathize with that. What if I were driven into the cotton fields to play dolls with sharecroppers' girls?"

"So, he didn't enjoy it?"

"He hated every minute. Brush Industries got bigger and bigger, but Sam was nothing but a mascot. He never got credit. The log lifting machine was his idea….and everything else came afterward. That machine was like Mr. Rockefeller's first oil well."

"And so Sam has been…sad?"

"Until now, but the new Sam Brush is here, where he belongs, in Society. The Clambake Club is a boost, and we are at work on his nomination to the Union Club and the Knickerbocker Club too."

Who, I wondered, was the "we" proposing Sam Brush for membership in New York's most prestigious clubs? Evalina's family? Perhaps Theo knew.

"Once we have ourselves a yacht—"

"I didn't know Sam was a yachtsman."

"Not just yet. But the New York Yacht Club beckons, and Sam will be handsome in yachting attire." Her smile was coy. "Seriously, Valentine, the contraptions on a steam yacht will draw Sam like a bee to honey. Just think, a yacht engine… so much better than fiddling with kitchen stove dials or air-cooled funeral coaches." She began to rise. "Just as soon as Sam gets the kennels and feeding stations designed for my French bulldogs, we'll start on the yacht."

Evalina stood. "Please don't stir, Valentine. I can tiptoe out." We looked together at the flowers. "A charming candle stand," she said, "just the thing to keep oleander away from Velvet. So far, I rely on mantlepieces, way up high."

"So that your little dog doesn't tip a vase? Or nip the flowers?"

Evalina looked at me strangely. "Surely you know about oleander?"

I shook my head.

"You don't? Why, Valentine, I'm surprised." She began to pull on her gloves. "I thought everybody knew. Oleander," she said, "...so dangerous."

"Dangerous?"

"Stem to petal, it's fatal. Beautiful to look at, but otherwise poisonous...a two- or three-day plunge from lightheaded to the graveyard. In a nutshell, that's it. Now you know, Valentine. And do tell your servants, just in case. Make sure Roderick knows. Take care." At the drawing room door, she turned. "I almost forgot...you and Roderick enjoy chocolate cake, yes?"

Cake? I could hardly focus. The dainty flowers on the candle stand blackened in my mind, and the furniture seemed to swim. Oleander, arsenic...two words that meant the same thing. Two words...different but the same. "Cake..." I said, my mouth so dry the word was barely spoken.

"From Cassandra's kitchen. Sam insists on fooling with the Seabright oven dials."

"Dials," I murmured, "dials...."

"And I told him that little Charles and Beatrice ought to get a treat, and their mother too. So, to my *Old Virginia* section on cakes, and Sam found one that calls for coffee grounds. 'Coffee grounds for little children?' I said, 'Perish the thought.' Cassandra's cook can find the best one and bake enough cakes for three cottages.' So, Seabright, Drumcliffe, and our Stone Point too. We'll all get a chocolate cake."

"When?" I managed to ask. "When, Evalina—?"

Through the open doorway I saw our maid bring my visitor's cloak and open it across her shoulders. "When?" she repeated. "Probably this evening. Sam will be in the Seabright kitchen later this afternoon. He never baked a cake in his life. I teased him about it. "Are you planning to supervise?" I asked him.

"What did he say?"

"He's so quick with a comeback. He said he plans to help out. He plans to tie an apron around his waist and help the cook every step of the way."

Chapter Twenty-eight

I STARED AT THE cane, speechless. "It's solid ash, Val, hardwood all the way. You can put full weight on it. Try it...the same wood as the Louisville Slugger baseball bats," he said.

Baseball bats. My husband's cheeks glowed from the out-of-doors. He held a walking cane like an offering. I didn't move.

"We can go to Stone Point this afternoon," he continued. "I understand that Sam will not be at home. We can find out about your bicycle.... Are you listening, Val? Please do try the cane. I bought a crutch just in case, but the cane ought to do it for you. What's that book?"

Stupidly I said, "Cookbook."

"Oh?" He blinked. "Meal planning? Feeling better?"

"Roddy, it's the *Old Virginia* book...Evalina's gift."

He heard the strain in my voice. "Something the matter in the kitchen?"

"Not our kitchen…Cassie's…Cassie's kitchen." I sputtered the message, like a telegram that barely made sense, my voice choked with "cakes" and "oleander."

Roddy looked behind me at the candle stand. "Poisonous flowers? Or is it the stems? Or leaves?"

"Everything, the whole plant. Deadly. I asked Calista which maid handled the vase, arranged the…." I could hardly say the word. "…the oleander. I'm having the maid watched. She's to wash her hands and rest up."

"So, we must go."

"Evalina said late this afternoon. And the cake…cakes. Three, and all chocolate. Roddy, it's one of these recipes." I thrust out the dark red book.

"Cakes…so many," he said, looking inside. "Silver cake, Mountain Ash cake…here's chocolate."

"It's got to be this one." I pointed.

"Grated chocolate…" he read."

"Eggs, sugar, chocolate," I continued, "and cinnamon, nutmeg, cloves. A few coriander seeds."

"All of which must be well powdered," Roddy read. It says 'well powdered.'"

We looked at one another. "'Powdered.'"

"Val, did Evalina say how much is fatal?"

"No."

"Is there an antidote?"

"Roddy, it was so fast I didn't ask."

He looked at the page. "What does 'quickly' mean? It says 'bake quickly.'"

"No idea."

A footman appeared to ask about lunch. "We ought to eat something. Let the kitchen send up something light." We paused while the footman bowed out. It was a lost hour.

"Three cakes, Roddy." My voice cracked "One for us, another for Cassie and the children."

"But Cassandra's cake," he said, "will contain the 'extra' ingredient." My husband's eyes had a thousand-mile stare. "Don't underestimate Sam Brush." He met my gaze. "We'll go to Seabright by...let's say midafternoon. I'll make certain that Dunlap is in the kitchen."

"And the 'groundskeeper,' Erbson?"

"Somewhere outside, no matter." He reached down. "Now, Val, you must try the cane. Come on, try your weight on it."

Too many hours on sofas made it a chore. But I stood, gripped the hardwood handle, and stepped down.

"Your ankle seems...."

"Sprained, Roddy. It's sprained, and it hurts. I'll have another dose of...what is it?"

"Aspirin."

"A double dose, and let's get ready."

Our plan was this: surprise Cassie and the children with an afternoon visit. Roddy would show interest in the new oven gadgets that Sam was working on. I would be curious about the preparation of a recipe from the *Old Virginia* book. We DeVeres would descend into the Seabright kitchen with one goal—not one single bite of the chocolate cake for anyone. We would confiscate the spice tins and the cake batter. We would witness the murderous plot-in-progress, as would Dunlap and the Seabright cooks and sculleries. Cassie and the children, all the while, would have no knowledge of the goings-on below stairs.

By two-fifteen, Roddy took the reins of a fast gelding to speed us to Seabright in a dog-cart on a fiercely hot afternoon. We wore sporting clothing, Roddy dressed for a country ramble while I chose a culotte skirt. We would need to move quickly.. The aspirin helped, but my ankle pulsed.

"The best laid plans…" I murmured when chocolate struck our nostrils the instant Cassie's butler opened the door.

"Chocolate…" I cried.

"A lovely aroma, Mrs. DeVere, is it not?" Hayes stood aside as Cassie stepped to greet us.

"Val, Roderick, how nice. Take a deep breath…isn't it heavenly? Dear Sam is at work in the kitchen. Our mechanical genius insists on helping the cook. Let's do sit down. Val, your ankle…that cane…?"

"A precaution, Cassie. A new pair of shoes…I'm just fine." The ankle throbbed.

"Cassandra," Roddy said, "We thought that Sam was to visit later on."

"Oh, he came early to inspect the oven dials and help the cook bake us all luscious chocolate cakes from Evalina's recipe book. We had a delightful visit. He brought the children marionettes devised from wood and wires. So very clever. Please, let's do sit down."

We followed like mannequins. The blue drawing room once again, and the chocolate odor grew stronger by the minute. "If miners out West could work through sprains and worse, I could surely ignore a wrenched ankle. Surely.

Cassie looked almost buoyant this afternoon. "You two are a tonic for my poor nerves," she said. "And Sam, of course...."

"Of course."

"And Evalina brought the most beautiful oleander bouquet this morning, and I showed Sam—"

"Showed him?"

"Actually, the bouquet was in the reception room, and he stepped in to take a peek."

"—before he went into the kitchen?" My "lilt" sounded choked.

"And may we join him downstairs for a few moments, Cassandra?" Roddy's haste caught Cassie's attention. "I am intrigued by his ideas for oven dials, you see, and Val is eager to know about the cakes. Aren't you, dear?" I managed a nod and smile. "We could send our cook to yours," he went on, "but you know my missus."

We had scarcely met the clock's quota for a social call. "And shall I accompany you?" Cassie asked.

"Don't give it a thought, my friend." She looked relieved. "We won't be long," I added, "but Roddy has a request—"

"Your footman, Dunlap," he said, "please send him with us to the kitchen." Her winsome face turned puzzled, then wary. "Remember, Cassandra, I must report to a certain New York office at regular intervals."

"Oh, yes, so kind of you, Roderick." She summoned Dunlap, who entered the space so fast he was doubtless within earshot. "Dunlap," said Cassie, "Mr. and Mrs. DeVere wish to go into the kitchen. Please attend to them."

His stiff bow better fit a prizefighting ring, but he stood ready. With a grimace masked as a smile, I proceeded slowly across the marble floor and down the dark metal stairs—too many to count, each one a ringing torment. The heat became intense, and the odor of chocolate an assault. The ankle pounded.

At last, the kitchen. Pots and pans hung from an overhead rack like a chandelier of gleaming copper. We scanned the scene. Kitchen maids wearing white muslin uniforms bustled about the sink and the cutting boards. At the near end of the vaulted room, two stout hands kneaded dough on a marble surface, while knife blades flashed a few feet away, chopping greens and peeling potatoes. Everything smelled like chocolate. The maids barely looked up, and we peered out to locate the cook or assistant cook. Where were the spice tins? Where was Sam Brush?

There, at the farther end of the Seabright kitchen stood Sam. Beside him, the cook. Roddy and I made our way along the flanking row of black, hot, coal-fired ovens toward the countertop that was set with mixing bowls and canisters.

Dunlap stationed himself behind us as we approached the aproned Sam, who flashed his warmest smile. "Roderick and Valentine, welcome to the shop floor...the center of dessert delights." His eyes inspected every inch of us and lingered on my cane without a qualm. My ankle thundered.

"Not to rival the throne of Escoffier," Sam said in jovial tones, "but I am assisting in the magical culinary arts. This afternoon I am apprenticed to Mrs. Forster's inimitable cook, Mrs. Brown."

"Green it is, sir. Mavis Green." The cook, a non-nonsense woman whose round face shone with sweat, offered a semi-salute with a wooden spoon. Her wide-set eyes scanned the kitchen, her command post shrunk to a duty station by a gentleman who fancied himself a baker. In short, a nuisance to be tolerated.

"Stirring up the batter," she said.

Or did I hear batters, plural?

We nodded, gripped by the sight of the large earthenware mixing bowl filled with thick brown batter that gave off chocolate vapors. Among the assemblage—a crock of butter, a canister marked SUGAR, a can of Hershey's Cocoa Powder alongside a huge block of dark chocolate that looked chewed at one end. Grated?

Not one spice tin was in sight. Where were they? Beside the bowl lay a wood box with a crank on the top. It resembled my papa's coffee grinder from our mining camp days. His one luxury was fresh coffee that he ground every morning from whole beans.

A second, smaller bowl lay to the side, a pale yellow liquid inside it. "It's chemistry, you know. Cooking is chemistry," Sam said. Cassie's cook looked pained. He went on with the lecture. I leaned on the cane, weight off the outraged ankle.

Sam pointed to the box with the crank. "Roderick and Valentine, I have brought my own small mill that can grind whole cloves, whole cinnamon sticks, and coriander seeds as well. As you might guess, I have designed the gearing of the mill to rival Mr. McCormack's. I can reduce spices to powder. From this little mill, think of it—to powder."

Roddy's voice sounded otherworldly. "And you'll patent the mill, Sam? A home appliance?"

"For the freshest spices, to rival McCormack's. I foresee a market, Roderick. "Indeed, I do."

The cook looked leftward at several greased cake pans. "We can get on with it, sir. You grated the lemon, and we're ready."

Lemon? What lemon? Roddy and I exchanged glances. "That bowl over there," I asked, "what is that yellow—?"

"Oh, that batter will be cake number three," said Mrs. Green.

"Not chocolate?"

"No sireee…." Sam spoke in a stage whisper. "It's a secret, a surprise for my bride. Guess?"

"Eggs?" I said.

"And sugar, flour, and the juice and rind of a whole lemon." He paused while we peered at the bowl. "My friends," said Sam, "you are witness to the making and baking of the official Robert E. Lee cake."

"Robert E...General Lee?"

"Hero of the Confederacy, yes indeed. Right out of *Housekeeping in Old Virginia*, Mrs. Samuel D. Brush's most cherished volume...after the Good Book, of course. My Evalina delights in chocolate, but this Robert E. Lee cake is a taste of home."

My ankle banged like a drum, and my brain roared with Roddy's warning about Sam. Then a kitchen maid's voice—"oven at temperature, Mrs. Green."

"To demonstrate..." said Sam. He slipped a leather bag, like a soft tobacco pouch, from inside his vest to produce spices, which dropped into the mill. I glimpsed a cinnamon stick, scattered cloves, seeds, something pink and green, something tan. He began turning the crank. "Want to give it a turn, Roderick? Valentine? No? You're sure? The gearing is very smooth, almost no resistance."

We watched his hand clasp the crank, his arm make circles in the air. We heard crunching inside the box. "Mrs. Green, would you care to try?"

She shook her head. "But thank you just the same, Mr. Brush."

A tableau of four—Sam, Roddy, the cook, and me—and the sole motion was Sam's circling arm with the crunching sound that softened slowly to a whisper. Standing aside, Dunlap leaned forward on his toes, his head cocked.

"Ready for the spices, sir." The cook's wooden spoon raised.

And still we stood, rooted in place while the little wood drawer was opened over the bowl and turned upside down. Ever afterward, we recalled the spiral of powder that was swallowed into the dark brown mass by the cook's wooden spoon and the sight of Sam's face turned away from the bowl as he seemed to hold his breath.

"Twenty-five minutes baking time, thirty at most."

The batter was poured slowly into two cake pans.

"Put the General Lee in too? There's plenty of room."

"No." Sam's voice rang like a sharp staccato thunderclap. "No, do not put in General Lee. Not with the chocolate. You must not."

A moment passed in dead silence, followed by the short nervous laughter of release. The rhythms resumed—and an oven door opened, a glimpse at the red pit inside, and the two cake pans were locked within.

Would we wait while the cakes baked? Thirty minutes of eternity? And then what? Meanwhile, the inferno of the oven and the hell of my ankle. I leaned against a wood counter, and Roddy struck a nonchalant pose, but tension knotted his neck and shoulders. We stood very still, both of us. Dunlap too. We stood and waited.

When does an animal feel trapped? Partnered with fear, that so-called sixth sense...when does it come to life? None of us moved physically toward Sam. No one took a step into the space where he stood between the oven and the table with the empty batter bowls. Nothing visibly meaningful stirred in that moment.

I know this: the kitchen maids and sculleries stood back. The cook too.

Dunlap, up on his toes, had balled his hands into fists but did not move. Roddy looked poised to pound a croquet ball through the farthest wicket, and I squeezed the cane until my hand went numb.

It was Sam who moved first, Sam whose eyes flashed and teeth bared without smiling, Sam who suddenly lunged with a poker at the oven door, pried it open and jabbed at the cakes inside, toppling the pans until the batter struck hot iron and hissed.

"Shut that oven door! Quick!" It was Roddy's voice, Roddy who sprang to slam the door shut with a kick—but not before Sam flung something inside...the little pouch from his vest. Apron thrown aside, he sprang to the stairs.

My cane shot out, and he tripped but did not fall. Dunlap plunged ahead and almost caught up, but the door slammed above and the bolt slid to shut us in the kitchen.

"Outside, outside...the service door...."

Was it three minutes to the basement door? Five? Dunlap beat us all and vanished. "Go ahead, Roddy. You go ahead."

He would not. His wife, the lame-and-the-halt spouse, was in his care. My sightline clouded, I nearly fainted from pain, but Roddy carried me in his arms up and outside to the garden.

The scene in the Seabright flower bed was two men wrestling, Sam Brush against an opponent in a denim jacket. The two had locked together and become one beast that tugged and grunted, that crashed into the rose bushes and disappeared in the wild grasses, then rose up and struggled against itself. Roddy whispered, "It's the groundskeeper, Erbson." We watched, helpless spectators amazed at the two-headed creature with four legs and arms.

The cook appeared and stood nearby, open-mouthed, a spatula in hand, and kitchen maids gathered on the sidelines. Dunlap got nearer to the tussle but backed away. Like tentacles, the legs locked and arms grasped and scissored until, at last, the entire body slammed down—no, the two bodies, one torso to subdue the other, to pin it down. The denim jacketed Erbson won out—

—only to be handcuffed by the Newport police who came running from the front gate, pistols drawn. Erbson's arrest was announced loudly while Mr. Brush was helped to his feet and asked, was he hurt? Roddy spoke, but Dunlap pulled a Pinkerton badge from his footman's waistcoat and said a second such badge could be found in the jacket of the handcuffed man who was, at the moment, too winded to speak.

Two Pinkerton detectives versus a Newport gentleman whose name was recognized worldwide—what was the outcome? For the moment, a stand-off. Mr. Brush was to be escorted home to Stone Point, with one policeman in attendance at his cottage, as Mr. Brush agreed. Free of handcuffs, Erbson rubbed his wrists, and the two Pinkertons prepared to go with a second officer to the Market Square police station to be interviewed. The cook and kitchen staff retreated to the kitchen—but not before Roddy insisted that the oven door remain closed and the burned remains of the cakes and other object or objects in the oven be undisturbed. Until further notice, the cake mixing bowl was not to be washed, nor the wooden spoon. The spice mill not to be touched or moved.

"Mrs. Green," Roddy said, "this matter is of utmost importance to Mr. and Mrs. Forster. Please give me your word." He added, "Your kitchen may be the scene of a crime." She promised, guessing the crime to be hot tempers and the theft of a prized recipe. We did not tell her otherwise.

Cassie was alerted, in the meantime, of a disturbance in the Seabright gardens. Slipping on a cloak, she tiptoed outside with her butler Hayes to see about it—only to find Roddy and me standing beside a bed of trampled grasses and a crushed rose bush. "My foot..." I protested before she could ask one question. "Oh, Cassie, I needed fresh air..." Then, to Roddy's astonishment and my friend's amazement, I pulled the stunt I'd seen countless times onstage at Piper's Opera House in Virginia City, Nevada. For distraction, and only for that purpose, I raised an arm slowly to my forehead, swayed unsteadily, and let myself collapse into a faint worthy of the theatrics of Sarah Bernhardt.

Chapter Twenty-nine

"YOU'RE CERTAIN?"

"Cassie, the chemists confirmed it. The residue in the bowl and charred scrapings from the oven—all deadly. Roddy has the report. Copies were sent to the Newport police, to the Pinkerton office and to your attorney."

"To Mr. Phillips," Cassie said.

"Other copies will be provided to the court as requested."

My friend looked away. "Val, must you?"

"I must. The facts must be clear, Cassie. No bonbons coated with...." I stopped. This afternoon, I had told the facts of the case against Sam Brush to my friend over tea that was served on a packing crate. I took her hand. "The trial is coming, and the newspapers will be full of it. You need to be prepared."

"No one can be prepared for this...this catastrophe." She dabbed a tear with a handkerchief as I squeezed her hand. Surrounded by crates and trunks, we were seated side by side on a settee in a Seabright reception room. Cassie's maids had draped all the other furnishings, and footmen on ladders had bagged the crystal chandeliers in muslin.

The Newport season was closing. Yachts weighed anchor daily and disappeared from the harbor, and the cottages along Bellevue Avenue and Ocean Drive were shuttered one by one. Except for a small "skeleton" staff who remained through the winter in each cottage, the annual household migration to the city was well underway. Cassie—Mrs. Dudley Forster—would depart tomorrow with the children and their nanny, as would Roddy and I. The telegram clutched in my friend's in hand told her to expect her husband at the Grand Central depot in three weeks' time.

"Dudley will be horrified."

"We're all horrified."

"But why, Val? Why would Sam do such a thing? Was he secretly brooding all these years?"

"Beyond brooding, Cassie. At the core, he was enraged. He felt betrayed by his brother and betrayed once again when the Brush fortune was left to Georgina, then to Sylvia, and then...."

"To me."

"Yes, Cassie, to you."

I hesitated to add the children, but my friend drew herself up on the settee, sipped her Oolong, and said the painful words aloud. "And if my children had eaten the cake, they too would be gone."

"—because Charlie and Bea could be the last claimants to the Brush fortune."

"What about my mother?"

"Rowena—?" I set down my cup. "As the late Georgina's sister," I said, "she might make a claim." I looked Cassie in the eye. "And we know she is fierce enough to do it."

"She is." Cassie shivered.

"But suppose," I said, "that Rowena were to be invited to dine with Sam this coming autumn, perhaps dinner at Delmonico's to console her for the loss of her daughter and grandchildren, all amid the travail of her divorce." Cassie's eyes widened. "And if Sam presented her with a gift, perhaps a piece of antique jewelry guaranteed to charm her—?"

My friend's eyes filmed with angry tears.

"And then, so soon after the lovely dinner, suppose she became terribly ill...."

Oleander," Cassie murmured. And once again, "Oleander," the word uttered with awe. "So, Sam might not have been finished."

"Not necessarily. If your mother needed to be out of the way, Sam could tend to her, then mount his campaign for the Brush fortune. New York lawyers would clamor to be at his service. At long last, Samuel Brush would rise from the communications committee of Brush Industries to become—"

"The president," she said softly. "To claim his birthright."

A moment passed, and a footman approached to inquire about a fresh pot of tea or refreshments. The kitchen was minimally stocked, he said, but a cold beef roast might be sliced.

"Roderick might welcome a snack," Cassie said. "He'll be here...?"

"Within the hour," I said. Roddy was overseeing last-minute details at Drumcliffe and planned to join us after a brief stop in town. A platter of cold beef was ordered.

Cassie crumpled her handkerchief. "I couldn't eat a thing. But I can read your mind, Val. I must fatten up before Dudley arrives, isn't that what you're thinking? My worries should be over because Charlie's arm is healing, because Dudley will be home soon, and because Sam Brush is locked up in jail. So it's now: 'Let Cassandra Eat Cake?'"

Our words hung for a moment. The room echoed with grisly laughter that could only be shared between friends. I did not remind Cassie that Roddy and I, too, were probably intended to be victims of Sam Brush. My sore ankle was a daily reminder, as were my missing bicycle and the contents of its basket.

Cassie's teacup rattled. "In all of this," she said, "it's Evalina I pity...poor dear. I understand she's with her parents."

"I believe they're taking her abroad," I said, "to Italy."

"Val, are we certain that she knows nothing about... about...?"

"About her husband's murderous schemes? Quite certain. Her family says she is 'indisposed.' I hear she has been heavily medicated."

"But she's innocent?" Cassie asked again.

"Evalina Sherwood Brush...yes, innocent, but an unwitting party to her husband's plotting. During their courtship, she entertained her fiancé with tales of the Old South. A good many stories were gothic accounts of jealousy and revenge. In every story, oleander played its deadly part, from the cotton fields to the mansion kitchens and boudoirs. When Sam courted Evalina, he learned the history that never appears in schoolbooks."

"And Evalina innocently gave him the plan."

"Not the plan, Cassie. Sam had the plan, but Evalina provided the method. She was Sam's fool."

In the silence, a slight "a-hem" announced the footman's presence with a platter of sliced beef, rolls, condiments, various tidbits on a silver tray. For sure, a work of decorative art, but I yearned at that instant for the iron skillet of a mining camp. The footman retreated. We ignored the platter.

Cassie sipped her tea. "Do you suppose Sam will be tried for Aunt Georgina's murder? Or for Cousin Sylvia's death?"

"We're not sure. That jurisdiction is New York." I refrained from the details of the burial vaults.

"He probably gets catered meals in jail because he's a Brush." Cassie sounded bitter. "And they'll claim it was insanity, won't they?"

"His defense will probably be insanity...mental illness. The prosecution will no doubt focus on the Brush fortune," I said. "However, a jury can easily follow the link between revenge and murder."

I squeezed lemon into my tea. "Roddy will testify, of course. And the cook and kitchen maids and sculleries will provide their eye-witness accounts. The Pinkerton detectives will also testify."

"Including my 'groundskeeper?'"

"The wrestler, Erbson. Yes, he'll testify that he stopped Sam's escape."

"I misjudged him, Cassie. It seems Erbson got interested in Judo, and he used it."

Before I could speak, Cassie burst out, "He murdered my aunt and her daughter, and he tried to kill me and my children. And to think, I should have known from the beginning."

"Known what, exactly?"

"That a poisoner threatened us. I should have listened to Madame Riva."

The moment was fragile, not the time to ridicule the gypsy with the nail files and séances. "Hindsight," I said, "is so often crystal clear...."

Cassie nodded, and we both sipped our tea.

COMING SOON

Murder, Murder, Murder in Gilded Central Park
(The 2nd Val and Roddy Devere Mystery)

Our footman fanned the half-dozen newspapers from the *Times* to the *Sun* on the breakfast table.

Park Police Baffled...Third Victim...Clothing Ripped Asunder... Central Park Strangler Strikes Again!!!

My husband pulled the paper toward him. "That vile nickname will stick. As of today, the killer will be known as 'The Strangler.' New York's Jack-the-Ripper is now in our part of the park."

A detective sergeant would soon put the case to us, point blank: "Mr. DeVere, this park got its start from families like yours."

His eyes searched ours. "So tell me this— how much more death and damage before you and Mrs. DeVere cooperate to save the park that your forefathers built?"

ABOUT THE AUTHOR

Cecelia Tichi is a native of Pittsburgh, the steel city of the Gilded Age, and is an award-winning teacher and author of numerous books focused on American culture and literature. Her most recent titles: *What Would Mrs. Astor Do? The Essential Guide to the Manners and Mores of the Gilded Age* was followed by *Cocktails of the Gilded Age: History, Lore, and Recipes of America's Golden Age* and the sequel, *Jazz Age Cocktails: History, Lore, and Recipes from the Roaring Twenties*. The "Val and Roddy DeVere" mystery series premiers with A Gilded Death.

Printed in Great Britain
by Amazon